The Treasury was dark. Nimnestl took a step in and stretched forward in the gloomy air. She avoided landing face first on an iron-bound chest by rolling to one side. Her saber knocked over a small table, sending a cascade of large silver coins across her body. She kept rolling until she was up on her knees, swinging her hammer up in the same motion.

The guard rushed in holding a torch. Nimnestl jabbed her weapon at the lump she'd tripped over, a crimson halo spreading around the victim's head. "What's he doing here?" she demanded.

"Not much," croaked her guide.

The Sure Death of a Mouse

A thrilling tale of fantasy and adventure in the treacherous world of Rouse a Sleeping Cat

Ace Books by Dan Crawford

ROUSE A SLEEPING CAT
THE SURE DEATH OF A MOUSE

THE SURE DEATH OF A MOUSE

Dan Crawford

ACE BOOKS, NEW YORK

Portions of this story appeared as "One Dark Falcon's Nest" in an insignificant fan magazine called "The Philomathean Press Presents" and are reprinted here with the Press's permission and rather to its astonishment.

THE SURE DEATH OF A MOUSE

An Ace Book / published by arrangement with
the author

PRINTING HISTORY
Ace edition / March 1994

ISBN: 0-441-00024-X

ACE®
Ace Books are published by The Berkley Publishing Group,
200 Madison Avenue, New York, NY 10016.
ACE and the "A" design
are trademarks belonging to Charter Communications, Inc.

PRINTED IN THE UNITED STATES OF AMERICA

10 9 8 7 6 5 4 3 2 1

Dedicated to those people in whose homes the manuscript was typed:

William J. and Amata I. Crawford

Kenneth F. and Evelyn J. Lampe

"Many cats are the sure death of a mouse."
—Kasper Hauser

CHAPTER ONE

Polijn

I

IT was a grey day. The rain had been cold and steady when Polijn got up that afternoon. The rain was still cold and steady, but not enough, in Ronar's opinion, to keep her from work. So at dusk, just after lunch, Polijn stepped out into the soggy city.

In two hours since, she had met just three pedestrians. Oh, it was early yet, but someone should have been abroad, on some errand. The rain had apparently chased even the alleydozers, not the most sensitive of citizens, to cover. Except for a few sodden rats, not so much as a corpse broke the monotony.

Polijn whipped around at the sound of thick wooden soles on the pavement to her left. A heavyset man slogged out of the shadowed alley and paused to adjust the pack on his shoulder. Polijn eased in his direction, sliding her thumb into her mouth.

Enough light dripped past the tapestries in the upper windows of the Thick Fleece for him to see this. He shook his head and raised his hands, fingers entwined to suggest something similar, but different.

Polijn smiled, and held up a number of fingers.

The man shook his head again, holding up fewer fingers. This prompted no response. He raised one more finger. Polijn watched water drip from the eaves of the Thick Fleece. The man made another gesture, suggesting alternate uses for Polijn's fingers, and sloshed away into the fog.

Polijn shrugged, but the shrug became a shiver. She didn't like turning customers away. That sometimes annoyed them. Whoever had taken Kronja apart and pinned the pieces to Jobafta's shutters must have been severely annoyed. That was another reason the streets were empty in the Swamp tonight.

Realizing this customer had been just a customer, though, Polijn kicked the wall of the Thick Fleece. She had lost him, and that meant, maybe, hours in the rain now until the next one.

"Faff," she told herself. "If it's so lintik early, why are you standing here?"

Ronar wouldn't come out in this to check on her. With an eye to the hiding places in shadows, Polijn scampered back to the rubbish heap at the back door of the inn. Someone before her had burrowed a cave into the broken chairs and benches on the stack. She peered into it, being sure it was vacant before she put so much as a hand inside.

If Ronar would pay the landlord's fee, she could work inside the Thick Fleece, dry and warm. That was fantasy, so half-dry and out of the wind would have to do. She spread her shawl over the splintered tabletop that formed the floor, and then climbed up to the hidey-hole. There was just enough room to stretch out, but Polijn did not do so. Warmer to huddle against one rackety wall, her fingers tucked under her arms.

When her hands had thawed some, she took her slide-whistle from its hiding place. After blowing on the mouthpiece to warm it, she tried the first few bars of "The Hot Featherbed" in a low, cautious tone. The whistle was the gift of an elderly peddler, a reward for fifteen minutes of concentrated effort. She was going to play it at the Palace Royal some day. She had heard of minstrels playing for kings and queens, and nothing she had ever heard from the broken-down, sixth-rate musicians who frequented the Swamp had suggested that lords and ladies would be uninterested in slide-whistle music. Fikemun always claimed the duchesses greeted him with open arms (and so forth) when he arrived, and he could never remember a song past the twelfth note. Polijn could do better than that, and one day she would leave the city of Malbeth and teach those dukes and duchesses about real music.

The music stopped. Something was jingling, above the sound of feet in leather-soled boots. Her slide-whistle was cached and her body stretching forward before she knew it. Those boots and that jingle meant possible profit.

The sound approached. Squinting, she could make out the man producing it, or at least the man's face, a pale white rectangle surrounded by swirling dark hair. The rain and mist seemed to part before deep, black eyes, making his face the only clear thing in the frigid fog. The rest of him was buried in a huge, black cloak. That cloak also marked him as a money customer.

Polijn slid farther forward. A splinter poked up through the thin shawl, and she jumped to the right. The tabletop moved with her. Polijn jerked away in surprise, destroying all chance of the tabletop balancing itself again. She landed in a puddle of mud and garbage. The slide-whistle bounced out into the alley.

Unstartled, and not even breaking stride, the cloaked man stooped in one smooth arc to pluck the whistle from the mud. "Yours?" he asked, extending it toward Polijn.

She rose to her knees, slapping her dress back down over her hips. Nodding, she reached for the instrument.

The man released it. "Are you available, oh infant of the evening?" he inquired.

The slide-whistle was quickly secreted, Polijn nodded again, the right thumb going to her mouth. The man did not appear to notice this. He put a hand under her nearest elbow and pulled her to her feet. "Come along, then."

He set off with a long stride and no apparent interest in accommodating Polijn's shorter legs. By moving at a half-run, she was able to keep up. This occupied her mind until she spotted Balwen's place and realized they were hurrying west.

"Where . . ." she panted, "are we going?"

"To my palatial chambers, of course," said the man, his voice a drawling sneer at the question. "To the Gilded Fly."

Polijn's heart was already pounding from the run, but this quickened it. Her mother had warned her never to go to the Gilded Fly; in fact, never to go near anyone who was in the habit of going to the Gilded Fly. During the recent killings, her mother had advised, when Ronar wasn't listening, that she ask customers if they had ever heard of the Gilded Fly, and, if they said yes, to find some excuse for walking away fast. And Polijn's mother was no coward, as anyone who had seen her act at the Yellow Dog could testify.

They rounded a corner and passed Denbover's, the shop that marked the farthest west Polijn had ever been. Somewhere among the half-fallen hovels ahead was the most thoroughly venomous, evil tavern in a city that held more pits of iniquity than pigeons. All her memories of brutality and near-tragedy swirled together into one lumpy fantasy of what was waiting for her in the fog.

She lost all control of her body. It tore from the man's grip and turned east. She had not thought of running. She didn't think of it now. She just ran, kicking off her cheap sandals for better traction on wet stones.

She tripped, passing Denbover's, and something just missed her left ankle, striking the pavement with a clatter. She didn't look down to see how close it had come. She wanted distance.

The man didn't shout. Strange: everybody shouted. Polijn thought she heard him say, "Perhaps a chaperone." And then he whistled. That almost made her turn around, a queer whistle, with melody in it. Hard to believe anyone who could whistle that way would hurt her. But Polijn was too old to cherish illusions about her customers, particularly those who lived at the Gilded Fly.

No footsteps came pounding behind her. That was also odd, but she didn't look back to check. Hard enough to keep running as it was, nearly falling at every fourth step as frozen feet kicked into irregular holes full of icy water. The man had already shown her he had a long stride. She'd need every advantage if she meant to escape.

The sign of Viglos's apothecary shop dangled from one ring, and she remembered his broken stairs. She dove for the opening, missed it in the dark, and cracked wood with her head. Her hand scraped along the splintered steps, finding the hole. She pulled herself inside, trying without much success to avoid any more splinters. Last year, she thought, she'd have cleared them easily.

Polijn crouched in the corner that could not be seen from the hole, gulping air to resupply painfully empty lungs. A pair of boots or a hairy head ought to have appeared at the hole, but neither did. At length, something did materialize out of the fog, but that was only a damp, draggled lump of fur. It spied Polijn and yowled something not readily translatable.

Polijn's reply was something like a gasp and something like a laugh. She held out two fingers.

The kitten stepped forward cautiously, shaking out each paw as it was lifted. "Come on," whispered Polijn. The animal eased up, accepting the attention as Polijn caressed a little water from its fur.

She could hear her sister now, saying, "Oh, you'll take in anything that's puny and miserable. I think it's some kind of self-pity."

"Oh!" she said, when the soaking bundle leaped into her lap. Her hand slid across the wet fur. "We night-walkers . . ."

She jerked her hand away from the cat. For it was cat now, no kitten, and growing by the second. Polijn tried to push the animal away, and then tried to pull herself out from under. The weight of the now dog-sized creature pinned her against the rough wall. A paw landed on each of Polijn's shoulders. The muzzle opened to meow sounds that became the words, "Will you relax?" as the cat melted into a human being.

II

THE woman was a bit taller than Polijn, and wore clothes even less suited to the weather. A strip of something here and a strip of something there: she could have been one of the dancers from the Horn of Drok. She certainly had the muscles for it.

"Really," said the woman, her only other movement an occasional adjustment of the arms to cancel Polijn's struggles, "we're nice people. Ask our friends."

She backed toward the tear in the wood, pulling Polijn with her. "Here!" she cried to the street.

The pale face of Polijn's customer appeared in the gap almost immediately. "Skbook?" it said.

Polijn doubled her efforts to break free. This was not noticed. The woman spun her around, so the man could gather up kicking ankles. Rain, now mixed with sleet, pelted her twisting body as they hauled her into the open. Her shift gathered up under her arms as she tried to at least avoid the splinters in the steps.

Her scream, more a matter of habit than of hope that someone would notice, was stillborn. Thick, heavy cloth surrounded her face. "Why," Polijn heard the man ask, "must they always do this the hard way?"

"I'd say it was your personality," answered the woman. "If you had any."

Curling, contorting, Polijn found the thick cape on every side. Her arms were pinned above her head and her feet were ingeniously tangled as they lifted her. From the slant, she could tell the man still had her feet and the woman her hands. The woman slipped now and again, letting Polijn's fingers, which stuck free of the cape, scrape on wet paving stones. It was Polijn's only experience of the world outside the cloth cocoon. As her hands numbed, she ceased to notice it.

She had also stopped struggling. No point trying to escape. She couldn't, for one thing, and she was so low on breath she couldn't run far if she did. And it was warm and humid here. She hadn't been so warm since summer. Her mind began to sway away from the holes someone had poked between Kronja's ribs and into the peace of sleep.

Kronja leaped back into mind as the slant of the bundle sharpened. This must be the Gilded Fly now, and stairs. Nightmares and forebodings returned, but, unable to run, Polijn had begun to think. Let them assume she was unconscious until they unwrapped her. Then she'd see.

The bundle was lowered to a hard, flat surface. Someone shouted, "Hype!"

There was a jerk. Sight and sound burst in on her as she spun free of the cloth, rolling across slick wood. A mildewed tapestry saved her from a cracked head as she skidded to a stop against the wall. Grabbing the cloth, she tried to steady the room around her.

"Long time no see," said a voice. "Where HAVE you been keeping yourself?"

The man stood across the room from her, hanging onto the voluminous cape. As Polijn's eyes came into focus, he yanked the cape into the air so that it fell around the small woman, burying her in its folds. Without glancing at the woman, he stepped to the center of the room.

Polijn didn't want to move. She wanted to wait until the room and her stomach agreed on their relative positions and stayed put. But as the man moved forward, she found her legs and forced them to act in unison. Using the tapestry for support, she pulled herself upright, her dress dropping back down over her damp body. No one complained about this.

The man came no farther than the center of the room. He wore an odd assortment of sixth-hand clothes, each an alarming, clashing, shade of brown. His face was no less unlikely indoors than out, particularly now that amusement flickered across all his features, and burned in the black marble eyes.

Polijn, born and raised in the Swamp, was careful to make only slow, noncontroversial movements. She bent to smooth out wrinkles in her shift, attending to this with more care than the rag deserved. Her eyes down, she nonetheless used them to study the room around her. It was bigger than the one Ronar rented; the rich could afford space. The floor was cluttered with large objects, which might be furniture, and small objects, which might be anything. The air was cluttered with the aroma of very bad cooking. The only thing out of place in this vast array of garbage was the glass in the window. Polijn had seen only five windows with glass, in the Swamp, and this was the first unbroken . . .

The window.

The man read her mind without any difficulty, and strolled, in a firm but casual way, to lounge between Polijn and the window. In doing so, he made a vague movement toward his vest. Polijn stopped pretending to fumble with her dress. Light from a lamp caught on metal in the man's hand.

Polijn took four giant steps back without asking permission. Her shoulder hit a doorknob. Her hands went to it, even as she decided it was surely locked.

The man stepped in at her, his hand free of the vest and the shaft of shining metal angled in at Polijn's chest. "You dropped this," he said, raising the slide-whistle, "during your headlong and entirely unwarranted flight."

The door Polijn had backed into now came open, and the woman walked in. Polijn hadn't noticed that the little woman was missing. With one hand, she took Polijn by the shoulder and forced their unwilling guest into the center of the room. With the other hand, she pushed a large, hot mug between Polijn's chilled fingers. Polijn eyed it dubiously.

"Have a seat," the man ordered, setting a lamp down on a five-legged table. "Have a couple. They don't all work."

Released, Polijn slid away to a chair with its back against the wall. She doubted even the walls at the Gilded Fly, but it was the best she could do. She let her weight down gingerly on the front of the seat, leaning toward the steaming mug as her fingers thawed painfully.

"Very good," said the man, dropping onto a large, elaborate tree stump. The woman seated herself on a malleable leather bag. "I," the man went on, "am the Vielfrass. Yes, I see this information renders you speechless."

Polijn nodded. She hadn't caught her breath yet. But, having been trained in diplomacy, she thought it best not to mention that she had never heard of the Vielfrass.

"I should perhaps state at the outset of our conference that I do not kidnap young ladies plying their ancient trade and cut them into easily portable pieces," he went on. He waved one long hand through the air. "How devastating it is to have to mention this!"

"Pooh," said the small woman, waggling her feet at him. "You like talking about it."

"Silence, faithful floozy, or I'll stab you cross-eyed," ordered the Vielfrass, not looking at her. "I have solicited your presence for an entirely different purpose. No. Take the thumb out of your mouth, drink your wine, and keep your ears active."

He pointed the slide-whistle at her again, and his bushy eyebrows crowded toward his round black eyes. "You," he said, "can get a job. You can be useful to several people at once. A friend of mine has need of a servant. I wish to place a spy in my friend's household. Perhaps the current of the conversation is not entirely a mystery to you."

Polijn didn't need all her fingers to count to five. "Why me?" she squeaked. She swallowed and started over. "Why not the, er, lady?"

"The what?" said the Vielfrass, looking confused. A slipper flopped against the back of his head. "Oh, the supernatural strumpet. Would you have me send mine own boon companion on a mission of peril? I never, infant, fish with a golden hook unless I'm sure the fish is worth it."

"A golden hook," sighed the woman, putting her chin down on her wrists. "You'd miss me, eh?"

"Not especially," the man replied. "But training replacements is so tedious."

"Why do you need a spy?" Polijn inquired further, taking a sip of wine.

"Why, small one," answered the unusual man, "I don't see that this is any of your business. A friend of this friend is a particularly revolting sorcerer, and would infallibly learn it if you had some plot in mind. If I don't tell you what you're doing, though, he can't find it out from you."

"That," replied Polijn, forgetting where she was and at whose mercy, "is crazy."

"That's the Vielfrass," replied the little woman, pointing her chin at the man on the stump.

"How would I know . . ."

"When you hear it," said the Vielfrass, trying to balance the slide-whistle on one finger. "You may hear nothing, in which case you'll simply have an indoor job, with winter coming on. And I predict a real pobble-freezer of a season."

This was the first sensible thing the man had said so far, but it did not really seem to weigh as much as the rest of the conversation.

"There are other details I will give you once you have said yes," the man went on. "You can say yes, I think? I imagine that some evenings it forms the whole of your conversation." He leaned forward. "What do you say, oh child whose mouth turns down at the ends?"

She looked into his eyes and saw nothing more encouraging than glittering madness. "I . . . I . . . don't know," she said, not sure whether it would be more dangerous to accept or refuse. "I'll have to ask my mother."

The Vielfrass sat back and raised crowding eyebrows. "You have a mother," he said, in wonder. "Well, go and ask her, little one." He raised the slide-whistle. "This shall be held hostage against your return. I will give it back whether your answer is yes or not. No one can say the Vielfrass isn't fair."

"What about me?" his partner demanded.

The Vielfrass stood and moved to the window. His voice seemed to come from far away. "Run along and slip into something more comfortable. A vat of boiling honey will do."

Polijn, though obviously dismissed, did not rise from her chair. She drained the mug first and then, encouraged by the heat in her chest, said, "I can't walk back alone." She said this quickly, to be done with it sooner. It went against her training, which was never to state a fear or a weakness.

"Hmmmm?" inquired the Vielfrass, not turning around.

"I can't walk alone through this part of the Swamp," Polijn admitted. "My mother said there . . ."

"Out there, child," said the Vielfrass, raising a hand to the window, "beyond the dirty walls of this dirty city, there are green fields, in which live bunnies. All around the countryside, infant, there are bunnies and bunnies. Those bunnies live in holes in the ground, without locks, and without doors. Predators get some of them, and others die of disease. And yet bunnies do not spend all their days in fear."

His voice rose as he went on. "In this city, there are rapers and murderists and other gentlemen and ladies of undecorative habits. Some are weak and some are strong; all are dangerous. But," he continued, lowering his voice an octave, "they will always be outnumbered by the bunnies."

Utter silence followed this. The Vielfrass turned to face the stares of both Polijn and the little woman. He licked his lips. "I perceive that philosophy is not your strong suit."

His hand slipped inside his vest again. This time he brought out a large round medallion on a shiny chain. He dropped the chain around Polijn's neck. "Here, child. While you wear this, you are not alone."

Polijn lifted the heavy talisman. On both sides she saw a circle crossed by a squiggle, and nothing else. The Vielfrass walked past her and unlocked the door. "I will, however, escort you to the door of this particular bin of iniquity. I know where the loose floorboards are, and you do not. Medallions are worth very little in such situations."

He bowed, and gestured for Polijn to precede him. She did so, keeping her face to him at all times. She had not lived with Ronar all these years without learning something.

The Vielfrass followed, closed the door, and set a hand on her shoulder. He kept it there all the way downstairs and to the door. Polijn saw little more of the fabled degeneracy of the Gilded Fly than she had on her way in. People drew back into the shadows as the Vielfrass passed. She couldn't blame them.

Outside the broken swinging door, on the sagging porch, the Vielfrass bowed again, tipping a hat he wasn't wearing, and then disappeared back into the inn, singing, "Sometimes I feel like a zorfleless plod."

III

POLIJN could see the docks from where she stood. She turned away from them, toward the east, and safety. A bulky woman wearing bladed wristbands was standing on the porch. Polijn took three steps to the left and ducked her head in deference, to go around. The woman took one step to the right, blocking her path.

Polijn did not change expression. North was nice, and she turned to the stairs that descended in that direction. On the top step was a man with a drooping mustache that looked as if it had bled across his upper lip. He was smiling up into the foggy sky. Polijn didn't even try to get around him.

She considered the west: she could walk toward the river just a little. Two men lounged along the wall there, cleaning their nails with long knives. Polijn knew all about that. Nobody in the Swamp cleaned his nails just to have clean nails.

She backed against the rotted swinging door, but it wouldn't swing. Looking up, she found three women who had come up behind it. Breathing faster, Polijn turned slowly to consider all directions. Now five men and six women formed the circle, casually reclining against this or that part of the Gilded Fly's decayed frame. The woman with polished cuffs was whispering, apparently to herself, about some method of rape Polijn had never even heard of.

The Vielfrass's medallion was inside her shift. Slowly, with great caution, she slid a hand to the chain. "Knife?" snickered a woman. "Use mine!" A dagger two feet long splocked into the aged wood between Polijn's big toes.

To her left, a man caught the sheen of gold and reached out to snatch up the talisman. His fingers didn't quite brush the surface. He leaped backward, dropping off the porch and out of sight as he hissed, "Vielfrass!"

Nonchalance went suddenly out of style. Two men got thirsty and pushed past Polijn into the Gilded Fly; the three women at the door had already vanished. The woman Polijn had seen first was newly alert, and spoke out loud. "That was, uh, a joke," she said. "Like to scare people. We never, uh, really, you know, um, do anything." Then she collapsed, her wristlets screeching against each other as she landed.

Polijn was impressed, but not convinced. This meant only that some people who hung around the Gilded Fly thought the Vielfrass was tougher than they were. Farther from the building, she might meet someone who wasn't sure.

So she kept to the middle of the streets as much of the way back as possible. The medallion gave off a little glow, enough to pierce the fog, and she held it high, trying to pick out the right path through the maze of streets and alleys. She couldn't ask directions, even if she'd been inclined to trust anybody. The few people she saw gave her room, no matter what else was occupying their attention.

Moving in a general easterly direction, she took bearings from the symbols and signs scratched on walls. She tucked the medallion away when she saw the stretched-neck insignia that marked the territory of the Long Haulers. This was getting to be home ground. Before long she had reached the Yellow Dog.

Polijn checked the street. There was no one to the left or right, but she could hear a good crowd inside. The show would be starting soon. She scratched at the wood below the iron lock. "Zhriacar!" she called, in a low, penetrating voice.

The door eased open enough to allow a hefty bale of a man to peer out and down. "Aw, klutsch," he said, seeing Polijn. "Go away, kid. The rain's keeping the Swampers uptown, and she's a ewe-dragon with her tail on fire tonight."

Polijn had never seen Karlikartis in any other mood. The woman's irrational prejudice against mother-daughter acts was what kept Polijn working outside in the weather. Karlikartis had forbidden Polijn to so much as exist within ten yards of the Yellow Dog.

"I just want to talk to her for a minute," Polijn told the doorman. "If the show hasn't started yet. It's important."

Zhriacar glanced back over his shoulder. "I can't . . . Wait. Make it quick. Glor, it's the kid."

Gloraida was in costume, and walked gingerly to the door so as not to displace any of the white ruffles on her gown. Real Silmariȅn lace was both rare and fragile, particularly those bits that made it to the Swamp, and Karlikartis had promised extra shows and double duty to anyone who broke so much as one delicate loop.

Behind her, the horse and pigs were being herded onstage, so there was very little time to go before the show began. This was not Gloraida's main concern as she confronted her dark, dripping daughter.

"Get out," she ordered, stopping three yards from Polijn so the skirts wouldn't be dampened. "Harliis was here tonight and upped the payment. She's got pepper in it tonight."

"But there's something . . ." Polijn began.

It sounded like a tree limb cracking. Gloraida ducked. Zhriacar cursed and grabbed his right ear. Once these were out of the way, Karlikartis had a clear shot at her main objective. Polijn was already moving, but had never yet been fast enough. A line of fire seared across her left thigh.

She thought about the Vielfrass's amulet, but decided immediate escape was more to the point. There were limits even to magic. As she scrambled away, almost on all fours, Zhriacar fell, still clutching his ear, against the door, slamming it shut on the braided leather of his employer's weapon. Polijn used this donation of time to skid around the corner and up the street. At the first alley, she ducked into shelter, stopping to catch her breath and listen for sounds of pursuit.

Too close to showtime, she decided; no one came for her. She sat on the tumbling stairway at Kyche's until she had all her breath. Then she used it up in a sigh. That left only Ronar.

She sloshed up the alley and down the street until she came again to the Thick Fleece. He'd be here if he was anywhere. With one shoulder she pushed the heavy door aside. She elbowed a path past the great tub filled with clay mugs. Murrisch was just behind this, and his eye fell on her immediately, but he made no move to have her removed. The Thick Fleece was too full of customers; he would have had to work to get through the crowd.

Polijn gave him no reason to eject her, not stopping to accept any invitations as she pushed through the damp, shouting crowd. She was looking for a particular tousled head, expecting to find it back somewhere at a table nearest the kegs. So intent on heads, she forgot to notice legs. One slipped into her path.

There was a general laugh as she sprawled out on the soaked wooden floor, and someone emptied the dregs from his mug onto exposed thighs. She rolled over and sat up. The owner of the intruding leg scowled at her.

"What're you doing here?"

"Ronar," she said, rising to her knees. "I . . . I have to ask you something."

"Eru save me, she has to ask me something," he told no one in particular, raising bony hands toward the ceiling. "Ask."

"Not here," she said, glancing toward the stairs.

Ronar produced four of his favorite obscenities and a blasphemy, and reached down to take her left wrist. He pulled this to the stairs, pausing only to smile reconciliation at Murrisch. He was behind in his rent. Murrisch grunted, and Ronar bowed his head before bouncing Polijn up the stairs.

He did not let go of the small wrist until he was in the room, and he did so then only because he needed both hands to box Polijn's ears.

"Now ask," he ordered.

Breathless, she began, "There was this guy . . ."

"There's supposed to be." Ronar found the only chair and sat on it.

"He wants me to do something for him."

"Nothing new to that, either." Humming, Ronar found a long, thin rod behind his chair and slid it onto his knees.

Polijn hunched her shoulders, but went on. "It might take a couple weeks. Or more."

Ronar stopped humming. "That's new," he admitted. He crossed his legs. "What's he want and what's he paying?"

Polijn explained as best she could. Ronar's face was non-committal, a bad sign, and he started humming again. The more she said, the more the story sounded to her like a dream, or, worse, a fantasy improvised so she could sneak in out of the rain. And not even as good as some of the stories she actually had made up. Long before she finished, Ronar had picked up the rod and begun to whip it back and forth across a table leg.

When her voice finally trailed away, he smiled, and rolled the rod between his fingertips. "Erumegard," thought Polijn, and closed her eyes.

But Ronar wasn't quite ready yet. "That does seem just a little lintik overripe, doen't it?" he inquired amiably. "Even to you? Doesn't it?" He stood up.

Polijn had a sudden snap of inspiration. "The Vielfrass," she said. "He said he was the Vielfrass, and he gave me this." She yanked the medallion from under her shift.

Ronar reached for it, but, like the man at the Gilded Fly, jerked his hand away before he touched it. He also dropped the rod. Polijn saw his face go pale as he bounced backward into the chair and raised his hands.

"You do anything the Vielfrass tells you," he said. His voice cracked. "Tell him whatever he wants to know. Er, did you mention my name?"

He perked up when she shook her head. "Good." He cleared his throat. "Um, no, the Vielfrass and me are old friends! Yeah. Trust him like you would me. Um. Yeah, he's a good man, the Vielfrass: the best. Just don't, uh, mention my name. In fact, if you meet me on the street, don't talk to me. Ever. He might be watching; you never know."

"Would he?" she asked. "Who is he?"

"You can't tell," said Ronar. He picked up the rod and tossed it onto the table. "That, er, nice young woman, Oozola, that works with him? Seen her, little woman, yeah? She's a shapeshifter. She could be a dog, or a leaf, or even this chair. Trust her, too: a real lady, she is." He rose from the chair as though afraid it might really be the woman.

"Um," he said, looking back over at Polijn. "So long. Don't make them wait."

Polijn moved to the stairs just a half-step ahead of the hands pushing her. She thought she heard "And don't come back" as the door thumped shut.

She stepped slowly down to the common room and pushed outside. It was easier to get out than in, perhaps because the Vielfrass's medallion was now hanging in clear view. The room seemed quieter now, too. Polijn didn't really notice. It was several minutes before she noticed she was outside, in the rain, headed west. She stopped. Had she been doing it unconsciously, of her own will, or was the medallion pulling her along?

She shrugged and resumed her pace. There was no decision to make now. At the Thick Fleece she would find a closed door, and Ronar, behind it, telling her to do whatever the Vielfrass asked. She would get worse at the Yellow Dog. She hoped Karlikartis wouldn't improvise anything tonight, just because she'd been there.

A bat flopped by. Did bats fly in the rain? This late in the fall? She'd never paid much attention. It might be a hibernating animal startled awake. But was it Oozola, the shapeshifter?

She found the Gilded Fly, with the medallion's assistance or not. Mistrusting the silence and darkness behind the broken door, she paused, her toes in a puddle of frigid mud.

"Have a nice walk?" inquired the Vielfrass, coming out of the shadows like a grey ghost.

Polijn was startled by the heat of the rage that bubbled in her throat, and had to choke it back before she could say, "All right. I'll try."

The Vielfrass pushed the swinging door to one side. "Fine," he said. He put out a hand. Polijn removed the heavy medallion, not entirely without regret, and dropped it into his palm. The Vielfrass set the chain and amulet inside his vest and brought out something else.

Polijn had reached to take it before she realized it was not her slide-whistle.

IV

SHE jumped back. "What?"

It was a long silver flute. Having seen flutes before, Polijn knew they were not, in the accepted meaning of the word, weapons, so she took a tentative step forward. The Vielfrass shook the flute, as if he intended her to take it.

"You . . . this . . ." she stammered. "It's not my . . . this is expensive."

He set the flute in her right hand and folded the fingers around it. Then he took her shoulder and escorted her inside to the same rubbish room she'd seen before. He pushed her at a chair.

"Sit down, small fry," he said. "We have smalls to fry. Listen to pearls of perfected wisdom from the oyster of genius."

Polijn sat down. The Vielfrass did not. "I heard music," he said, "from an alley. Or what passes for music in the alleys of our garden city. You will work for one Ynygyn, a minstrel. He uses a number of instruments and knows many tunes, but his specialty is the flute. Can you play a flute?"

She goggled at him. "I've seen people play flutes."

"How's it done?"

She ran a finger along the shiny surface, assuring the flute that, given her choice, she would not soil it with her lips. Then she said, "You twist up your mouth like this and blow over the hole." She set actions to the words. A low, clear note quavered from the instrument. Polijn nearly slid off the chair.

"Nice start," said the Vielfrass. "We'll make a silk purse out of you yet. Now. You will work for Ynygyn. You will not play for him. You will not mention that you own a flute or a slide-whistle." He took this second instrument from his vest and set it on her lap. Her hands still stroked the flute.

"You will not so much as hint that you can even hum. He is expecting a peasant clod; you will be one. But you will take this flute and, in your spare time, if any, you will find the most hidden hidey-hole, the most secluded cranny, a place where he can never find you, and practice your flute-playing."

This made no sense to Polijn and, rather to her surprise, she said so.

"I have faith, me," said the Vielfrass, splaying a hand on his vest. "You will hide in order for him to find you. If you tell Ynygyn that you have a flute, he will have you tossed out on your ear, probably from the highest tower. Presumptuous scullery-slut, to mention your ridiculous music to him! And more, much much more, arrogant remarks of a like nature. But he has a hearing ear. You hide, and he will find you. That will make you his discovery. How clever of him to have seen a musician in such a pitiful specimen! And you will have demonstrated a becoming humility suited to your lowly station. Beyond this, I guarantee nothing. He may be interested enough to try to make a minstrel of you; he may not. But you will be in a position to listen to what goes on around him; he will most likely show you off to his friends. What do you think? Don't be afraid to say it's genius; I won't hit you."

Polijn felt the whole business was very iffy, but did not say so. The man had just given her a flute. "Scullery-slut" did bother her some; scullery work was hard labor.

"What would I have to do, working for him?"

"Light housekeeping," he said, shrugging. "Menial, but not taxing. He has a valet to mind his clothes, and he eats with the others. But he doesn't trust his patron's servants, and is hiring a few of his own. You may be shamefully overworked during the day, and it's always possible that he may have other duties for you by night. But I don't think that will trouble you much, hmmm?"

Polijn didn't think so. As he had said, it would at least be indoor work and to work indoors, without kneeling, was one of her great dreams. "But you aren't going to tell me what I'm supposed to be spying for?"

"No," he said. "It might prejudice your ears. Keep in mind, child, that very often, and, in my case, always, what appears to be idle eccentricity is really the mark of an inhumanly clever mind. Just do what I tell you, infant. You've heard that before, I suppose. Ronar is your business manager, isn't he?"

"I . . ."

"Never mind, never mind. Beside the point. I knew it when I saw you out in the rain. Now, what are you going to do?"

Polijn wasn't sure what he wanted. "I don't know."

The Vielfrass shook his head. "If you were really a musician, you'd have better ears. Listen this time. You will do whatever Ynygyn wants. In your spare time, you will go into hiding and practice this flute. Is this difficult? Is this a source of pain? Is it going to be less fun than standing in the rain sucking your thumb? You should be paying me for this, whereas all I ask is that you keep an ear open for anything not quite right and square while you do your daily do."

Polijn nodded. "How do I report it to you? Will you be there?"

"Ah!" cried the Vielfrass, both hands shooting into the air. "The little persimmon shows signs of higher intelligence. You do not report to me, thank you very much for mentioning it. You will take your information to a woman called Nimnestl. Oh, you know her?"

He had moved behind her, so Polijn had to twist her head around back. "I've heard of one."

"There is just one in Malbeth," he said. "Met her?"

"But," Polijn objected, "she's the King's . . ."

"Chief Bodyguard to the King and general errand girl for the Regent," he said, obviously enjoying himself. "Then you do know her."

Futile fury burned through Polijn again, pushing prudence aside. "Of course not! She lives in the Palace Royal!"

"So does Ynygyn," the Vielfrass told her. "So will you. Don't look like that; your face will freeze that way. Then you won't be able to play the flute, I'll have to get someone else, and Ronar will rent out your head as a birdhouse. If you don't know Nimnestl, then, I'll have her call on you some time. I'll pass the word to Kaftus."

Polijn was now risking dislocation of the jaw. "Kaftus! You . . . you know the Regent?"

"Oh, I sometimes drop over to chat when I'm slumming," admitted the Vielfrass. "I have no idea why I get no respect until I mention this. It just shows that it's not your personal magnificence that counts, but whom you know. If you're ready, then, let's go."

"Where?" asked Polijn, as her brain spun.

"My child," said the Vielfrass, with weary exasperation, "if I have to repeat one more thing that I have hitherto made perfectly clear, I shall assuredly beat you. To the Palace Royal."

The prospect was unnerving enough without the suggested beating. At the height of Malbeth, on four hills, rose the Palace Royal, home for centuries of the ruling family of Rossacotta. To Polijn, and to other inhabitants of the Swamp, it was an abode of dread to rival even the Gilded Fly. Terrors tangible, in the guards and officials who sometimes penetrated the Swamp in search of a specific offender, lurked there, as did terrors intangible, with all the storied horrors conjured by the necromancer Kaftus. But the castle was older even than Kaftus, and everyone knew that within the walls crawled ghosts of horrible, aged secrets.

Polijn knew now she was to be sent into great danger; she recalled, suddenly, that she was in danger now. But the Vielfrass had already donned that huge travelling cloak, and was gesturing to the door. Polijn slipped the flute and the slide-whistle back into the hidden pocket in her shift, and followed him.

She moved as if she were dreaming, or just sitting somewhere else watching Polijn move. Or perhaps it was just distant memory: there she was again, in the wet streets, running to keep up with the long strides of the man in the rich cape. The only difference was that now it was darker. Night was fully fallen, the weather was worse, and the lights in the better inns were being extinguished.

They were nowhere near the Palace Royal when the Vielfrass came to a halt. Polijn sidestepped a grimy pool and looked up at him. The strange sorcerer was studying the black sky. "I wonder what chance there is of snow, this early," he mused. "Come here."

To her surprise, he led her to the Yellow Dog. The show was obviously nearly over, because half a dozen large sedan chairs and their heavily armed bearers waited by the big door. The Yellow Dog frequently saw customers from the more respectable parts of town, and such visitors like to take their precautions. Many had their own chair-bearers call for them. Polijn saw none of these; this crowd was all free-lancers, hoping for a large commission. This was as far west, though, as such men came, and even though they could obviously travel only in groups and were thus relatively safe from attack, they held large knives and hammers for defense.

The Vielfrass raised one hand in summons, and a plain brown chair was brought to him at once. The bearers looked dubious, but his cape and boots won them over. In silence, the Vielfrass checked inside the chair for roof leaks, and then motioned Polijn up ahead of him.

"This is easier on the feet," he told her. "And, in some parts of this blurry city, a better way to travel."

The thick, hard seat was dusty but even so, Polijn hesitated before settling her own dripping person on it. The Vielfrass showed no such doubts. "Down, child, down. It's a rule I live by: do not stand while the coach is in motion."

This made no sense to Polijn, but she was getting used to that. She plopped onto the cushion just as the lead bearer peered through the door. "Where, Master?" the man asked.

The Vielfrass looked across at Polijn and nodded toward the man. Realizing what he wanted, Polijn ordered, "To . . . to the Palace Royal." She bit back a laugh to hear herself say it.

The bearer stood where he was. "You heard?" demanded the Vielfrass.

"Yes, Master," said the bearer. "I . . ."

"Then move," suggested that bizarre gentleman.

The bearer shrugged and disappeared around front. "You can't get good help any more," the Vielfrass confided to Polijn, as they were picked up. Polijn nearly released a giggle. Things had become increasingly unreal.

The chair and its contents moved eastward up a sloping road. The Vielfrass told an absurd story about bunnies and oatmeal. Polijn passed the time by not listening. She watched out the window for bits of the city that showed through the fog. Architecture was the key to location in the city of Malbeth. The main style up here was massive: squat boxes with thick stone walls designed to offer no grip, with windows few, narrow, and barred. Doors were set back into walls, so callers could be observed through any of a dozen peepholes before the door was unfastened. Each home was a little fort.

What must it be like to live safe behind such walls? Things were different in the Swamp. You knew your door would be broken down, so why spend money on a good one? Wood made the houses and doors in the Swamp; it was plentiful and easily replaced. Wood did not reappear in Malbeth until you passed this fortressed neighborhood and reached the richest part of the city. Here were more windows, with more ornate bars, and even balconies. The rich could have long, gaudy houses that attracted attention; they could afford private armies to repel any attention that became intrusive.

Polijn didn't admire these nearly so much; they didn't look safe. Then came another zone of massive stone boxes, and then a few streets littered with frail wooden shacks. Then there was nothing; they were nearing the first outer wall of the Palace Royal.

Once they had passed this low barrier, the main castle could be seen as a huge shadow against the sky, another stone box, master and ancestor of all lesser copies. Everyone in the Swamp could have been housed in the gigantic gatehouse; some officials at court would have considered this a good idea.

The drawbridge was down. Polijn had never seen it up. A few ancient crones in the Swamp could, if in the proper mood and required state of saturation, recall the blood and fire of the last civil war, when the bridge had been raised.

The great gate at the end of the wooden bridge was locked at dusk. The bearers halted at the near end.

"Forward, forward," ordered the Vielfrass.

"The gate is closed, Master," called the lead bearer.

"I wondered why it looked closed," mused the sorcerer, "and then I thought to myself, 'Perhaps it is closed.' Thank you for solving this for me. Forward, now, and stop when you reach this closed gate."

There came a heavy sigh, and three lesser sighs, and the bearers moved ahead. They could predict that they and their intoxicated customers were going to be whipped from the gate by castle guards. Polijn wondered about that, too.

As they neared the gate, though, the Vielfrass jumped from the chair, his cape swirling around to slap Polijn above the eyes. He strode to a small guardhouse and spoke in a low voice to the guard on duty. The door to the little sentrybox opened.

The Vielfrass returned and extended a hand to Polijn. "You'll wait," he told the bearers.

The lead bearer said nothing. He was impressed.

Polijn jumped down and followed the Vielfrass to the door. They passed a castle guard, his oak leaf badge shining on his gold-grey tunic. Polijn had seen the man before, but did not mention it. She had visited the Palace Royal just three times before, drumming up business in the courtyard on holidays. The fees, however, that this guard and his companions charged to allow this had finally risen beyond the reach of Ronar's never very expandable pocket.

The Vielfrass led her through a low, dark passage, lit only by a pair of torches, and then up a steep, narrow staircase. The wind whipped at their ears as they emerged in the main courtyard.

The vast field was empty, huge and terrifying to Polijn, who had seen it only when it was packed with people. Her world was one of alleys so narrow that Ronar, standing in the middle, could touch the walls on opposite sides at the same time. She shrank back, a reaction to the courtyard as much as to the two men who were stepping across it: soldiers, no doubt, with the power of arrest.

She was just recalling her most recent brush with prison when a new hand slapped down on her shoulder. "Is this the one, then?" a voice boomed.

V

POLIJN turned automatically under the hand and twisted away in the direction of the stairs. The Vielfrass interposed a leg, pushing his knee up into her stomach for added stopping power.

"Good evening, Aesernius," he said.

"Hardly," replied a caped, hooded man. "Shall we go inside?"

"Can't stay," the Vielfrass replied, turning Polijn toward the newcomer. "Left an alligator on the fire. Just dropping off the merchandise. How's tricks? Nimnestl well, I hope?"

The other man snorted. "She grows more regal every day," he said, his voice lower. "Next she'll be demanding to be borne in a litter."

The Vielfrass shrugged. "Most cats are."

The second man's laugh was cut short by a quick glance over the shoulder. "I'd be careful, brother," he told the Vielfrass. "She doesn't like jokes being made at her expense."

"No expense," drawled the Vielfrass. "Perfectly free."

"Most cats are," said Aesernius. "I like that. It was an unlucky day for Rossacotta when that black cat crossed our path."

"Of all the people to be superstitious," sighed the Vielfrass. "Well, I must get back before the building boils over. Child, this is Aesernius, Ynygyn's confidant. You may trust him as you would me, that is to say, not at all." He stepped toward the passage, but looked back. "You know where to find me if there's any question?"

"Yes," said the other man.

"Fine," answered the Vielfrass. "I won't be there."

As he moved off, the cape flailed up again, snapping at the backs of Polijn's legs just where Karlikartis's lash had left its mark. Polijn was inclined to believe this was intentional, but before she could think much about it, Aesernius had taken possession of her shoulder again.

"Let's be in, girl," he said. "The Vielfrass can love this weather, but I cannot. There is more than a little strange about my brother sorcerer. He expects to be Regent one day, I think. The wise do not get entangled in his schemes."

Polijn had reached that conclusion already. Aesernius ushered her toward a door and into the main building complex of the Palace Royal. She had never been inside before, but she'd heard all about it. Obviously, the people she'd heard all about it from had never been inside either. Where were the stacks of gold and silver? Where were the stately villains in silks? All she saw was a grimy stone floor, running with half an inch of water near the door, and a lot of muddy footprints farther along. She shrugged, too sensible to be disappointed. Surely no one stacked their gold and silver by the door.

"Ah," said the man. "Much better." He threw back his hood to reveal a face like a good-natured skull. Bright eyes hung back in deep sockets, and his skin was tight and pale. But laugh lines bunched around the eyes, and dimples hid under the ends of his mustache. His hair looked too sleek, too blue-black to be quite real, but that could have been from the rain.

"Personally, I think everyone tolerates him in hopes of getting to the Lady Oozola," he went on. "Why she tolerates him, I couldn't say, but they do tell me you can't tell how far a rabbit will jump by the length of his ears."

This watered version of an old Swamp saw was incongruous in this setting, and Polijn smiled. Aesernius smiled back. "Let's keep moving. Ynygyn will have a fire in his rooms to chase out the damp. How did you get involved with the Vielfrass, young one?"

"I don't know," said Polijn, in perfect truth.

Aesernius laughed. If nothing else, he was a good-natured soul.

He led Polijn up a winding staircase. Polijn counted the landings they passed; she might need to know the way out in a hurry. At the third landing, Aesernius turned away from the stairs and moved into a corridor. He knocked at the first door he reached. There was no answer, but he took the handle and lifted it.

The room behind the door was small, but more heavily furnished than any Polijn had ever seen. On every side she saw ornate chairs and small tables. A fire burned in a small hole in the wall at the far end. She saw no sign of the promised minstrel.

"Yes, Aesernius?" demanded a low, smooth voice.

She realized that all these chairs faced the center of the room, where sat a massive wooden block. A long, thin hand dangled from the right side of it, showing that it, too, was a chair.

Aesernius ushered her inside and closed the door. "This is the one the Vielfrass suggested. From the Swamp. I find nothing in her worries but old plots and a vague fear that we'll find out what she's been up to lately. Harmless."

"Hardly harmless, in the Swamp." The hand flipped over, palm up, and one finger rose to beckon. "Here, please."

Polijn followed Aesernius around the massive seat. A slim blond man slouched in the hollow of it. His face was ageless, bland: he could have been twenty or sixty. The features were cold, cut from marble. It was not a face that could show affection, or rage, or any of the warmer passions.

"A thick-fingered clod like the rest, I suppose," he was saying. "Not much difference among them. This is it?" Pale blue eyes pierced Polijn's body. The man's eyebrows rose, but just a little, not the grotesque grimace of the Vielfrass. "But no," he said, his gaze fixing on her hands. "You must have noble relatives."

Polijn shrugged. Thin lips rose at the ends. "And you have been in service before?"

"Yes, sir," said Polijn. "I . . . I worked for the Paryice. For two years."

Ynygyn's eyebrows rose a little higher. A small army of

collectors from the Ministry of Taxes had overrun the castle of that bandit chieftain some years earlier, revealing massive amounts of hoarded treasure. To judge by just that portion that was actually turned over to the Royal Treasury, the whole hoard had been enormous, and the Paryice was known as an easy spender.

"Not recently," said Ynygyn.

"Four years ago," Polijn replied.

"Ah," answered Ynygyn. "You are . . . nine?"

"Eleven," Polijn told him.

Ynygyn did not respond to this. Those cold eyes ran up and down her body again. When his hand moved, she jumped.

"Have you anything better to wear than that rag?"

"Oh . . ." she said. "I . . . not . . ."

In a burst of exertion, the man raised both his hands and clapped twice. A thick man with a solemn manner but a turned-up nose stepped into the room from a door on their right. He stepped noiselessly, but Ynygyn seemed to know when he reached the chair.

"Imidis," said the minstrel. "You see what Aesernius has brought us. We will be using it. Find her something to wear. Blue, I think. No green to it. Just blue. Not too long."

The servant bowed and stepped away. Polijn watched him go, wondering how so large a man could move so silently, but was recalled by Ynygyn's voice.

"Your duties are easily outlined," he said. "The floors, walls, ceilings, and furniture: keep them clean. The palace servants are fools, individually and collectively. You do not look like a fool. If this proves to be correct, and you can do as you are told, you will be paid. If you prove to be a fool, a thief, or, in short, like nine-tenths of the population of this nation, you will be expelled in poor condition. Like Jurafta, you will 'howl when the wind touches your skin and cry aloud when a glance bruises your cheek.' Sleep where you will, so it is out of my way. I prefer not to see my servants at all, and if I do see them, I prefer to see them working. Sleep where you are well concealed. I must come and go at all hours, and would be grieved if I stepped on a fool in the dark. If I need you, which I doubt, I will call for you. You have a name?"

"Polijn, sir," she told him.

"It will do," Ynygyn replied. "A marked improvement over

'Girl!', which is . . . ah, Imidis. Yes, that will do. And a blanket. How clever of you to think of it. I have remarked what a wonder you are. So clever. Perhaps you can show her a place to sleep. You, Polijn: sleep."

"But I'm . . ." Polijn began.

"I expect you to be working early in the morning," he told her, closing his eyes. "And silently, as I sleep late. Go away." He waved one finger toward the door. "Aesernius, did you have speech with the Vielfrass?"

Polijn looked up at Imidis, who nodded at the door. She tried to walk as silently as he did. The room he showed her was dark, but he lit no light. "Here," he said, tapping the top of a wooden floor cabinet attached to the wall.

He had left the door open, and enough light came from the next room to show Polijn a door in the cabinet. She knelt to slide it open. The cabinet was empty but for a flat mattress slightly thicker than the blanket Imidis held. The man handed the blanket and the blue shift down to her.

"The last girl slept here."

"Oh," said Polijn. "Er, thank you." Imidis did not move. Polijn could think of nothing to do but crawl into the cabinet.

"You'll start cleaning here in the morning," said the servant. "If he didn't say so, you'd better know enough not to touch anything hanging on the walls here. The last girl did. She doesn't work."

Polijn realized that was the whole sentence when he closed the cabinet door. She wondered what was hanging on the walls.

Nothing was to be heard from outside the cabinet. Deciding that she'd probably continue to hear nothing, she stripped off her drenched shift before it could soak the mattress. The slide-whistle plopped out onto the mattress but the flute, sliding after it, hit the door.

The door was opened by Imidis. Polijn snatched up the blanket, as if in modesty, covering the instruments. "He wants it quiet," said the servant.

"Sorry," said Polijn, knowing this would be the only warning. "I'll be careful." She made as if to throw her wet shift down toward her feet, but Imidis took it from her hand. "Er, thanks," she said. He didn't take the thanks. The door was shut again.

Polijn tucked the flute and the slide-whistle under the mattress for the night. Later she'd find a better hiding place. She rolled the new shift under her head and arranged the blanket around thawing feet. It had been little more than eight hours since she had been pushed out of bed by Ronar, and she didn't expect much sleep.

But it had been a cold, bewildering evening. Exhausted by confusion, warmed by the blanket, she was asleep in minutes. Fortunately for her job security, Polijn did not snore.

After years of twilight existence, it seemed horribly unnatural to be required to rise, eat, and work with the sun still in the east. Imidis made it clear, however, that her regular habits were no concern of his. He was to see that she worked, and was prepared to back the schedule Ynygyn decreed by force. He did not demonstrate any force this morning, though whether this was a matter of consideration or fear of waking Ynygyn, Polijn did not waste time worrying. Having already made observations about the man's size and physique, she made no complaints.

When she had finished her bread and cheese, he brought her a pail and a rag, and suggested that she begin by washing away the mud she'd tracked in last night, and why not scrub the whole floor while she was at it. Polijn was inclined to regard this suggestion as law.

Enough light poked in around the tapestries over the windows for her to see that this room was a kind of study. A bookpress stood in one corner, and hooks on all the walls held stringed instruments and drums. A rack of flutes and a few other instruments sat on the cabinet in which she had slept. She saw no slide-whistles.

The room was perfectly silent, unnatural to someone who lived among the screams and alarms of the Swamp. Imidis had disappeared after further suggesting that she wash her feet before starting on the floor, and Ynygyn was still abed, apparently. If there was anyone else in the Palace Royal, Polijn heard nothing that let her know it.

In an hour, she managed to dampen the entire floor. She had no experience in floor-scrubbing, and had no idea whether she was doing a good job. She straightened up when she heard a soft footfall, and turned to receive Imidis's orders.

But it was Ynygyn who entered the room. He did not appear

to see Polijn, but strode directly to a table where a rolled sheet of paper and pot of ink sat. He slid into a chair, took a pen from a nearby stand, and unrolled the paper, his quick, purposeful actions a marked contrast to his languorous lounging the night before.

A movement at the door caught Polijn's attention. Imidis was there, jerking his head toward the next room. Polijn nodded and rose, lifting the pail carefully so that no clink or slosh would alert the minstrel.

"Good," said Imidis, in an undertone, as he closed the door. "Now in here."

With some dismay, Polijn studied the footprints of Aesernius, as well as those of her own feet, covering most of the floor. Before she could decide where to begin, however, there was a thump at the door.

Imidis strode to the door, but it flew open before he got there. Into the room stalked the tallest, most massively muscled woman Polijn had ever seen, even among the bouncers down at the Broken Halter. The huge, dark woman filled the doorway, adding to her mass with a quantity of dark leather armor. At her belt hung a long hammer, and around her throat she wore a high leather neck-guard.

Imidis made a token protest and then stepped aside as she came in. She stopped a few yards inside the door and glared at Polijn.

"What," she demanded, "are you doing here?"

CHAPTER TWO

Nimnestl

I

FOR its age, it was the smallest, most bloodless creature Nimnestl had ever seen, even among the slaveys in the scullery. It wore a thin blue shift which was perhaps long enough for decency when it stood up, and, above this, a face of utter terror.

"What," Nimnestl demanded, though she knew, "are you doing here?"

Ynygyn answered, leaning on the door that led into his study. "Must you inquire into the affairs of every menial in the Palace Royal? What is it: an ingrained tendency to pry or simple nostalgia?"

Nimnestl did not mention her true admiration for Ynygyn's ability to come up with a rude comeback for any occasion. "There is, Minstrel, a law," she told him. "Just a little law, but a law, nonetheless, and it requires residents to bring new servants to the authorities for questioning. I am surprised that anyone of such renowned memory should have let it slip his mind."

The minstrel's face grew blander. Nimnestl thought sometimes that one day it would become so smooth and expressionless that it would slide right off his head. "One would have thought, my darling, that one in my position would be exempt."

Milk and honey poured from his voice, but it went down the wrong way. Nimnestl's hand fell to the hammer hanging at her belt. “One could suppose that,” she said, her voice matching his for unconcern. “Could one also suppose that one has something in particular one wishes to have done with one’s remains?”

Ynygyn sighed a gentle sigh of genteel oppression and beckoned to his new servant. She gave Nimnestl a glance of uncertainty and rose to join him. The minstrel stooped and, pointing up at the Chief Bodyguard, whispered in a trained whisper that could be heard in the corridor outside. “This is Nimnestl, child. She watches us all as we sleep. Go with her. She will ask you questions. Answer them. Tell her the truth. Lies upset her, poor thing. She was not raised, you see, to court life.”

“Not at a white court,” Nimnestl replied amiably, “The ode for the King’s Birthday is complete by now, I suppose?”

Ynygyn straightened, but his face and voice lost only a small part of their nonchalance. “Coming, my darling, coming. You know the difficulty of finding rhymes for the barbaric names of his companions and bodyguards.”

Nimnestl decided to concede the game; she didn’t really have time. Turning, she strode from the room, the idea that the girl might possibly fail to follow her never entering her mind. What was the Vielfrass up to? Did the Vielfrass himself know what he was up to? She did not condemn all sorcerers and magic-mongers to perdition; she had done it so often that there was no fun to it any more.

She turned in at a room similar to Ynygyn’s study. It was her “office” but served primarily as a symbol of rank. Considerable personal sway was required to draw a suite of rooms for one’s private use, and the Head Bodyguard could not do without this mark of status. That she was seldom actually in the rooms, and used them primarily for storage, was irrelevant.

Nimnestl waited for the girl to enter, and shoved the door shut. She hunted for a chair, and found one near a table stacked with dented scabbards. Even seated, she wasn’t low enough to look the girl straight in the face.

She tried to modulate her voice to make up for this. “You’re Polijn, are you?” she asked.

“Yes, Ma’am,” said the girl. She did not move from the spot where she’d stood when Nimnestl closed the door.

"Who sent you?"

Terror increased in the girl's eyes. "The . . . the Vielfrass, Ma'am."

Nimnestl nodded. "Very good." The thin shoulders seemed to unbunch. "Now, did he tell you why?" She tapped one forefinger on the table.

Polijn's eyes went to that finger. "N-no, Ma'am."

The fingertapping turned into the thump of a heavy fist. Three scabbards bounced to the floor. "Lintik blast the man! Didn't he even give you a hint?"

Thin shoulders hit the door as if the girl was trying to melt back through it. Nimnestl clamped her teeth together and ground her fist against the table. Closing her eyes, she took a long breath.

"Here," she said. She stood up and swept aside a rack of quarterstaves that concealed another chair. "I won't hurt you, girl. Not today, at least. Sit down."

Nimnestl returned to her own seat, putting the table between herself and the chair she had cleared. She hoped the girl could see over the top of the table. Polijn inched her way across and perched on the front edge of the seat. Nimnestl had an urge to snap her fingers, just to see what happened.

Instead, she said, "All right. What did the Vielfrass tell you?"

"Just . . ." She had to stop and breathe before going on. "Just to listen and report to you, Ma'am."

"He didn't say anything about what you were to listen for?" asked Nimnestl. "Or give you an idea whether there was some person you were supposed to watch, particularly?"

"No, Ma'am," said the girl.

Nimnestl didn't care to be ma'amed quite so much, but she preferred it to being miladied or my darlinged. "Very well," she said. "Go back to Ynygyn now. I don't need to ask you not to mention anything we've said."

The girl shook her head; she was obviously in the grip of acute awe. "If anything comes of it," the Head Bodyguard went on, "you can find me by coming here. You remember the way? Two flights up, the door to the left. If I'm not here, wait. There's a spell on the rooms, and the Regent will know. He will either come to you or bring you to him."

Nimnestl thought for a moment that the girl would collapse. Reassurance, however, would spoil the healthy state of terrified respect, so she said no more, rising to open the door instead. Polijn came right behind her, but paused, uncertain, as Nimnestl held the door open.

"Out," ordered the Bodyguard.

The girl jumped to comply, nearly tripping up a man who was striding to the stairs. "What's this?" demanded Aesernius, pulling up short. "Ah, good day to you, Milady Bodyguard. And is it . . . yes, Ynygyn's new cleaning girl, Polijn. Shall I escort her back, as long as I'm pointed in that direction? Let's go by way of the Great Hall, shall we? I'll show you the Banner of Kairor. Never too early for the young to learn about the heroes of old."

The sorcerer pushed Polijn ahead of him to the stairs, producing a continuous stream of chatter. Nimnestl wondered how anyone could be so obvious and still feel he was fooling somebody. When he judged himself to be out of earshot (he was wrong), he paused to tell Polijn, "I hope she didn't terrify you too much. We've had another big killing, and she's young and jumpy. In the end, it'll turn out to be what the little boy shot at. Er, what did she want with you?"

"She asked what part of the Swamp I was from," Nimnestl heard the breathy voice reply. "I said east. That'll be all right, won't it?"

Nimnestl nodded. The lie had fallen readily and smoothly from those thin lips. Of course, they were born to it, in the Swamp, but the child might have her uses, if the Vielfrass was on a true scent. Among the few people in the Palace Royal that Nimnestl might have been inclined to trust, Ynygyn was foremost. The minstrel was insolent, but he was insolent to everyone alike. He was not known to have ever involved himself in any of the castle's sexual intrigues, and had never shown any interest in politics beyond what he needed for his acid satires. The satires were what had raised him to his position as one of the King's three Chief Minstrels; fear of those had served him as sex and politics served others.

Nimnestl locked the door of the room, but stood where she was, waiting for the footsteps echoing in the stairwell. This time it was General Ferrapec, with three or four of his soldiers. His errand was apparently farther down the hall, but he turned aside when he saw the Head Bodyguard. Nimnestl grimaced; she had rehearsed the impending conversation six times and still didn't like it.

Ferrapec had begun as a young man of leisure, living off the money his father took from his uncle and passing time hanging around prisons offering his services to female prisoners hoping to get a lighter sentence through a plea of pregnancy. He joined the Army on the reputations of his father and uncle, and made his own by wooing his commanding officer's wife. Promotion and popularity came his way when it was discovered he was sleeping with the man's mistress as well.

Now, grey and fiftyish, he was second in command to Gensamar, commander of the companies stationed in the city. He had abandoned the image of wild womanizer (without quite abandoning the womanizing) in favor of a more dignified persona. It was concerning a matter of his dignity and reputation that he wished to question Nimnestl.

"Bodyguard," he said, striding up to her, "I must have a word with you. You have been asking the servants questions about my uncle."

"Yes," said Nimnestl, her voice neutral but not encouraging.

"Tell me why. Arnastobh was an ancient man and doddering; when he spoke at all it was about the dear old days when the pines were draped with gold and the firs hung with silver. It was past time for him to go: his mind wandered and his joints were swollen double with age."

"They were swollen more than that when I saw him, General," Nimnestl said, breaking into what sounded like a rehearsed speech, "and they were turning purple. It was not age, but poison, and no very subtle poison, either. Any case of poisoning in the Palace Royal is my concern."

"Why?" Ferrapec demanded. "He was dying in any case. The investigation is unnecessary, of no interest."

This was the wrong thing to say to Nimnestl about the death of Arnastobh, Count of Bonti, hero of Kairor. He had secured the northern border from the rebels of oh-one, crushed a major insurrection in Malbeth itself, and had been one of the chief architects of the city that rose from the rubble of the war. Now a forgotten man, his achievements taken for granted or claimed by others, he had fought to the end. When the pain forced him to bed, contradicting his determination to die standing up, he had forbidden his granddaughter to undress him or even take his boots off. Only the granddaughter and the Head Bodyguard had been present when the end came.

"It may seem unnecessary," she replied. "It must be of interest, however, to the new Count of Bonti, and his son. No man is so great but that the vultures, at least, are glad when he dies."

Ferrapec was inclined to take offense at this proverb. His hand dropped to his dagger. Nimnestl's was already on her hammer. Ferrapec's personal bodyguard braced for action.

"You are offensive," spat Ferrapec, thin nose rising.

"We are both offensive, General, but I have to work at it and you can't help it." The hammer was unhooked now from the belt.

Ferrapec sneered and, whirling, moved down the stairs. Nimnestl watched him go, exuding triumph for the benefit of the men who followed him. Inside, she felt only relief. In fact, she was exceeding the bounds of her office by asking questions about Arnastobh. Her only real duties were to investigate such matters as had a direct and demonstrable bearing on the security of the King. If Ferrapec chose to question her activities, and the other generals backed him, she could be forced to call off her investigation, which would not only allow the murderer to get away with it, but strike a blow at the prestige of the government.

She had wanted to keep Kaftus out of it, but she'd better go see him now, before Ferrapec accosted him, too. Not that the Regent was likely to listen to him, any more than he listened to anyone. But if Ferrapec made enough noise, Kaftus might order her to cease and desist simply to remove the cause of the nuisance.

She took the stairs down to the next level and turned toward the central section of the keep. Where the corridor broadened, five men tussled, one being throttled, and two others banging a third's head on the floor. Nimnestl's eyes skimmed over the brawlers, checking first for any of her own men. Any members of the Royal Bodyguard wasting their time this way would find themselves patrolling the beach. Then she looked for knives unsheathed; security as a whole would suffer if any guards were seriously damaged.

Seeing nothing worthy of comment, she passed on without a word. But the five men had pulled back on recognizing the Head Bodyguard, and a fight interrupted would probably collapse. Inevitably, a similar one would break out elsewhere. Brawls were continuous in the Palace Royal, where the heads of the main branches of government met and schemed and wrangled. If the masters couldn't get along, who was going to keep their dogs in line?

There were more armed men in the Palace Royal than in any other spot in the country, perhaps in the world. Besides the men of the regular army, there was the palace guard, marked by its oak leaf badge, and the more elite King's Bodyguard, with its silver pine branch. Both were under Nimnestl's command, and each had some excuse for existence.

There was an excuse for the Treasury Guard, too, but not for the number of men enrolled in it, beyond aggrandizement of the Lord Treasurers. There were almost as many armed Tax Collectors, who, as the government had been organized, were not commanded by the Lord Treasurers but by the First Minister. Few of these men actually collected tax, and speculations on the fate of what they did collect was always a good way to start a brawl, particularly if a treasury guard did the speculating.

Even the housekeeping staff had its private army. Forokell, First Housekeeper, controlled not only supply, cooking, and cleaning, but also all skilled labor in the Palace Royal, from doctors and minstrels to torturers and dungeon guards. These last existed in large numbers and were often idle, as were the surplus treasury guards and tax collectors.

There could hardly be a better breeding ground for turmoil, for even within divisions of government there were differences, as generals vied for control of the army and ministers sent their bodyguards after their rivals. Within limits (it did result in an appalling turnover rate), Nimnestl approved. As long as the Lord High Treasurer and the First Housekeeper and the rest were busy with infighting, they could not combine to attack their common foe: Kaftus, the Regent, with his "black dog" Nimnestl. And as long as Kaftus and Nimnestl existed, Forokell and Ferrapec could command what and whom they wished. They would not command the King or the kingdom.

II

EVERY person in the Palace Royal knew the words blazoned on the wood of the Regent's main door. Their meaning was taught to the illiterate within an hour of their arrival. Anyone who forgot received a second lesson from Kaftus. No one who survived that forgot again.

STOP
Ask Yourself Four Times If You Should
Disturb Him, Five Times If You Would
Risk His Wrath

Like many sorcerers, Kaftus required privacy. And he could afford to have it. In theory, as in practice, he was the greatest power in Rossacotta, perhaps in this corner of the continent. He had been powerful enough in his bizarre, secluded castle away to the north. Then Queen Kata had declared he would be Regent if she should die while her son was underage. She had known she would die too soon; it was that kind of job. She had selected Kaftus on the basis of his power, rather than for any other good points. Kaftus had no other good points.

Nimnestl knocked twice and then pushed the door open with one foot. A bat hissed a warning, as it always did.

Apples sat in a plain silver bowl near the door; it was Kaftus's only concession to sanity. Next to the bowl, a skull wore a tasselled headdress, while below the table a human hand reached from a spiny seashell. The rest of the suite was filled with ornate objects of gold, human hair, ivory, silver, and materials about which Nimnestl wanted to know nothing. All that was lacking was taste.

Kaftus stood at a bookpress next to the shadow of a black cat. He turned when he heard heavy footsteps, and looked into Nimnestl's face; he was one of four or five men in the Palace Royal who could do that without tipping his head back. He was long, thin, and deceptively ancient. It seemed that a single slap would have sent his withered grey body flying into flinders. Nimnestl had tried something like that when they first met. It hadn't worked.

"Well?" he demanded.

"Nothing. Just that she was to listen and report to us. Or so she says."

The necromancer turned back to the book he was examining. "It will do. The Vielfrass is . . . Trustworthy isn't the word. But he is on the King's side, insofar as he is on anyone's."

Nimnestl preferred a predictable enemy to an erratic ally. "Couldn't it be a plot? On his own side?"

"The Vielfrass doesn't plot," said Kaftus, his mind really on the book. "He wanders, he ambles, he meanders. To plot would be to pick out what he wants and walk straight at it; he can't do that."

The Chief Bodyguard shrugged. "You're the necromancer. Isn't there some way you could read his mind, or check the omens, or some such? A hint would do. And he might know something about Arnastobh."

Kaftus turned the page and flicked away a small spiderdragon that had crawled from the binding. "You," he said, not looking up, "are like a little dog who has chased a rat into a hole. You will sit by that hole even though the rat raced out the other side of the wall hours ago. The man's food was poisoned. No one went near his food but the woman who cooked it and the girl who served it. If you'd let the torturers do what we pay them for . . ."

"No," Nimnestl broke in. "I'd rather work on it myself." She had meant to ease into it, but there it was.

Kaftus shrugged. "As you will," he said. "Remember, you have sometimes failed to find the guilty party. The torturers have never failed."

"That's because I insist on getting the right one," Nimnestl replied. She sat down in a polished wooden chair, bypassing one of bone. She had known the original owner of the bones, and though she hadn't much liked him, she still felt uneasy about sitting in his remains.

"Arual and her mother had no reason to kill the old man," she told Kaftus. "But Jintabh did, and Ferrapec, and even Kodva. There may be some other old enemy we know nothing about."

"He may have done it himself," suggested the necromancer, flipping back two pages. "He was old and tired, as men judge old and tired. Maybe he got too tired and decided to quit. Think about it."

Nimnestl thought about it. "Life," Arnastobh had said to her not many weeks before. "Life's a great mug of cold beer on a hot day. Mine's nearly empty, and not a barman in sight to refill it." And, just a week ago, laughing outrageously at one of his own outrageous stories, he had banged both gnarled fists on the table and gasped, "Eru, I LIKE being alive!"

"No," said Nimnestl. "He didn't do it. And he was afraid of someone. He always had that dagger by him, with a hand at it if anybody came near, even when he ate."

"I know a number of people who keep knives by them while they eat," the necromancer told her, smoothing a wrinkle in the page.

"Oatmeal?"

"Maybe he thought he could ward off death if he saw it first." Holding one hand on the book, Kaftus reached out another for a skull under the nearest table. "Some men do, toward the end. There's hardly anyone else in the castle old enough to care whether he lived or otherwise."

That was true enough. They had cared in oh-one, when he came back waving the torn Banner of Kairor. Nimnestl remembered sitting with Arual in the old man's room high in the tower, hearing the story four, five, six, who knew how many times.

"Were many of you killed?" Arual would ask.

Arnastobh would raise bushy eyebrows, still veined with black hair, but he would take her youth into consideration and reply, "Of course. That's why they cheered us."

"How many did you kill?" his granddaughter would ask next.

"Well," Arnastobh would say, stroking a chin invariably coated with thin white stubble, "I was fair. I killed as many of them as they did of me."

Nimnestl always liked that, but Arual thought it smacked of nonheroism. "Did you win the battle?" she'd persist. "You, the leader, I mean."

"Me personally?" the old man would say. "Why, that I couldn't say, now that I've heard all the songs. But I do know that if we'd lost, I'd've gotten the blame."

They would all laugh and Arnastobh would forget, for a while, that he couldn't walk from his bed to the table without a shoulder to lean on. With an audience around him, he was again bold and undefeated, his legs still strong, his eyesight clear, his hearing acute.

At fifteen he had entered the army, becoming an officer on his grandfather's reputation. For five years he did little more than attract the loathing of his commanding officer. One evening, hearing rumors of a rebel force massing at Kairor, on the northern border, he had forged his grandfather's seal to a series of orders and taken a company of his friends up to see. His commander declared the whole band outlaws, but news trickled south of a hideous battle. News continued to trickle, but neither rebels nor Arnastobh's company came with it. A sharp, martial song mourned the heroic last stand of Arnastobh, and the massacre of his men.

The song was still around, despite the fact that Arnastobh turned up six months later, with over half the men who had been presumed massacred. There was no sense, everyone said, in cutting down a perfectly good song simply because it wasn't true.

But the rebellion had been well planned, and hardly anyone believed Arnastobh when he declared the traitors at Kairor were just a ripple of the larger stream. His commander made noises about the forgery, and there might have been trouble and even disgrace for the hero had Theybal not decided to launch his coup early despite the losses at Kairor. Arnastobh was instrumental in securing the Palace Royal in the face of Theybal's assault, as well as in salvaging what remained of Malbeth after the holocaust.

He was chosen to help redesign the city, and the Swamp had been one of his ideas. "You will never rid Rossacottans of rascality in one generation," he said. "The best thing to do for it is march all the biggest rascals into one district, where they can practice their arts on each other, leaving us to deal with the aristocratic rascals in the Palace Royal."

At twenty-four he was one of the mightiest men in the country. No longer one of the daring young men who forged orders to run off to battle, he had become one of the officers charged with catching and punishing such men. From a world of amiable scheming and easy camaraderie, he had risen to the murky heights of intrigue and power. He had withered a little in the shade.

The great shadow was the discovery that Jintabh, his brother, was plotting to overthrow him. The wound never healed, though Arnastobh, refusing to retaliate, had turned over to Jintabh his lands, his income, his office, and even Kodva, his wife. What Jintabh wanted were Arnastobh's rank and title and repute, and these were not in the older man's power to give. Jintabh had rank of his own, having made an heroic stand at Southgate during Theybal's Rebellion, but only now that Arnastobh was dead could he revel in the title.

"There were still people who wanted him dead," Nimnestl told Kaftus. "Jintabh might be too old, or even Kodva, but Ferrapec would care about the title, since it comes to him next."

"Only Arual and her mother came near the food," said the necromancer, his voice sharp with impatience. He checked the book again. "I've confiscated some of Maitena's keys."

Nimnestl's jaw dropped. "Took her keys? You might as well accuse her openly. In fact, it would be better. Now you've got one more ranking Council member who hates you."

"Pity," Kaftus replied, tracing some design on the skull with his little finger. "If she goes to the scaffold for murder, she can hate me as much as she wishes. If not, I still have the keys."

Maitena's personal prestige, her life, was wrapped up with those keys. They indicated both power and rank. And Maitena was not a forgiving person. She had never spoken to her father once she learned he had given away her mother to conciliate her uncle. But she had allowed Arnastobh to speak with his granddaughters, particularly Arual, the youngest.

Maitena always prepared her father's meals personally, though no one ever dared ask why she'd feed him if she wouldn't talk to him. Arual always carried the tray up. The day the old man was poisoned, she had met Jintabh, Elgona, Frowys, and Hopoli on the way. Each had confided to Nimnestl that Arual had been hiding something under the tray. Elgona had been in too much of a hurry to see what it was; the others found excuses to rush away when the girl asked for help carrying the food. Arual had certainly known that none of the three would have helped her in any case. Her uncle Jintabh despised her, while Hopoli and Frowys were just too important to be bothered. It was an obvious ruse to keep them at a distance.

Worse, one of Ferrapec's silver spurs had been found in Arnastobh's room. Ferrapec had his spurs made to his own design, and this was unmistakably his. It was also unmistakably one of a pair that had been stolen a week earlier, and Ferrapec had been out all that day anyhow, inspecting guard houses at Southgate. And what would Ferrapec have been doing in his uncle's room anyhow, after forty years or more of neglect?

The clumsy attempt to attach blame to Ferrapec pointed more than Kaftus's finger at Maitena. The contest was close, but no one hated Ferrapec more than his cousin did. The spur could easily have been carried wrapped in a napkin, under the tray.

None of this made Arual, who now sat on the straw-covered floor of a dungeon cell, guilty. Nimnestl refused to let the torturers touch her, because of that and because the eleven-year-old and her grandfather reminded Nimnestl too much of a darker eleven-year-old and grandfather farther north.

"Well, I'll find out what I can," she said, "But Ferrapec may . . ."

"Do you know, woman, how little Ferrapec interests me at all?" Kaftus demanded. "Take your little hammer and bat his head open; you may find naughty thoughts therein. I would like, if possible, to finish this research before luncheon and the attendant ceremonies. I will get little enough opportunity to work in the next thirty-six hours."

"I'd better go," Nimnestl agreed, rising. "The luncheon has been moved up an hour. Nurse insists she needs the extra time to get the King ready for the oath."

The necromancer raised his hands above his head and Nimnestl felt, rather than heard, what he was calling down on Nurse's head. None of this came to pass. It was merely an expulsion of wrath, and the only actual power exhibited was that which raised the temperature of the room.

"Are there any other changes I should have known about?" he demanded, teeth clenched.

"Oh, yes," said Nimnestl. "Someone seems to have left Arberth out of the planned entertainment. I put him back in."

Kaftus was amused, as Nimnestl had anticipated, and the room returned to its normal temperature. "When?"

"Luncheon," Nimnestl replied. "First."

"Excellent," said the necromancer. "They won't be so picky at this end of the festivities. Do you think we can convince him to sing 'The Lovesick Bull' for you?"

Nimnestl was prepared to sacrifice Arberth to mollify Kaftus, but not to join in the fun. "I'll see you at lunch," she said, and marched to the door.

III

EVERYONE who lived in the Palace Royal was entitled to eat in the Great Dining Hall. This did not mean that everyone did. It was becoming fashionable—they called it civilized—to have a fire and a meal in one's own room, with a few friends.

But on a major holiday, the yew decorations were polished, and brackets were hung with torches, lamps, and candles. And everyone entitled to dine there did so, along with many who usually were not. Courtiers who owned houses in the city and commuted to court (also "civilized," though foolhardy for anyone who aimed at real power) were present, with many of the most important merchants (some said bandits, some said both) of the city. At the other end of the social scale, beggars and pickpockets pushed in to join the crowd.

Blades glittered everywhere. Each diner carried at least one knife openly; it was the standard eating utensil. (A few had begun to pack forks, as well, but this was so far too civilized for most.) Many displayed additional knives, and it was a good bet to go along with the Rossacottan proverb that claimed, "Who carries three knives in his belt has six under his shirt." Frowys, for example, carried a dozen, but most were specialized knives, which made her the star attraction in one end of the room. Small children attending their parents drifted over to watch her carve hounds or stags from scraps of wood she carried in her purse. She had worked six months on a hunting scene with moveable figures for the King; it waited now in the Royal Reception Room with other gifts.

Each veteran diner, in anticipation of a long, varied meal, had arranged for a pot under the chair. Some had two. The King, however, would have to be whisked away early, to don his robes and regalia, so there were no such pots at the head table.

Nimnestl sat at the head table, between the King and Nurse. Kaftus sat at the King's right, obviously irritated at this interruption of his work, and declining most of the food. The King, however, ate freely and readily, despite Nurse's frequent warnings, or because of them.

The Head Bodyguard shut out the running argument between the King and Nurse, and studied the crowd. The new Count of Bonti sat not far away, wearing all the trappings of his inherited title, though he was not entitled to them until the succession was confirmed by the King. Jintabh was a fragile man, with just a little of the family looks left in the brightness of his eyes and the cleft in his chin. The last of his hair glistened in the flickering light like streaks of paint on a yellowed skull. A great choking cough threw him against the table.

"Oh, lad," he told a soldier close at hand when he had his breath, "don't ever get old. Or at least stop at seventy-two."

The young man nodded and laughed politely. With Arnastobh gone, Jintabh was the greatest of the surviving war heroes in the Palace Royal, victor and sole survivor of the battle at Southgate. His commander had resolved on a major stand against the rebels at the southern gate of the city, less to crush the revolt than to assure himself of a place in story and song. When things went wrong, only Jintabh had escaped to get help, in a dash through the blazing streets of Malbeth.

It had ever rankled Jintabh that he was remembered for running away, even for such an heroic run. The memory twisted him; he never allowed anyone to forget how rich he was, how powerful, how blessed with goods, which would not have bothered anyone in the Palace Royal, surely, except that they all knew everything he had was a gift from his brother. Songs survived from his scandalous middle age to tell of his habit of ripping away his wife's gowns at Palace celebrations, the better to show off the treasures that belonged to Jintabh and Jintabh alone.

Kodva sat near her husband, tall, straight, serene: hard to fit her into the songs. Nothing could be read in the face but calm superiority; Nimnestl never saw anything there beyond the pride of someone who has little besides her pride to be proud of. She seemed to pay no attention to her husband or her children.

Maitena was required by etiquette to sit with her mother and her stepfather/uncle. She was as silent as Kodva, but sullen, fuming. The Third High Housekeeper, she was also unofficially known as First Lord of the Kitchen. Maitena was an imposing power in her own right, as tall as her mother though less austere, with a body that implied that she had no bones at all below the neck. But there was enough hardness in her for two-thirds of the Royal Bodyguard. Only recently a stablehand, attracted by the tidy plumpness of her figure, had attempted to make known his affection in a forceful manner. The organic utensil with which he had attempted to express his emotions was found pinned to the kitchen door with the skewer Maitena had unfortunately been carrying at the time.

She wore a long white dress embroidered with gold thread, and quite civilized and striking it would have been had she not also worn an obviously antique apron over it. Maitena still lent a hand in the kitchen on major feast days, and was even frequently to be found in the kitchen when the occasion didn't call for it. Generally, upon reaching the level of High Housekeeper, a woman relied on underlings to keep her informed of work in progress and never troubled her hands with it again. But Maitena somehow enjoyed kitchen work, and until recently had cooked at least a little every day, for her father.

And for this reason she now sat glumly beside her mother, the ring of keys she had gloried in now diminished, and her youngest daughter enjoying much sparser fare several yards below ground level.

Her next youngest daughter, Einoel, was near her, waiting on her relatives and serving from trays that lesser kitchen help carried in. Einoel was even taller than her mother and grandmother, but awkward, not used yet to her own proportions. She was cute in the way a colt is cute: innocent and dependent, yet determined to stand alone. She was not so much pretty as adorably grotesque.

This was the first time she had been allowed to serve at a table so near the head table on a feast day. Naturally anxious, she tried to keep her hands moving all the time, pulling on her dress when there was nothing else for them to do. She could not see the view this offered to those behind her when she was standing, the fabric stretched tight across her backside. Nimnestl doubted she would have understood. She was being courted by at least two of the palace guards, Elgona and Borothen, but Maitena had made no commitment yet.

Attracting more attention than Einoel's stretched gown were the thin, nearly transparent wrappers worn at the table across from that graced by the Count of Bonti. These were a concession on the part of Iranen, whose servants these women were. In Iranen's service, one wore nothing at all, to save time when one was invariably found guilty of causing irritation to one's mistress, and summoned for punishment.

Harliis sat at this table, idly thrusting his eating knife at thighs and elbows as Iranen's servants waited on him. Harliis had no title, and no official identity at all, but he would have sat at the head table had not cooler heads advised against it. He had a long face and blond hair worn rather long in back and rather thin in front. Two wisps curled up like horns at each end of his forehead. There were big round eyes and a tiny nose with a tiny red V of a mouth far below it. Between nose and mouth was something that didn't look so much like a mustache as a lonely lip yearning for a mustache. For no reason Nimnestl could think of, it always reminded her of cats. Nimnestl liked cats, but she did not like Harliis at all.

Most of the inhabitants of the Palace Royal—indeed, of Malbeth—shared her opinion. He was the latest favorite of Kaftus, though, and one spoke well of the Regent's favorites, even in one's sleep. What riches and power Harliis could not get from Kaftus (and the Regent was surprisingly stingy in this respect) he gouged from anyone who would take him at his own valuation. And virtually everyone who owned a building in Malbeth also paid rent to Harliis, simply because Harliis told them to. He referred to this as a tax, and everyone in Malbeth politely called it a tax, too. They understood these taxes.

Harliis had carried his family up to power with him. His sister Hopoli, sitting next to him, was officially First Assistant to the Fourth High Housekeeper. She was more familiarly known as Hopoli Feetintheair. Palace rumor had her trying to work her way to the top as her brother had, but Nimnestl could not believe this. Hopoli indulged her tastes when and where she felt like it, without regard to political expedience. The jolly little woman was not nearly so bright or scheming as her brother. Nimnestl had nothing much against her except that she was Harliis's sister, and had a tendency to bobble. The front of her gown always stopped moving half a minute after she did.

"Like working these hours?" whispered a voice at the head table.

The whisper was not meant for Nimnestl, so she did not turn. Sliding her eyes toward the voice, however, she saw that First Lord of the Treasury Garanem had turned to chat with Elgona, one of the palace guards on duty at the table.

"They're all right, My Lord," Elgona replied.

"Odd," mused the Treasurer. "Now, almost all of the treasury guards are given time off for the King's Birthday. I find it raises morale. I worry that someday, the . . ."

"Elgona," Nimnestl called, "take up a post at the other end of the table and stop worrying Lord Garanem, will you?" Elgona grinned and moved off. He had been complimented twice, by Garanem's attempt to recruit him for the treasury guard, and the Head Bodyguard's interruption to forestall this. There was always competition for good men.

"You see?" Garanem demanded, all outraged innocence. "One can't even hold a private conversation any more without interference. That woman has her fingers in everything!"

Flact, the Minister of State, nodded. Nimnestl shrugged. "Not unlike your wife, My Lord."

Hopoli giggled, and the treasurer's wife stiffened in her seat. "What's that?" demanded Garanem.

"That's what worries me, My Lord," the bodyguard went on. "Don't those long nails occasionally do some damage?"

The First Lord Treasurer threw his chair back from the table and stormed from the hall, kicking a beggar who had had the misfortune to be in the way. Einoel ran to set the chair back up, but Elgona reached it first.

"Bedsniffing?" inquired Kaftus, leaning forward the shake his head at the Bodyguard. "I thought you were above that."

"I am," said Nimnestl. "His wife never washes her hands." By this time, Garanem's wife and several of his assistants had left the room in sympathy. Others remained, preferring to offend the treasurer rather than offend the King.

Unoffended was Garanem's father, Eldred. "Ha!" the old man exclaimed. "That's got him his own! I told him not to marry one of Ipzemadel's daughters or he'd never hear the end of it. Ha! I was wrong. That was the end right there!"

Those who could hear this laughed at it. The King joined in, not because he'd been paying attention but because it was right that everyone should laugh on his birthday. Nimnestl, struck by sudden memory, leaned forward to call down to Eldred, "You were at Kairor with Arnastobh, weren't you?"

Eldred's dislike of his daughter-in-law did not make him an adherent of Nimnestl's. "Why?"

Nimnestl shrugged. "I'd like to hear about it sometime. Nothing important." Eldred could be difficult if pressed.

"You wouldn't think it was important," the old man replied. "Just killed a bunch of brown, half-breed border guards."

The Head Bodyguard let that slip past, and shrugged again. "Well, if you don't remember, I'll ask Dahil instead."

"Dahil!" spat Eldred. "That long-legged, pixy-faced . . ." He remembered the Regent was within earshot and choked back the noun. "He never got within ten miles of Kairor! He was an outpost runner when I was second sergeant of the White Wolf! He don't know any more about that battle than . . . than Ipzemadel! Dahil! Ha!"

"Well, if you can't tell me anything . . ." Nimnestl began.

"Who said something like that?" Eldred demanded, reaching for a dagger. "Did Dahil tell you that? Listen, you come around after the Oath and I'll tell you anything anybody knows. And what Dahil tells you, you can pitch that over your left shoulder into the sewer. Dahil! I never heard . . ."

Nimnestl had heard what she wanted to hear: the invitation. She sat back in her chair, and took a drink. When she lowered her cup, a series of bells announced the beginning of the day's special program.

"Who's starting?" the First Minister asked Flact.

"Arberth, I heard, My Lord," Flact replied.

"Fine, fine," said the minister. "I like a nice nap after my meal."

Arberth was a long, lean jester with a long, lean face. Mustache and mouth drooped alike, providing a theme continued in a long, limp nose and dejected eyebrows. His divided tights, the right side black, the left in blue and white checks, were an incongruous contrast to this study in melancholy. He pushed through the gap in the lower tables, dodging the housekeepers reaching out to pat his thighs.

He tripped, of course. If he had not tripped, it would not have been Arberth. His flowered hat swirled away from his limp, colorless hair and landed in Trioafmar's soup. The act could begin with at least one laugh.

Rising to his feet, Arberth retrieved his hat and slapped it, dripping with grease, back on his head. Then he stepped up on the long central platform to begin his anticlimax. (This stage sat where the central hearth had once been. Central hearths were no longer considered civilized. Fortunately, the rash of colds had coincided with the introduction of the extremely civilized handkerchief.)

"Greetings, Your Royal Highness," said the jester, bowing to the King. His hat slopped off onto the floor. "And greetings to His Royal Regentness and to his pretty girlfriend as well." A few titters, more of thrill than amusement, rose from the crowd. It was daring to the point of foolishness to make any public reference to the Regent's private habits.

Arberth frowned. "I refer, of course, to the pale, delicate, vulnerable wisp of a girl seated by the King," he declared. "Yes, fair Nimnestl, as pale and delicate and fragile as . . ." He put one hand to his greasy forehead as he struggled for the proper comparison.

"As Kwaimor Mountain," he concluded.

The audience registered approval and pleased surprise. Arberth usually launched into endless, pointless tales of obscure people and distant lands. A good snap at the Head Bodyguard was preferable, and unprecedented.

"You know my mule kicked her once and broke both its hind legs?" the jester asked, following up on his triumph. "I was that mad I was going to beat her black and blue." A laugh he hadn't expected threw him off for a second. "Well, er, blue anyhow. But someone stopped me."

"Who would do something like that?" demanded the shrill, nasal voice that could belong only to Harliis.

"She did," Arberth sighed. The King banged his mug on the table in approval as laughter rolled through the hall.

Arberth seized his chance. "Now that we're on the subject, I'd like to tell a little story. I'd use a harp, like Ynygyn or Laisida, but how could you believe what you heard from a lyre? It goes back to the days of Ruril and Rurik, when Russ was King of Rudimin."

His epic began with the audience amusing itself in various ways. Some ate, some drank, many were passing gossip, some in dark corners were creating gossip to be passed at the next meal, and others were filling the time in their own little ways. This was to be expected. Arberth was just another attraction of the feast, like the gilded pheasant or the boiled potatoes.

As the story of Ruril and Rurik advanced, however, Arberth attracted more and more attention, all of it bad. Gossip died and eating stopped as people turned to glare at him. Each humorous sally was greeted with sullen silence. The torches and lamps even seemed to dim a little.

Unconscious of any imposition, Arberth's cracked voice wrested the story around to its climax. "And so Rurik replied, 'I can't sell those: they're too floppy!' "

He struck a dramatic pose. A full second passed before he peeked at the silent crowd. His eyes were uncertain; even he couldn't believe he had entranced them so completely. Someone yawned. He looked grateful for the sound.

"Um," he said, coming out of the pose. "How about a little song? And you minstrels keep out of it. You're always butting in, trying to tell me what key to sing in. If I could sing in one key, I wouldn't be a jester."

Without further ado, he launched into, as Nimnestl had feared, "The Lovesick Bull." Arberth's songs were, if anything, more pointless than his stories, and the little dance that accompanied them made them perfectly pathetic. It was not the kind of performance that would conciliate a Rossacottan audience. She gestured a few of her men in closer to the King. The audience would not sit still for this, and the air would be cluttered.

A gob of gravied bread started it, followed by cups, plates, potatoes, and medium rocks. Arberth held his position as long as he could; it was his job to entertain the crowd, and that included entertaining them by taking a bowlful of boiled beets in the face. But when the first knife lodged in the wood of the platform, he ducked aside, slipped when he stepped on his hat, and went for shelter headfirst.

The King applauded the dive, at least, but Nurse took advantage of the diversion to bustle him out of the built-up chair and out of the room. His Highness protested loudly, for Arberth's place was being taken by Bilibi, a less ambitious artist favored by the crowd for his ability to swallow live mice. After displaying this talent once or twice, and pulling the mice out again by the strings attached to their hind legs, he raised the intellectual level of the program further by sexually assaulting one of the statues near the door. His technique was interesting enough to make Nurse pause, and the King jumped back up into his chair.

The audience was in a good mood again. Now Ynygyn took up his lap harp and prepared to sing. Nimnestl saw a long scratch along the back of his neck. She couldn't see Ynygyn getting into a fight, and wondered if a snapping string could dig so deep. Not that there was a lack of reasons to attack him; the minstrel always performed at least one ode to the sexual practices of high court officials, describing half a dozen or so popular perversions with contempt, and sometimes breaking the news about the bedchamber habits of someone hitherto considered secretless.

It seemed he was going to begin with that selection this time; he announced a new song called "The Hunt That Never Ends" and passed a few more hints as he tightened a harpstring he had loosened beforehand. Nimnestl could not follow the opening strains because Nurse and the King were holding a whispered debate. When Nurse whispered, only the deaf could fail to hear her from sixty yards away. They had to be leaving now, and didn't anybody remember there was a ceremony this afternoon, and what if the robes weren't even set out yet, which was very likely, since last year the lazy sluts hadn't even set out the proper shoes and . . .

In her youth, according to Arnastobh, Nurse had been a woman of unusually clear complexion and calm features, the quarry of many a young buck and the subject of a popular love lyric entitled, "Cool Serenity With a Big Nose."

Only the nose remained.

The Head Bodyguard nodded to her men and joined them in their escort. Kaftus glowered as the little group moved off. He would have to stay for the entire meal.

Nimnestl's patience was long, but it had its limits. She had no choice but to stand and take it while Nurse and her equally fussy, and ancient, companions, the obscure Keepers of the Robes, attired her in the long gowns of ceremony and strapped a belt and saber around her waist. But when they started in on the King's robes and accoutrements, she gave a whistle and headed for the door.

A large black bird sped in through the window. "Where you go?"

"To check arrangements on the balcony," she told it. "You stay here."

Nimnestl strode from the room and closed the door just as the argument began over where a bird should sit in a room filled with ancient heirlooms. She shook her shoulders, trying for a more comfortable way to carry the numerous heavy garments, decided there wasn't one, and strode for the Main Balcony, which overlooked the courtyard.

She was almost there when a figure dressed half in black and half in blue and white checks darted out in front of her. "My Lady," it said, "I was coming directly to apologize for telling jokes about . . ."

"You know that's the only reason you're still alive, don't you?" Nimnestl demanded. "You should have done more of that. Instead you made a fool of yourself. It's a good thing nobody knew you were sober."

Arberth flushed. "In Gilraën, to the south, the story of Ruril and Rurik . . ."

"Is probably as popular as it is in Reangle, where, I may tell you, it is a favorite," said Nimnestl. "But we are in neither of those places, and, even if we were, it has to be told right. How did you get to be a jester, anyway?"

"I fall down a lot," Arberth said. He spread his hands out before him. "An exile must do something for his money, and I'm not the soldiering type. Why don't you marry me and take me away from all this?"

Nimnestl shuddered. The worst of the joke was that Arberth meant it; he had proposed nine times, to date, and had written "The Lovesick Bull" just for her. There were honors Nimnestl could have done without.

But she felt a certain sympathy for her fellow exile, so she just said, "Certainly not while your face is stained with beet juice. If you're trying to dye it, let me tell you that won't work. And if a drop of juice gets on these cuffs, the Keepers of the Robes will have us quartered. Go away."

The jester sighed, but saluted her as he sloshed down the hall. Nimnestl growled and tugged at her collar. It was hot.

IV

NIMNESTL put the curtain aside, letting a cold wind slap at her. She inhaled gratefully.

The crowd was fidgeting in the courtyard. It had stood in that wind for hours now. Fortunately, this was the warmest Nelvère since the civil war. Things would have been worse with snow.

From the Main Balcony, Nimnestl could see the courtyard as far as the massive gatehouse. She could make out enterprising pickpockets working the crush of spectators under the V.I.P. gallery. Near the stairs, Flact was selling seats in the gallery at horrendous prices (as good a way of ensuring exclusivity as any). Lesser thieves were at work on the corners and edges of the main crowd.

In the center of the audience was a brown mass of Ykenai, the sect which met at unknown places at unknown hours to work on a necessarily short song to be sung at the end of the world. The brown robes of the members flopped back into other members' hoods. Farther back, near the gatehouse, some mercenary soul was either auctioning or raffling off a brown-haired woman. General Gensamar also saw this. He waved an arm, and five men rode over to disperse the group. They rode with bare swords, not watching what or whom they slashed in the process. They also had been waiting in the wind.

Where Nimnestl came from, this would have started a small war. Here, men and women used to dodging for safety scuttled into any shelter available, to the delight of the pickpockets, and slid back out when the soldiers had passed.

Nimnestl let the curtain drop, not overly interested. This was what Rossacotta was, particularly in Malbeth. She ran a hand over a torch bracket in the wall, noting absently how crudely it had been made, though it was made of gold.

Rumor made Rossacotta the wealthiest nation in the world, insisting that nine-tenths of every treasure, of every hoard ever plundered, of every herd ever stolen, wound up in Rossacotta. If encouraged, rumor could go on to explain that Rossacotta was the center of all sin and depravity, handling the wholesale wickedness business for the known world. Murder was born there, said rumor, and rape had its early training in Malbeth. When other countries turned too unfriendly for thief or thug, said rumor, there was always a place in Rossacotta. The first person to steal something and then explain, "I bought it Rossacotta-style" was long dead, but his little joke was an accepted part of the language.

Rumor called Rossacotta, and Malbeth, its capital, the home of sadism and sudden death. No one who died violently in Rossacotta was so very much astonished by it, said rumor. People in Malbeth took murder the way other people took rain and slow drizzle. One could expect to die young in Rossacotta; one could bet on it. Said rumor.

And rumor was uncharacteristically accurate.

For fifteen centuries, Rossacotta's government had offered sanctuary to any knave or scapegrace who would pay a percentage of the loot in return. The rulers of Rossacotta saw little of this money. The kings and queens of Rossacotta had been allowed to exist only because the bureaucracy needed a stable royal succession to insure its own security. In grand, beautiful, windowless kennels, members of the royal family had, for a millennium, been kept in seclusion, bred like prize dogs, and displayed when ceremony required it.

The kings became kings again a century before Nimnestl's day. Escapees from the royal breeding pens had at last gathered enough of a following to topple the ancient aristocratic families who had held the ministries as personal possessions. But the power of fifteen centuries had not wholly died with the passage of one. The last major outbreak of the bureaucrats lived yet in the memories of those who had fought the battles of oh-one.

The queen who reigned in the wake of that civil war had ordered a general house-cleaning. Rossacotta reopened regular trade with its neighbors, promising long and irksome death to any who dared molest the brave merchants who ventured into the country. Merchants did come, for Rossacotta still had its reputation for being the wealthiest land on the continent, and they were glad to risk its other reputation for a shot at the hoard. Rossacottans discovered that civilization had passed them by. Queen Aleia issued hundreds of laws, doubling her efforts to make a new, well-scrubbed Rossacotta that was honest, clean, and, above all, civilized.

Sixty years had passed. It wasn't enough. Even Rossacottans from the Court in Malbeth were considered crude by the standards of such backward nations as, say, Turin. Rossacottans wore torn shirts, or no shirts at all, under cloth-of-gold capes. They picked their noses with silver spoons. They had skinned knuckles and polished nails.

They were wood that had been varnished before it was sanded. Nimnestl didn't understand any of them.

Nimnestl came from Reangle, to the north. Varnish was hereditary and ancient there. Everyone in Reangle could sing brave old epics, though few could read them. People were killed, sometimes by violence, in Reangle, but they generally died face-to-face with their attackers. Natives of Reangle, particularly those born in Nimnestl's circumstances, might be unlettered, but they had more potential for civilization than anyone in Malbeth.

Nimnestl's grandfather was a baron. This did not make her singular; ninety-odd children in the castle and surrounding countryside could claim the same relation to the same baron. This had turned to their misfortune the day Nimnestl turned eighteen. A new baron had chosen that day to take office, wading in through a swamp of noble blood. Nimnestl had been down by the river, in the smithy, at the time. She was able to escape with a large hammer, a small pack of items useful for living off the land, and a lover who carried similar supplies.

The two years that followed had been filled with rough camping and hurried moves through the countryside around Koanta. She had lost the lover, found him again, avenged her grandfather, become Baroness of Koanta in his castle, and finally lost both barony and lover in a second, more conclusive massacre. The nobleman responsible for this was dead now, too, but she had not been invited back. Her name was still inscribed on the stone that marked the boundary between Reangle and Rossacotta on Strayhorn Pass, warning that it meant death for her to cross into her native country.

Left with only her hammer, she had been skulking through the mountains on the frontier when she was reunited with the necromancer who had casually, almost accidentally, made her Baroness of Koanta. He had changed little and improved not at all, but he was on his way to Malbeth, to become Regent of Rossacotta.

Queen Kata was dead, leaving a one year-old son to become King Conan III. She had chosen Kaftus to be the barrier between this child and his adult subordinates. The Regent, requiring a few assistants on whom he could depend, picked up Nimnestl and took her along. She had no friends at the Court of Malbeth and, being a foreigner, probably never would have. He offered her the post of Head Bodyguard, and, though Nimnestl would ordinarily not have taken so much as directions from the ancient magic-monger, she accepted when he assured her that the post meant sure death within a year or so.

Eight years now, and death had so far disappointed her. But she had grown into the job for its own sake. A truce had been declared between Kaftus and the Bodyguard, each distrusting the other less than they distrusted everyone else in the Palace Royal. Kaftus did the actual ruling, making sure that the King knew as much as a boy could take in about what this involved. Nimnestl helped the King reign and tried to make sure he would live to handle the ruling as well. At all opportunities, she and the Regent had him display himself to the populace to reaffirm the fact that, yes, he was King, and his health was fine, thank you.

Today was one of those opportunities: not a major state occasion, but a national holiday. The celebration of the King's Birthday traditionally began in mid-afternoon with the Oath of the Pearl. The King went before his people to swear on the ancient and unlikely Pearl of the Adriack that he would see to it that the farmers had enough rain, the miners enough ore, the soldiers enough exercise, and so on. The ceremony took a bare fifteen minutes, and hardly one in a hundred of the crowd would actually hear it. Preparations for this had taken six hours so far, exclusive of time spent in planning and purchasing.

What was delaying the King? Nimnestl turned to go find out what Nurse had thought of to slow things down this time, but heard steps. Kaftus pushed aside a curtain and stepped into the anteroom.

"Where . . ." Nimnestl began. Then the King entered, followed by four bodyguards.

Conan III, King of Rossacotta, Lord of the Mountains and Rivers, was heavyset for a nine year-old. The thick robes really billowed him out, until he looked almost perfectly square. Glancing at the curtain in front of the balcony, he expelled a long breath. "Is there any breeze out there?"

"And then some," answered the Head Bodyguard.

The King saw her there, next to the curtain. "Oh, Nimnestl!" he called, his breath hard and fast. "Did you see all the presents? The Reception Room's almost full!"

"You peeked," she replied amiably.

"I did," he declared. "I can peek. I'm the King." Contemplation of royal perquisites occupied his mind for a second. Then, grabbing one of her thumbs for emphasis, he went on. "And there's a black horse, from Kaftus. You have to come down and look after they put the Pearl away."

Nimnestl glanced at the Regent, raising thin eyebrows. The Council had considered the matter for three weeks before deciding that the Regent would be most proper in presenting the King with a golden hunting horn.

Kaftus's eyes dared her to object. "I thought it was time. And it was not paid for out of the Treasury. This horse is on me."

"I'd like to see that," Nimnestl replied. She turned to the King and opened her mouth, but then frowned. The King frowned back.

"Haven't you brought up the Pearl yet?" she demanded.

"No," replied the monarch. "Kaftus said I didn't have to. He sent Harliis." The King wrinkled his nose. He didn't like Harliis.

No more did Nimnestl. Her eyes measured Kaftus for caskets. The Regent looked as worried about this as the tapestry on the wall. "The women were fussing with his hair again. Nurse was more excruciating even than usual. I thought it would hurry things along. I was evidently incorrect."

The tradition that the King himself must bring the Pearl from the Treasury was not very important or, historically, well observed. Nimnestl let it pass. "How long ago?"

"Some time," said the necromancer. "He must be dawdling."

Nimnestl whistled. The large raven that had been preening itself on the balcony pushed through the heavy curtains, pecked playfully at the King's sable collar in passing, and settled on Nimnestl's shoulder.

"What you want, Missy?" it inquired.

Apart from Nimnestl, Mardith was the only survivor of the old court at Koanta. As an old retainer, he was firmly attached to the service of Nimnestl, fearing nothing but his "Missy" and Kaftus.

"Go down to the Treasury," she ordered. "See what's keeping Harliis."

Mardith, glancing at Kaftus, muttered something uncomplimentary about Harliis. "Tell him that," said the Regent, who had excellent hearing. "I'll have something to say to him myself."

The bird took off and sped toward the hall. He was by now familiar with even more secret passages through the Palace Royal than was Kaftus. He would reach the Treasury before any other courier.

Nimnestl pulled off her hat and fanned the King, gently, not wanting to dislodge any hairs of the royal coiffure and set the ceremony back another hour. She would have done this even had Nurse not suddenly appeared and ordered her to be careful and did she know what she was about and please try to remember how susceptible the King was to colds.

Nimnestl's reply, fortunately perhaps, was cut off by the return of Mardith. "Come, Missy!" the bird cried. "Trouble!"

V

NIMNESTL was out of the room in seconds, one hand diving into her robes for her hammer. She could have drawn the ceremonial saber instead, but she never thought of it. The hammer was her weapon, and had been since the blood-spattered afternoon her grandfather died. Ynygyn had a song that speculated how much blood and hair had been wiped from it.

It was in her hands as she and Mardith scudded around a corner and reached the main door of the Royal Treasury. Orifel and Troan were on duty at the door, and Elgona was chatting with them. The sight of the Head Bodyguard in full regalia, braced to scatter someone across the floor, was obviously the last thing they had prepared for.

Nimnestl could see nothing amiss. "What are you doing here?" she demanded of Elgona, coming to a stop.

The guard eyed her hammer. "He with Harliis," Mardith answered. "He not know."

"Not know what?" Elgona demanded.

"Where's Harliis?" snapped the bodyguard.

Elgona's hand was on his sword now. "Inside, getting the Pearl."

"If you were sent to guard him, you were sent to be with him," she said. "Why aren't you?"

"I went in," Elgona answered, apprehension hanging on his

face. "Those were my orders. But then he ordered me out." He looked to the Treasury guards.

Elgona was well liked, and the two were prompt in coming to his defense. "We heard him," Troan agreed.

"The . . . Harliis threw something," Orifel added.

Elgona was startled by that. "Did he?"

"We saw you duck," answered Troan, "And then something hit the wall."

"I didn't see it," said the guard. "I was bowing my way out."

"How came you to leave him?" Nimnestl demanded, her hammer still ready to be raised and lowered in somebody's body.

Elgona raised both hands in the air and shook his head. "He . . . said something about ceremonies: something old and sacred that had to be done before taking up the Pearl. I wasn't fit to witness it, he said."

Nimnestl snorted. It sounded like Harliis. She knew about the ceremonies he referred to; they hadn't been used in sixty years. But Harliis was always grubbing in the old books, and liked to claim a superior education. He would want to reinstate the tradition, to show off that he knew about it. He'd tried the same thing with an ancient ceremony for swearing in palace guards. The resulting assembly was so filled with archaic grammar, obsolete words, and Harliis's own improvements that the guards had their toughest assignment just keeping their faces properly solemn.

Nimnestl had been present. When Harliis intoned, "Remember, mighty ghosts look upon us," she had added "and giggle" without even thinking. It had at least cut the ceremony short, if it had not endeared her to Harliis.

"They not know nothing, Missy," scolded Mardith, perching on the door frame. "What name you not hurry?" He shot up to the crack in the ceiling that would take him inside the Treasury.

Nimnestl, unable to go in that way, had to search a bit under her robes to find a ring of keys. She selected an ivory-colored one that was heavy with filigree, and unlocked the door.

The Treasury was dark. That was wrong, to begin with. The torches were special ones, made to last, and installed on a staggered schedule, so they wouldn't all burn down at once.

Nimnestl could not remember whether darkness was essential to the ceremony.

"Harliis!" she bellowed.

The name echoed, but there was no other answer. She took a step in, peering at bundles and boxes stacked on shelves, barely visible in the light from the hall.

"Lintik blast you, where . . . hopitok!"

She stretched forward into dark air. By rolling to one side, she avoided landing face first on an iron-bound chest. Her saber knocked over a small table, sending a cascade of large silver coins across her body. Her heavy robes caught on a casket and tore.

Nimnestl rolled until she was up on her knees. The hammer came up in the same motion. Nothing charged her.

She jabbed the weapon at the lump she'd tripped over. "What's that thing doing across the doorway?"

"Not much, Missy," croaked Mardith.

The relish in the bird's voice gave her pause. "Light!" she demanded. "Elgona, now!"

The guard rushed in holding a torch lifted from its bracket in the hall. He was reaching to help the bodyguard up when his eyes found the barrier across the doorway. His face spread open at the sight of the red halo around Harliis's head.

"Not . . . not dead?" he rasped.

"Sure enough dead," called Mardith, in glee.

Nimnestl rose slowly, her eyes on the body. Harliis was lying on his stomach, as if asleep, his head turned to the left. He had fallen into a stack of horned helmets with bulbous insect eyes of silver. Several had dropped with him on his way to the floor. The horns had been kept sharp; three had penetrated his ceremonial vestments. Other points might be concealed somewhere in his person. But they were not responsible for the dent in his skull.

A small, lumpy bag had fallen between his legs. She knelt to this and found it filled with pennyetkes, coins of little value. It might be more debris that had fallen with the helmets, or it might be the murder weapon.

She turned slowly, studying the shadows and dark hiding places among the royal treasures. Even though she knew no one could be there, she started back among the shelves to hunt. Then she stopped.

"Mardith!" she ordered. "Search! Elgona, with me."

Five chests sat on a small altar in the center of the wall to her left. From the fourth of these she brought out an ancient leather bag. She checked inside. The Pearl of Adriack, a glistening lump the size of four fists, lay quietly inside. She fitted her hammer back under her robes so as to be able to carry the bag with both hands.

"To the balcony," she ordered. If the ceremony were delayed much longer, rumors of bad omens would start to circulate, and there would be trouble. Time enough for trouble after the Oath.

CHAPTER THREE
Polijn

I

DINNER had proven to be an ordeal for Polijn. As personal servant to one of the King's High Minstrels, she had found herself seated at a low table in the Great Dining Hall, when she had expected to scrounge for scraps down in the kitchen. Not used to eating this early in the day, she had indulged sparely in bread, cheese, milk, and beer. This had added to her novelty as a new face in the Palace Royal, and she was relieved when she could sneak back to Ynygyn's suite, to sweep down the walls and change the dried moss under the windows to catch any rain that blew past the winter tapestries and loose sash.

Ynygyn was there, too, sitting in the quiet of his study and strumming a tune Polijn recognized, the tale of the great hunter and tracker Kaimon, how, seven years before Kaimon was born, his father's pigs were stolen. At fifteen, Kaimon heard about this, tracked down the pigs, and brought them home.

Polijn was glad the minstrel was there, and not just for the music. All morning, when the minstrel was out, a creeping, uneasy silence had pressed in on her ears. She felt as if she were being watched, but Imidis was not in evidence, so Polijn decided she was just nervous about doing well on her new job. Imidis might well be in hiding, watching for mistakes. He seemed the type.

Besides that, she wasn't dressed for all this stooping and stretching. The shift Imidis had handed her was thick, and well made, and it probably cost more than Ronar invested in food in a month. But it was lintik short. As Polijn heard the door open, she rose a bit and pulled the hem down. She had no objection to putting on a show, if necessary; she just preferred to know about it in advance.

Aesernius stepped into the study, and Ynygyn let his hands fall to the base of the harp. "Not watching the Oath?" drawled the minstrel. "I thought you'd be there with your fingers crossed."

"More trouble," snapped the sorcerer. "Ah, they say trouble is friendly, and never travels alone. No sooner does Arlmorin's paper go missing than . . ."

The minstrel held up a long, pale hand. "Wait."

"That's what broke the bridge." Aesernius's eyes followed a long finger pointed at Polijn. "Ah, I see. A good pair of ears can drain a thousand tongues. Run along outside, will you, child? Go watch the Oath. It hadn't quite started yet when I left."

Polijn stooped and patted another handful of dry moss into place before looking up at Ynygyn. The minstrel nodded and waved her toward the door, one corner of his mouth crooked up.

"You know how to get to the balcony?" Aesernius asked. "You won't get lost?"

She nodded, pulled her shift down again without much result, and moved out into the corridor.

Polijn would have liked to go watch the Oath of the Pearl, but decided against it. The walk down to the courtyard was not a short one and she, like the rest of the servants at her table, had been warned by Iranen not to show a face on any of the balconies "as happened last time," under pain of her displeasure. Iranen was First Assistant to the Second Chief Housekeeper, which made her displeasure worth avoiding.

One or two of the inevitable wags at the table had tried to convince Polijn that it was her duty as a new resident to go introduce herself to Lady Iranen and ask if she could be of service. Even without the gleam in their eyes, Polijn had known Iranen for a decidedly dangerous creature. As far away as the Swamp, everyone knew at least one version of the story of the court official who wore, next to her ring of keys, a cluster of severed dog heads. The usual story was of a fiancé giving her a puppy as a betrothal gift but then marrying someone else with more social value. Iranen could be seen in the Swamp herself, now and then, looking for suitable servants, and her name often came up during discussions of the mutilation murders. Iranen was a woman who bore watching, if only to keep out of her way.

Polijn came to the stairs, and took the set that went down. In time of war, she'd been told, having two flights of stairs simplified things for defenders, as did the wide central channel down the center of the tower, used for hauling boiling oil or other dainty weapons to the top. Polijn stayed in, near the wall, as she went down. The railing around the stairwell looked flimsy to her, and heights were unfamiliar. Few buildings in the Swamp rose above two stories.

Aesernius had taken her past the Great Hall on the way back from the Bodyguard's office, but not inside; there had been too much work going on. But Polijn remembered where it was, just a flight down from Ynygyn's suite, and surely it would be empty while everyone was watching the Oath of the Pearl.

At the next landing, she could tell she was on the right track. The hangings on the wall were thicker, heavier, less faded. The torch brackets were hung with gold. She stepped from the landing into the corridor, which did seem to be empty.

No. To Polijn's right, tucked onto the sill of a tall, narrow window, sat a crying woman, half-concealed by the braided edge of a tapestry. Polijn slid past, trying to avoid notice, but the woman glanced up.

"Arual!" she cried. Her hands came up, but dropped as Polijn took a step back, into the light.

"No," she said, slumping back into the sill. "I'm sorry. I thought . . . you're like my sister, a little."

Polijn did not know what to say to this. They looked at each other in silence for a moment. "Did you . . ." the woman went on, "did you ever have a sister who was . . . in trouble and no one could hel-help her?"

Polijn took another step backward as the woman plunged into a semi-liquid, incomprehensible tale of poison and prison, death and dungeons. Polijn listened, without wanting to. But she didn't know who this woman was, and didn't care to offend anyone important by just walking off.

It so happened that Polijn had had a sister. They had worked for the Paryice together, under the patronage of a supposed aunt. The work was light and the Paryice had liked them. This did not please the putative aunt, who decided to become a more distant relative. She had the girls ejected from the castle, just before the Paryice fell to royal displeasure. No one had heard since from the aunt.

Mokono had not taken the return to the Swamp well. Getting older, and near auctionable age, she began to wander from her appointed routes, north and south, as if seeking a route of escape. One day she wandered too far west, to be pinned down in an alley and raped with a broomstick. This wiped out Ronar's expected profit from the spring auction, but the damage went deeper. Brooms in the Swamp were no better made than anything else, and this had been a cast-off: broken, splintered. Pinaci the Apothecary hadn't been able to save her. He hadn't much tried. There wasn't much money, and what was Mokono to him, or Polijn, or Gloraida? A collection of warm, wet holes, of which there was no shortage in the Swamp.

Words gave way completely to sobs in the woman's speech. Who was this? What would have become of her in the Swamp? Tall, awkward, young, a little helpless-looking, she would probably have been another Ynfara, finding a protector in one of the local strongmen. Not that the protection of Treyn had been much of a blessing: Treyn took payment by alternately battering and bartering Ynfara. The woman became a symbol of stupid devotion, at least until the day she doused the dozing Treyn with oil and set him alight.

For no reason at all, Polijn thought of the Vielfrass and his homily on bunnies. Some impulse unfamiliar to her made her reach out and pat the sobbing woman's hand. At the touch, the woman leaped from her seat and, casting Polijn one look, too quick for Polijn to tell whether it was shame, anger, or gratitude, rushed for the stairs.

Polijn shrugged and licked her upper lip. Then she turned toward the corridor again, in time to bump the hip of an elderly man hobbling in the opposite direction. For a moment it seemed he must fall, but Polijn grabbed his nearest arm and pushed him into the wall, where he took hold of the fringe of the nearest tapestry to steady himself.

Once he had his equilibrium, he turned to Polijn and snapped, "Don't touch the Count of Bonti! In my day, servants knew enough to turn their faces to the wall when we passed!"

"F-forgive me, My Lord," Polijn, tucking her chin against her chest in case he felt like hitting somebody. "I didn't know."

One bony hand shot down to her wrist. "Aye," he said, his voice lowering. "I am. He is dead now and I am Count of Bonti. He is dead, lintik blast and burn him. It wasn't my fault. It was Hombis's fault: his and Oc's. But he is dead and the rest with him."

"Y-yes," said Polijn, feeling that this was not the best of corridors for her to go down.

"Why for Southgate?" the man demanded, shaking her wrist though he was obviously not talking to her at all. "I was young. I'd have done better, given time, given duty. They should've known. He should've told them. You see that!"

"Oh, yes, My Lord," Polijn replied, taking her cue promptly. "I . . ."

The Count of Bonti became aware of her wrist and tossed it from him, nearly throwing Polijn to the floor. "You know nothing!" he roared. "It's a waste of time talking to you!" He strode to the stairs, stumbling but catching himself before he fell.

They were all crazy. With a shrug and a sigh, Polijn moved on. Maybe it was the smell of all the gold in the Palace Royal. She'd heard that did strange things.

She didn't get far. Seeing the three women before they saw her, she engaged herself in a thorough examination of the fringe of the tapestry, taking the Count's suggestion and turning her back to the corridor. She recognized Iranen immediately, and Maitena a fraction of a second after. Either woman had the authority to demand to know what Ynygyn's servant was doing on this floor.

"First the bread, and now this," the shortest woman was saying. "It's the judgement I knew would come on them for taking your keys, Maitena. Remember? I think you should go directly to the Regent and tell him . . ."

Polijn did not know who the woman was, but did know what she was. Chin high, her nose slightly raised, she had a set, determined expression that was repeated in her stride. This was a woman who knew what she wanted, and was prepared to make trouble if she didn't get it. There was less hope trying to explain anything to someone of that type than to Maitena or Iranen, so Polijn went on trying to blend into the wall until all three had passed.

Then she moved on, stopping once or twice more to duck aside for other richly dressed courtiers. Wasn't anybody out in the yard watching the Oath?

Four guards stood duty at the doors to the Royal Reception Room. Polijn knew without checking that eight eyes were on her, so she stepped right along, sparing just one quick glance for the broad table surrounded by birthday gifts. The look didn't last long enough for her to recognize what anything was: she got only the impression of massive piles of gold, silver, and dark, shining wood.

The next door was larger, but only two guards stood there. They lowered ceremonial spears as Polijn came up to them, to bar her progress and to leave a hand free to slip back to less ornamental and more functional weapons.

"Is this, er, the Great Hall?" Polijn asked, taking two steps back.

"It is," said the guard to the left of the door. "What's your business?"

Polijn hadn't thought she'd need any, to just go in and look. Before she could think of an answer, the other guard provided one. "Don't tell me Lady Iranen's thought of something more that needs adjusting!"

"Well . . ." Polijn began.

"Yes, don't tell him that," agreed the other guard. "He just finished sliding the heralds' hangings around to suit her. And he's only about seven feet too short for that."

His partner amiably condemned him to awkward sexual acrobatics in the underworld, concluding, "These ceremonies are a lintik waste of time."

"You say it now," replied the guard on the right side of the door. "Someday you'll get in on one and we'll have to kiss the floor and say 'My Lord' when you come out."

Polijn had laughed in all the proper places in this conversation, proving herself the right kind of person. The spears came apart, therefore, and she was allowed to pass into the Great Hall.

This was obviously the best time for sightseeing. The King's Birthday would naturally include a grand ceremony for the rewarding of those subjects to whom he was most grateful. The yew ornaments gleamed, and dust covers had been removed from all the artifacts and treasures (she could see the dust covers stacked behind a statue). Three-legged "frogs of the moon" stood silent watch by the door into the reception room, their brass-noses shining.

Polijn didn't even try to think. She turned, letting the room soak into her. There was too much to look at now to allow for thinking; she could do that later, in her dark little bedcloset. The room was bigger than the Yellow Dog, and packed every inch with ancient wonders. She turned her head slowly, eyes wide to record everything, mouth wide in the only possible reaction to the splendor.

She turned to the throne last, the old stone chair never touched by any but the greatest officials at court. The sides were rough, but seat and back were polished by millennia of use. The mighty stone sat unchangeable, with a will of its own surpassing those of mortals who used it as a seat.

Above it, high on the wall, were reminders that anything mortals made could be changed: the relics of the Battle of Kairor. Polijn knew what they were and could name every one. When Arnastobh returned unforeseen from the battle, some poet had added five stanzas to the song of his heroic death. They were an awkward little appendix to the main epic, but they rattled along nicely, and even Fikemun could remember that part:

> "The shield of Zoénoxi, the spear of Foroched,
> On left and right, the broken sword of Klee,
> And on the top, its place secure, the tattered banner red:
> The tokens of a mighty victory."

Seeing them was anticlimax to having seen the throne. Apparently not even the guards pressed into service could reach that far to polish them. The old green shield looked dusty, and the spear was just a dull wooden rod dotted with metal studs. The broken sword was a dead, useless thing, and the banner wasn't even there.

Polijn stepped forward to see if the banner had fallen down. But there was really no place for the thing to be, she realized, unless it had dropped behind the throne. And she wouldn't go near that throne for crowns.

To be sure, the banner might have been moved for some part in the King's Birthday ceremonies. Or perhaps it was to be buried with Arnastobh. She had heard the old hero was dead now: another disappointment. She had looked forward to seeing him among the other famous folk of the Palace Royal, perhaps at the head table, near the King.

She thought about the famous people for a moment and then thought, unwillingly, of the Vielfrass. He had ordered her to report anything unusual to Nimnestl. If someone had stolen the Banner of Kairor, that certainly qualified. She didn't like the idea. What if this wasn't unusual? Maybe the Banner had been lost years ago; she'd look stupid reporting that. And it was obvious that the Head Bodyguard wasn't the type to humor stupid people, any more than Ynygyn. She would look like an alarmist, someone not to be trusted. The Vielfrass had surely sent her to listen to Ynygyn, or, more likely, Aesernius, and not to take inventory in the throne room.

But maybe it would show that she was doing her job. And maybe this was what the Vielfrass had expected. Who could tell what he had in mind? At any rate, Ronar had always told her, "It's by taking chances that great profits are won." He always said this to convince her to take a chance. Ronar himself took no more chances than baths.

She left the Great Hall. "Everything's okay," she remembered to tell the guards on duty. "For now, anyway."

A mass of people was passing toward the stairs, but they were all going down. Polijn went up.

II

WHAT she had seen of the Head Bodyguard's office before had been cramped and cluttered, but Polijn was sure there were other rooms behind the front one. There would be rooms for giving orders and asking questions, probably beautifully appointed rooms, probably fine rooms.

To stay out of.

Every ounce of instinct told her not to knock on the door. But Polijn had done so many odd things in the past twenty-four hours that her instincts were muted. She knew she had gone utterly, hopelessly mad when, there being no answer to her knock, she tried the handle. The door was unlocked, and she slid her head just far enough around the door to peek.

She had braced herself for anything, but she was not particularly prepared for nothing. The room wavered before her eyes, and then disappeared. Her hand had been on the door; now she saw neither door nor hand. There seemed to be nothing left of Polijn but a pair of eyes, floating in a gray sea. She spun, arms and legs flailing. But she touched nothing, couldn't even feel whether her arms and legs were moving.

"What is it?" asked a voice from far away. It seemed to be that of the Chief Bodyguard.

Polijn tried to float toward the voice, wondering whether, if she answered, any sound would come out of her.

"Nothing," answered a high, slow drawl. Polijn stopped. Rumors in the Swamp said the Regent could freeze a bird in flight with his voice. Polijn believed it. "Something up in the office, a small creature who probably wandered in by mistake. I'll hold it for a while and later we'll see what it knows."

Polijn didn't like the sound of that, but the Head Bodyguard said, "All right." There was a long pause.

"Well?" demanded the Regent "There are eight other places I should be right now."

"Who did it?" said the Bodyguard.

There was no answer. She went on, the voice sharper. "If you were any kind of wizard, you'd cast a spell on something and find out."

"But I am no kind of wizard," drawled the Regent. "I know it's hard for a layman to tell the difference, but I am a necromancer. I could bring Harliis to some semblance of life for a moment and ask him. But since he was certainly struck down from behind, he'd have little to add to what we know."

Harliis dead? That explained the crowds going for the stairs. Polijn wouldn't have minded seeing that herself. She'd have paid admission. His "rents" had meant longer hours for Gloraida and longer walks for Polijn.

"You, on the other hand," the Regent went on, "are our chief intelligence officer, and ought to have a clue."

"None," said the Bodyguard. She sighed. "All right, we know nothing. We'd better start learning. Who could have done it?"

"The guards on duty," suggested the Regent.

"No," answered the Bodyguard. "They could see it wasn't the King. If they'd been after Harliis, there were easier chances outside the Treasury. It had to be someone inside, lying in wait for the King, assuming he would be the one coming for the Pearl."

"The guards at the hidden door," said the Regent.

"They'd have had to come in. And the hinges still squeal; the other guards or Elgona would have heard it. We are trusting Elgona?"

"I wouldn't have sent him otherwise," the Regent replied. "He was ripe for promotion."

"Then, unless someone materialized inside the Treasury . . ."

"Impossible."

"Your business," said the Bodyguard. "Very well. Someone must have gotten in while the guards were being relieved. Whoever it was waited in the dark, and struck out at Harliis, assuming it was you or me, with the King."

"That means a key," said the Regent.

"Hmmmm," said the Bodyguard, her opinion obvious in her tone. Polijn agreed. Keys and locks were no more than jokes.

"The Treasury lock is specially constructed," the Regent explained. "It's easy enough to pick, but it takes time. It can't be done in under an hour, and the guards are never away from the door for more than five minutes. By the way, how did your someone get out of the Treasury afterward?"

The Bodyguard's voice was thick with disgust. "Joined the crowd of sixty or seventy who pushed in once the news got out. Half of them were probably inside before Elgona and I reached the balcony. Garanem found out, and ordered the guard to let him by; the others pushed in after. What's this? Is this all the keys there were? That simplifies matters some."

"It simplifies them considerably. Those are the only keys there are. Each Treasury key must be made of copper and human bone, each bone being two thousand years dead. Imitations wouldn't work."

"But it isn't impossible to duplicate?" the Bodyguard inquired. "Could the Vielfrass have done it, say, and sent one with that girl?"

Polijn had feared the Bodyguard wouldn't remember her, but was not gratified to learn she had been mistaken. "No," said the Regent, to her relief. "It isn't in the Vielfrass's line. One needs the proper book, too, and I have both copies."

"Yes, this is simple. No one's reported losing a key, though I'd better check. Very nice. Cross off my name; I knew the King wasn't there. You . . ."

"Knew it, too," said the Regent.

"Ye-es," admitted the Bodyguard. "But weren't you planning to dump Harliis? I had an idea that Adimo was . . ."

"But to do it this way," said the Regent, his voice oiled silk. "So crude: a hundred things wrong with it. And you, woman, never liked Harliis. I have only your word for it that he was dead when you walked in. You could easily . . ."

"Peace, peace," said the Bodyguard. "I'll cross off your name if you cross off mine. Back to the list. Besides, Harliis must have been using your key to get in."

"You grow in wisdom every day."

The Bodyguard growled a little. "The list," she said again. "General Gensamar was in the courtyard; I saw him. Lord Garanem and Lord Isanten were there as well. We were considering the other Lords of the Treasury loyal, I think?"

"Except Trioafmar," said the Regent. "Yes. I had that from Elgona. He has been investigating on his own, in hopes of earning promotion to the King's Bodyguard. Trioafmar is an Ykena."

"The Brown Robes have been increasing," noted the Bodyguard. "And quickly, for a reclusive sect. We may have to make them our winter project."

"You might," the Regent replied. "They use a sympathetic magic that feeds on power. The more potent the magician they face, the more potent is their defense. You would be immune; I would be in deep woods."

"Never heard of it, but good for them. Now, Lynex and Iranen we were considering loyal for now."

"It would have taken some force to kill Harliis with one blow that way," the Regent put in. "Forokell and Kaigrol are a little old for it."

"Good, good," answered the Bodyguard. "Then if we're right, that leaves just . . . Patrak, Borodeneth, Flact . . . no, Flact was selling seats in the gallery and Borodeneth was counting the take. They couldn't have made it in time. Just Patrak then, General Torrix, Lady Kirajen . . . she's too small."

"She could have thrown something," said the Regent. "She would have, too. Don't neglect Trioafmar. Now what? Order all four to the dungeons for questioning and await results?"

The Bodyguard's voice was stiff. "I will investigate, and see which can account for their movements after dinner."

"In that crush?" demanded the Regent. "I wish you well. I will have the torturers heating their irons just in case."

"Every fence has a rotten plank somewhere," said the Bodyguard.

"Yes, yes," soothed the Regent. "And if enough people beat their heads against a wall, it may crack. But by all means, go gather some smoke and see if you can make any wood of it. It will keep you out of mischief."

There was a sound of wood hitting wood, and the scrape of boots on the floor. "Ah, ah, ah," said the Regent. "Don't go away mad. And we are forgetting the guest we've had out of sight and sound all this time."

Polijn had forgotten it, too. Now, around her in the gray limbo, her arms appeared, then her body, and then her legs. All were falling and, with them, her eyes and head. They hit a wooden floor and rolled together.

"How kind of you to drop in," said a cadaverous figure above her.

III

POLIJN did not like the room. She was sure she wasn't supposed to. No one, surely, would own a jade grasshopper with six-inch orange fangs unless it was meant to terrify visitors. She looked away from the leering insect only to be confronted with a brass rat, dangling by its tail from the ring in a silver dog's nose. Behind it, on the wall, hung a skull-headed bat with a two-foot tongue. Polijn nearly dove for shelter behind the Bodyguard when the Regent raised a hand.

"Yes," said the large woman. "This is Polijn, the girl sent us by the Vielfrass. This, if you hadn't guessed, is the Regent, Lord Kaftus, Guardian of the Palace Royal."

Polijn had indeed guessed this, but she was in no position to curtsy. So she just flattened herself a bit on the floor.

"Good afternoon, Polijn," said the necromancer. "My, you're looking well today."

His voice held the mocking menace of one who knows he is in command of the situation. It reminded her of the Vielfrass, or of Ronar when no one bigger was in the room. Those two men inspired irritation, but in the presence of the Regent, Polijn was willing to concede the point.

"You have something to report?" Nimnestl demanded.

Polijn tried to remember what it was. "Ye-yes," she said, raising her head just a little. "It may be nothing, but the Vielfrass did tell me to report anything unusual." There. That shifted the blame outside the room. "Ynygyn gave me some time off."

"That is unusual," said the Regent. "Make a note of that, woman: an occasion of unprecedented importance."

The Bodyguard ignored this, her eyes on Polijn. "Why?"

Polijn, not bold enough to ignore the man, glanced at the Regent. What was he wearing around his neck? Maybe she'd be happier not knowing. Looking back to the Bodyguard, she went on, "Aesernius came in and wanted to talk in private."

"Less unprecedented," noted the Regent, folding his hands. "Make no notes."

"Could we let her talk?" the Bodyguard inquired. "I, at least, have other things to do."

"What, watch the King open his presents?" demanded the Regent. "He can wait a little longer. It's good for him."

Polijn glanced at the thing around his neck again, deciding first that whatever it was had fur, and then that it had feathers. Noting that the Bodyguard's lips were pressed thin against each other, she hurried on. "I wanted to see the Great Hall, and thought everyone else would be out watching the Oath of the Pearl. So I went in, and . . . the Banner of Kairor is missing."

There. That was done. She looked up into the Bodyguard's large brown eyes for reward or reprimand. Neither was there. Instead, she saw just what she'd feared: nothing at all.

"I see," said the woman. She tipped her head back a little. "It may have fallen behind the throne during cleaning. Or do they ever clean back there?"

Polijn had already wondered these things, and was now busy wondering what the penalty might be for wasting the Regent's time. It was her first day in the Palace Royal: would they go easy on her, taking that into account, or would they be sure to do something she'd remember for a while?

"The ladders have been up for three days, if anyone wanted to take it," the Bodyguard mused. "Well, I'll have someone look into the matter. You may go, Polijn."

Polijn rose to her knees, shrugging a little to remind everyone that she had started by saying it might be nothing. But neither was looking at her.

"I couldn't see the Vielfrass being interested in the Banner of Kairor," said the Regent. "Or anyone, for that matter."

If this was aimed at Polijn, it passed over her head. She was too concerned with getting out of the room. She stood up carefully, and was searching the door for a handle that was safe to take hold of when someone cried, "Faff!"

She and the Regent turned toward the center of the room, where the Bodyguard stood staring at an immense ivory beetle. "That's what she was carrying!" the woman exclaimed.

The Regent glanced down at Polijn. "Don't let it disturb you. She becomes cryptic at certain times of the month."

"Arual!" the Bodyguard exclaimed next, turning to the Regent. Her eyes were bright now. "Under the tray," she went on, her voice designed to pound comprehension through thick skulls. "She was taking the Banner to her grandfather! Not Ferrapec's spur!"

"Not impossible," said the Regent, hiding his lack of interest not at all. "Then where is it?"

"In his chambers." The Chief Bodyguard strode to the other side of the room for no apparent reason. "She took it up the day he died, but in the uproar after his death, she couldn't put it back. She had to hide it. That's why she's being so stubborn under questioning: she stole the Banner of Kairor. Of course. That's what Arnastobh said just before he died, when we thought he was raving; 'It is death to take the Banner of Kairor.' "

The Bodyguard strode back across the room, reminding Polijn of Ronar the day Polijn brought him word of auditions at the Yellow Dog. Polijn found herself breathing deeper. Her news had been of some great significance, even if she did not herself understand what it was.

The Regent was immune to the excitement. "Has a search been made of his rooms?"

Nimnestl strode back to the center of the room. "There will be one now."

"Good luck," said the Regent. "Maitena and Kodva were going to sort and split the estate in his room today."

"I'll go now," said the Bodyguard. "They'll all have to be in attendance on the King. Mardith can take my place." Expressions Polijn couldn't read passed across the faces of both the Regent and the Bodyguard. Then she ducked out of the way as the Bodyguard stalked among the hideous curios to the door.

A large hand caught at her shoulder and pushed her ahead of the tall, dark woman. "Be off with you now," said the Bodyguard, her voice cold as she thrust Polijn into the corridor. "And stay where we can find you, should further questioning be necessary."

Polijn shot off down the hall as soon as the hand released her. Surely the Bodyguard couldn't suspect her of taking the Banner! She shook her head. Of course not. But if she was to continue spying in Ynygyn's room, there could be no gossip that she and the Head Bodyguard were on friendly terms. The chill in the voice had not been for her, but for the active eyes and ears of any passersby. At least she hoped that was the story.

She glanced up and down the corridor. That was all very well, as far as it went, but Polijn could have used just a few more seconds of conversation. She had no real idea where the Regent's quarters were. The necromancer's spell had plucked her from the Bodyguard's office and set her down in a part of the Palace Royal she hadn't yet seen.

Courtiers passed her, but it never entered Polijn's head to ask directions. No one dressed that well would stop for the likes of her. And in the Swamp, you didn't ask for help: it was never much good, and what there was of it cost too much. She just struck off to her right, assuming that sooner or later she had to come to one of the towers.

A long gallery branched off the busy corridor. Tall, narrow windows opened on both sides, making it bitterly cold, though well lit. Glassed winter sashes had been set up in the openings, but these were old, gapped and patched, and the wind could pass through without check.

Even cold, the lonely sills made excellent trysting places for lovers and plotters. A couple stood whispering in one, the woman apparently objecting to the overeager explorations of her partner: her collar was halfway to her waist, and she was shivering. Polijn had learned her name at dinner: she was Aleia, another High Housekeeper on the kitchen staff. The man had been at dinner, too, sitting at one of the highest tables. Polijn had remarked him because of his bright red hair, a rarity in Rossacotta.

The couple was whispering as lovers do, not necessarily to keep secrets, but because lovers felt some things sounded better in whispers. They were generally correct, too. Polijn hurried past, offering them little attention.

The gallery ended at another corridor, this one lit by only a few torches, and doorless. Polijn hesitated, and then turned right again. There had to be a clue somewhere. Perhaps those lights at the far end meant a more heavily travelled passage was up ahead.

Her footsteps sounded terribly loud to Polijn, but she didn't even notice those of the second person until the figure of a small woman dressed in a minimal black costume flashed past. Pale, muscular legs shone where the light hit them.

"Lady Oozola?" Polijn called. The figure didn't pause.

Reaching the end of the corridor, the woman skidded to the left. Polijn ran after her, but didn't call the name again. It might not be Oozola; Polijn couldn't recognize a moving person from the back in these shadows. Anyone might wear one of those tiny suits. And if it was Oozola, she might not want it known that she was acquainted with Polijn.

Polijn reached the end of the corridor and sped left. She pulled up short, her face smothered in a thickly starched apron. A large, strong hand fastened onto her neck.

"I'm sorry," said Polijn, trying to move on without waiting to see what or whom she had hit. The hand did not release her.

"Milady," she added quickly, looking up and seeing that it was Maitena.

The Third Chief Housekeeper was scowling down at her. "This is the second time I have seen you roaming the halls," said Maitena, her voice a deep growl. "Have you nothing better to do?" She shook the neck she was holding.

"I . . . I am sorry," Polijn repeated. "I was just going there now, Milady."

"Where is it?" the houskeeper demanded. "Whose are you?"

"This is, though I blush to make so presumptuous a claim, mine, my lovely Maitena," drawled a new voice.

They turned as Ynygyn and Aesernius completed their approach. "Yours, Minstrel?" demanded the Housekeeper. "Then take care of it and don't leave it to wander about." She gave Polijn a shove as she released her grip, and marched away.

The push was not enough to throw Polijn off balance, so

she turned to her rescuers and executed a clumsy curtsy.

"Imidis is out," said Ynygyn, looking at empty space above her head, "Doing my business, but I want those back shelves in the study cleaned. The empty ones. The ones with nothing on them. Just those. I will be in and out for the rest of the day, so strive to keep out of my way."

"Yes, sir," Polijn replied. "Is . . ."

The minstrel, having spoken to her as much as he cared to, was walking away. Aesernius chuckled as Polijn allowed herself one grimace.

"A new broom sweeps clean, but the old one knows all the corners," he said. "Turn right up there and go to the end of the hall; you'll see the tower from there."

"Aesernius?" Ynygyn inquired.

The sorcerer hastened after the minstrel and they moved off the way Polijn had come. She shrugged and started for the tower and work. There was no sign of the small woman in the smaller costume. It was probably no more than a dancer who was part of the celebration, lost, or plotting, or on some innocent errand. But where had she gone? Maitena would have said something, surely, at the sight of a grown woman so scantily clad? Or not? Or maybe not to Polijn?

She was still considering this when she found the stairs and mounted them to Ynygyn's rooms.

IV

THE only light in the room was provided by a small lamp in the study, the fire in the anteroom, and what rays of sun sneaked in when the wind hit the window tapestries just right. Polijn slid the cloth across dark, empty shelves, whistling for comfort what she recalled of Ynygyn's tune that afternoon. The sense of being watched had passed, but she was still uneasy, unnerved both by the dark silence of the chamber and the aftereffects of all her encounters with Palace staff.

The shelves looked clean enough; it was hard to tell in the darkness. Now what? Imidis and the minstrel were still out, so she had no orders. There must be work to do somewhere, but she could not see a thing that needed to be cleaned, adjusted, or arranged. Her work for the Paryice had not included house-keeping, and Ronar was never fussy about order in his rooms.

She walked around the suite, and came around to the cabinet where she slept. Her time was free, then, so far as she knew. The cabinet, she had discovered, was fastened to the wall. Polijn had some experience of panel houses, and furniture that was fastened in place aroused her suspicions. In the course of the morning, under pretext of arranging her things in the cabinet, she had been able to verify these. The back of the cabinet slid into the wall, quietly if not easily.

In the wall, behind the cabinet, there was a moderate chamber in the stone, large enough for Polijn to stand up. It was the perfect hiding place for her instruments, and she felt it would be a good place to practice as well. She crawled inside now, slid the door nearly shut behind her, and found the flute and slide-whistle by feel.

She no longer needed the Vielfrass's orders to hide. She would have done it at any rate. Having heard Ynygyn play now, she would have shrivelled in shame to have anyone hear her fumbling, even with the slide-whistle. It was hard enough to even think of her own playing. And she had a pretty fair knowledge of people: she knew what Ynygyn would say about it. Oh, he might use more refined terms than the ones she was thinking of, and he would say them in low, even tones, but they would draw blood just the same.

Still, the Vielfrass had ordered her not only to hide, but to play the flute. Try to play it, anyhow. She took up the instrument and tried a note. The result echoed in the little room, and she quailed before it. The sound was harsh, ugly, cluttered, compared to Ynygyn's clear, professional tones. She chewed her upper lip a bit, and shifted her shoulders. Even the professionals had to start somewhere. She thought back, very briefly, to early days with Ronar, and then blew across the flute again. The same horrid sound rattled around the chamber. She braced herself and shifted her fingers, hunting for the next note up.

She found it on the fourth try and then attempted to fit the three false tries into places on the scale. Fikemun had given her some instruction, not without price, so Polijn was not quite groping in the dark, dark though it might be. She had six of the notes in proper order and was pretty sure where she could find the seventh when the darkness was split by light, and a hand reached into the secret chamber to fasten around her left wrist.

Without thinking, she struck at the hand with her flute. In return, the hand pulled her hard against the sliding panel. Polijn had just time to turn her face before her head hit the wall. Her chief pain, however, was in the wrist, now being crushed in a grip without mercy.

"Every palace guard is looking for you, did you know that?" demanded the owner of the intruding hand. The voice was a hiss of hate. "Thief. The Banner of Kairor and a flute as well."

The owner of the hand dragged Polijn free of the hidden chamber, through the cabinet, and into the study, showing a minimum of interest in her comfort. His free hand took her right shoulder and raised her a little above a standing position. Polijn expected, at this point, to be rattled a bit, but instead Ynygyn forced her shoulder back, until her face was pointed into his.

This face was as cool and unlined as Polijn had ever seen it, except for a brightness about the eyes and a gentle, sideways motion in the lower jaw. "I did think," said the minstrel, his voice low, "that even someone from the Swamp would be wise enough to keep her hands from . . ."

He spared one glance toward his rack of instruments. His grip loosened, becoming one that was strong by normal human standards. Polijn was able to set her feet on the floor.

When Ynygyn looked at her again, one eyebrow was lifted and his eyes seemed almost to have changed color. "It isn't mine," he said, tipping his head to the left. "Where did you get it?"

He released her. Polijn took a step back and rested against the cabinet. Her wrist radiated agonies, but she didn't touch it. She was waiting for Ynygyn to move, preparing to dodge out of the way.

But the minstrel took a step back himself. "Perhaps that's indiscreet, asking anyone from the Swamp where she found something." He put up a hand to wipe sweat from the back of his neck. "Let me hear what it sounds like without the wall in the way."

Polijn was alarmed at the change in his voice which held now neither menace nor boredom. And her hands were shaking. But she had been trained to do what she was told, without hesitation or demur. She raised the flute to her lips and, after one wince at the pain in her wrist, eked out a trembling scale. That seventh note was right where she'd expected it; the eighth followed as well.

Ynygyn leaned on a writing table. There was no emotion in his face as she finished. "Have you played that before today?" he inquired.

Polijn braced herself. That was the first line of the speech she had imagined he would make. "No. Not . . . not really."

He nodded. "Very good. Now, a fingering that works better on the . . . here." He plucked a silver flute from the rack nearest to hand and repeated slowly the scale she'd just played. Then he lowered the flute and looked to Polijn.

The pain in her wrist seemed to have run off somewhere. She raised her own flute and went through the scale, copying his fingerings as best she could. When her flute came down, Ynygyn inclined his head.

"You," he said, "may be able to learn something." Polijn blinked.

"Now, come stand over here." He waved a hand at the floor next to him. She stepped over to it and, at his nod, raised the flute again. "Not like that," he said, putting down one finger to adjust her hand position. "Try it now."

What followed was not so much a lesson as it was a series of pointers. The minstrel told her how to breathe, how to stand, how to sit, how to rise, and even how to look at her audience. "Play lightly," he told her, "even on the low notes. The listeners don't want to know how hard a flute player works. They want someone who looks as if she's about to take off in a romp across green hills. If you do play a tragedy, twist your head to one side so they can't see your face full on. The expression spoils the mood; some fool is certain to laugh."

Polijn nodded, and engraved his instructions on her memory. But she wasn't really there. She was in limbo, as much as she had been in the Regent's grip, or in the Great Hall. With so much or so little all around her, she could do no more than let it soak in, for her mind to sort and store later.

Ynygyn was explaining the breathing patterns in a simple little melody about King Birulph when the door to the room shook under thunderous bumps. The minstrel sighed.

"Close the cabinet," he ordered.

Polijn slid the little door shut just as the one out to the hall banged open. "Here!" exclaimed Nimnestl, seeing Polijn.

"Would you mind closing that door behind you?" Ynygyn asked. "No, no, my darling: from the outside."

Polijn turned to stare. She had forgotten that the drawling, sneering Ynygyn existed. With the eye farther from the door, the minstrel winked at her.

"It no doubt slipped your vaunted memory that I was looking for this one," snapped the Bodyguard. "And on suspicion of a serious state charge: the Banner of Kairor is nowhere in the Great Hall."

"Of course, of course," Ynygyn responded, raising long, pale hands. "I recalled it, certainly. But I hesitated to try to capture so dangerous a criminal without assistance. These villainous banner-stealers are not to be trifled with. You have only to look at her to see how fierce and lawless she is."

Polijn turned her eyes up toward the Bodyguard's face. She wanted to run, but she also wanted to see if the big woman could turn red.

Whether Nimnestl could turn red or not, she didn't. But she did grind her teeth a little. Then, parting them, she stated, "The girl reported a crime and then vanished. This was highly suspicious behavior."

"Now, another thing you should try to avoid," Ynygyn said, crouching as if to speak confidentially to Polijn, "is talking just to move the air around. When you are in a room and discover there is nothing for you in it but the exit, you should, if you are sufficiently civilized, take it and go."

Something in Ynygyn's drawl struck Polijn on its way to slap at Nimnestl. The minstrel was defending her! And from Nimnestl: the Head Bodyguard, the highest, most powerful (biggest, most muscular) officer of the law in all the country. Things did not operate that way in the Swamp. Ronar would have handed her over in the blink of one eye, and asked Nimnestl if there was anything else he could do while he was up. Polijn choked a little.

The Bodyguard did not choke. She took four steps toward the minstrel, pushed Polijn to one side, and stopped. Polijn expected murder, and wondered what you did about that in the Palace Royal. But the Bodyguard then turned her back to Ynygyn. Polijn was utterly confounded to receive a wink from the Bodyguard now. Then Nimnestl resumed her ferocious stride and passed from the room with a slam of the door.

Ynygyn sighed. "If she's thinking about me what I'm thinking about her, I fear we shall never meet in heaven."

The tired Ynygyn was back. His eyes, previously so alive, were again hooded, secret, and amused at some joke the rest of the world wouldn't understand. He nodded to Polijn.

"That is enough for one day," he said. "If you do not agree, you have nerves of iron and muscles of tempered steel. I have duties this afternoon at the singing contest. You may wish to attend, but it will drone on for hours. There is no need for more fortunate individuals to hear the whole contest; the better performers and the king will not appear until later."

Polijn nodded. Ynygyn lifted his flute from the table where he had set it and replaced it on the rack. "Keep your instrument where you will," he went on, "so long as it is out of my way. I need not warn you to put it where it cannot be found by any of the regular thieves and prostitutes who work in the Palace Royal."

He took up some papers and turned to go, still talking. "It is the King's Birthday and, as such, a holiday. Further, you have earned some time for resting. Go somewhere and think; then come back and practice. Watch for the Bodyguard and her husky crew, or you may find yourself in a cell like little Arual."

He reached the door and passed through it, pausing only briefly to add, "If Imidis is here when you return, have him show you how to dust shelves. Be sure to mention I said he was to show you how: the easy way. They're filthy. The Paryice, I am sure, would not have stood for it."

"Yes," said Polijn as the door closed. "Th-thank you."

He hadn't heard her. Polijn sat down with a thump on the hard floor, feet wide apart, the flute clutched fiercely to her chest.

V

AFTER Polijn had sworn a bit, and wiped her face with the hem of her shift, she got up and tucked the flute back into place in the hidden room, next to the slide-whistle. She noticed she was shaking as she closed the sliding panel. She swore a little more, and felt better.

Imidis had not returned. Polijn flattened the wrinkles in her shift, shook her head, and started for the Great Dining Hall. She had heard at dinner that there was to be a singing contest, but hadn't expected to get any chance to hear much of it. She hurried to the stairs, lest Imidis turn up suddenly and take her back for a lesson in dusting shelves.

She found her way after only a few false turns. Courtiers and townspeople packed the room, some to compete, some to hear the others, and all chattering, jostling, and looking for a quick profit. Near the door, an old man with a box and a black bird was offering to tell fortunes for a pennyetke. "Dozens of predictions for lords and ladies," he called as Polijn pushed past him, "handed down by the oracles at Ushmaal. One coin, Missy, one small coin, and the Sacred Bird of Ushmaal will pluck out a scroll never before seen by man nor woman, set down for you alone by the oracle, to guide one so enlightened for all futurity."

Polijn could see the papers were tattered and well thumbed, and did not look for help from the Oracle. She continued to push her way through the lowing herd.

"Did you see Jintabh when the King declared him Count of Bonti? I thought he'd fall on his face, he had his chest sticking out that far."

"Quick, gimme the bottle back. He's almost done and I didn't bring anything to throw."

"Let's slip into the hall, pal-o-mine, and we'll discuss what that hand's doing in my pocket."

"Ah, I say she could do it with both hands tied behind her back. In fact, she'd prefer it that way."

Polijn worked far enough forward to get a look at the judges, sitting at a high table to one side of the now-vacant head table. The King and his party would not arrive until mealtime. Ynygyn was there, more bored even than usual, with his colleagues, Tarobbin and Laisida. Somewhere in front of them a thin, reedy voice made some complaint about some lover who had done something unkind at some time. Polijn couldn't see the singer, and dodged back through the crowd to seek a better vantage point.

"Kirajen's really going to do that ballad about Forokell? She's got nerve. No brains, maybe."

"When they started in, the guards just opened the cells and told us to hide where we could. I think they did it just so they could watch us scramble, but it was a good turn for me!"

"Look at that gown, now! She looks like a featherbed tied in the middle!"

It was that jester who had been pelted from center stage at dinner. As Polijn reached the front of the mob, he hit a high concluding note, covering the crack in his voice by reaching into a deep sleeve for a handful of flower petals, which he flung over the judges. This novelty amused some of the crowd, and hardly anybody threw anything back.

This was to be his only triumph, however. Tarobbin held up three fingers, Laisida two. Ynygyn, after a pause for suspense, sighed and raised one.

"Two!" cried a herald.

Arberth shrugged and stepped off into the crowd, to mocking congratulations. The herald consulted a long list on the table and called, "Yslemucherys of the Palace Royal!"

A small, colorless man wearing bright, colorful clothes struggled through the crowd, being pushed and tripped impartially by members of a crowd wearing green and gold badges, and those from a mob with badges of gold and purple. Badges worked the same way here as in the Swamp: not so allies could instantly find each other, but so rivals could see how numerous and powerful the green-and-greys, for example, were.

The little man wore no badge. He was one of those who belonged to no party and played no power games, hoping the storm would pass over him without doing any damage. He was careful to do no more kicking in reply than was required for him to reach the stage.

"I thought I saw you over here!" a small voice piped. "You didn't have to work after all, huh?"

Polijn turned to look down at a small, dark-haired girl with a face that would probably be startling as she got older. Iúnartar had sat next to Polijn at the dinner, chattering all the while and passing judgement on anyone and anything that caught her eye. Only seven, she was theoretically Polijn's inferior, being too young to have an official identity. However, she was also the youngest daughter of Colonel Tusenga and Jilligan, Fourth Chief Housekeeper, which made her an acquaintance for servants and even low-level courtiers to cultivate.

Iúnartar didn't bother about any of this when she had a willing listener. Polijn would have preferred to hear some music, but did not try to shush her self-appointed pal. It would have done no good, in the first place, and every bit of knowledge that she could pick up about life in the Palace Royal could be useful.

She was informed that Yslemucherys, who had chosen to perform a lyric on the beauties of spring, was Keeper of the Privy Purse. This should have made him a power to be reckoned with. But Polijn could have guessed even before Iúnartar mentioned it that Kaftus liked to handle the privy purse himself, leaving Yslemucherys very little to do. Contests like this were his only chance to draw attention. That was the chief reason behind the crowd at the contest. Courtiers who could show off their wit and versatility in performance stood a chance of bypassing some work and political footing on their way to the top.

Yslemucherys was not going to make it. He was accompanying himself on the flute at breathy intervals. Polijn thought she could have done better herself on the slide whistle. Fikemun could have competed on an even basis here, between Arberth and Yslemucherys.

The song went on and on. Iúnartar did the same. One person Polijn had never heard of had received this honor earlier, and this other person Polijn knew nothing about had received a parcel of land and was furious because it meant he would have to leave Malbeth for a while and that person over there . . . Polijn let her eyes travel over the crowd, listening just enough to nod or smile whenever the girl paused for breath.

She was surprised to find someone looking back at her. It was General Ferrapec, the son of Jintabh, standing with his wife, Raiprez. Raiprez had eyes like half-moons of crystal. The colored center was small, though; little goldfish in big bowls. When she turned her eyes to look at something, everyone in the room knew it. Her husband whispered something, and those eyes slid toward Polijn.

Iúnartar saw it. "She has pierced ears," the girl announced gaily. "They say she poked the holes in them as punishment for spying, and the diamond earrings are the bribe she gave them to spy some more."

It was an old joke, but Polijn laughed just to be friendly. Raiprez shrugged and turned away, but Ferrapec kept his eyes on Polijn for some time. Not wishing to get into a staring match, she turned to look where her friend was pointing. She identified the man with red hair for Polijn, calling him Arlmorin, "the ambassador." Next to him was "Aunt Frowys," who had seated herself on a table and was carving up a lump of light-colored wood.

"She's got strong hands," said the girl, with some awe. "Once when she was Head Cook, and the Lord Executioner was sick, she had to cut the hands off two Lord Treasurers who got caught. She just whomped them right off. Everyone said she was so good at chopping meat, she should take his job."

Polijn saw Nimnestl not far from that grouping, talking earnestly to a tall, square man with close-cropped hair. Iúnartar obliged with an identification before she could ask. "That's Lord Patrak. They say he never goes out with less than ninety gold pieces in his purse, and one of his horses is always saddled and carries a bag with nine hundred gold pieces, just in case he has to get away. That's Harmtha snootching up to him; she used to be Ledbria's lover. But Aperiole saw . . ."

Iúnartar attached a name to every face they saw in the crowd, generally adding the name of a spouse, at least one lover, and passing some judgement on their personal habits. At least three of the men waiting to sing, she speculated, were former favorites of Kaftus who had somehow lost face and were at the contest in hopes of regaining it.

Yslemucherys's own attempt fared badly. The amiable Tarobbin rated him at no more than two fingers, while Laisida ventured only one. Ynygyn, apparently affronted by the flute-playing, raised both fists over his head in a double zero.

"One!" announced the herald.

"This is the worst contest they've ever presented," growled Yslemucherys, pushing quickly through the crowd in hopes of disappearing.

There was a general laugh. "Ah, yes," said a voice Polijn knew. "Each man will speak of the fair as his own market has gone in it."

The two girls turned around to look up at Aesernius. "Good afternoon," said the sorcerer. "I was looking for this little one in hopes of having a private word with her."

"What for?" demanded Iúnartar.

"Cat fur," answered the sorcerer. "To make kitten britches for inquisitive little girls who need to have their seats warmed."

"Foo," she said, not at all intimidated. She put an arm around Polijn's waist. "You go away. I'm talking to her now."

"I think . . ." Polijn began, trying to work her way loose politely.

"Oh, go on," Iúnartar told her, letting her go. "He's so mean, he'd probably turn you into a frog or something. I'm sure I don't care."

Aesernius grinned and took Polijn's hand. "I'd more likely tell one of your sisters on you," he said. "But it would be a bad time of year to be turned into a frog."

He took Polijn through the crowd to the corridor and then along this hall to the nearest tower, keeping up a stream of chatter as inconsequential as Iúnartar's, or almost that bad, concerning the weather and minor methods of foretelling it. They moved on up several flights of stairs until he pulled off onto a landing and led the way to a wooden door.

"After you," he said, unlocking the door and pushing it open.

Polijn turned slightly to one side and preceded him into the room. It was high in the tower, and should have been cold, but several large braziers burned brightly, in various colors. She supposed it was Aesernius's own apartment.

The sorcerer pulled the door shut and stepped over to one of the braziers. Polijn felt a quiver of apprehension as he drew out a long hunk of metal, but saw that it was a ladle. Raising a mug from a nearby shelf, he poured some liquid in, and passed the mug to Polijn.

"Drink up," he said. "There's more down cellar in a teacup."

He took a second mug for himself and walked across the room to sit down. Polijn stood where she was. A sip of the heated wine reminded her powerfully of a similar scene less than a day earlier. She waited for Aesernius to say something strange and unexpected.

He did. "Do you think you'd like the King?"

Polijn put her head to one side and stared at the lined face, hoping to prompt a little explanation.

"Hmmmm," he replied, folding his lips in. He shrugged. "They're always looking for a few new members for the King's Companions. I thought he might like you, and it would be nice for you not to have to work so hard. Not that Ynygyn's the slave driver some courtiers can be, but he makes no allowances for human weakness, he having none himself. You, er, aren't any taller than the King is, really, and you're smallish. Positively elfin, with those ears."

Polijn had been hearing about her ears for years and wasn't much interested in the subject any more. She wanted to know what Aesernius was up to, and how much danger she was in as a result. "What are the King's Companions?"

He stared. Then he shrugged again. "They may not have heard, in the Swamp. A small group of children has been approved by the Council to associate with the King, so he knows people his own age. The membership changes from month to month depending on what they think of the parents: the usual ups and downs at court. I could probably put in a word for you. Anyone who lasts in the Companions is bound to be somebody if the King ever shakes off the, er, older generation and comes to power on his own. So I thought I'd ask: would you like the King? I could get you into the

Companions, maybe, but it would depend on you and him whether you got to be special friends."

Polijn felt she could see behind this. "He's the King," she said. "I think I'd be . . . scared of him, as a king. I wouldn't know how to talk to him. And he's only a little boy. Not old enough for me to . . . if that's what you meant, I mean. I don't . . ."

Aesernius waved a hand to cut off the sentence. "Of course, of course." He took a sip of wine and sighed. "It was just an idea. It's the wrong age, really, to go trying to introduce a lot of girls into the King's circle. I thought it might be a way for me to get an arm through the window. I can't compete with Kaftus in the magic line; I know that as well as a squirrel knows a hickory nut from an acorn. And when it comes to politics, I'm just a small dog in the long grass."

Polijn said nothing, trying to look sympathetic. "Ah, well, I'm keeping you from the contest." Aesernius jumped out of the chair and unlocked the door. "No, no; take it with you. It's cold; land, it's cold. That's the real reason I want Kaftus's job, you know: so I can get a room down farther, out of the wind. Joke, that: if the big bad bodyguard takes you into custody, you don't have to mention it."

He locked the door behind her and Polijn started back down for the Dining Hall, wondering whether she had just turned down an offer to be made Queen of Rossacotta.

CHAPTER FOUR

Nimnestl

I

"NOT there," said the Head Bodyguard, stepping into the Regent's chambers.

The Regent was grinding something in a mortar. "Pity."

Nimnestl sat against the edge of a silver-streaked table. "Kodva says there's a curse on the banner, but that doesn't explain the poison."

"It doesn't do, does it?" Kaftus answered, adding a spoonful of red powder to what was in the mortar. Nothing happened.

"Are you listening to me at all?" Nimnestl inquired, out of idle curiosity.

"No," said the Regent. He reached for a flask of yellow liquid. "I gave it up years ago." He added two drops of this to the mortar. "I know the chances that you'll say anything worthwhile. I may have a bare hour to finish this before it's time to . . ."

Someone knocked at the door. "And I may not," the Regent went on, rubbing his thumbs in irritation. "Enter, if it's worth your miserable life to do so."

The door swung aside and a large, square man stepped into the room. "Your pardon," he said, bowing. "I did not think to find Your Excellency here at all during the contest. But I saw that you were not in the hall and dared to hope."

"Lord Arlmorin," answered the Regent, with a nod as Nimnestl returned the bow. "Come in, by all means, and join the interruption."

The man smiled, and obeyed. Lord Arlmorin was a big, cheerful man, with a tremendous red mustache and hair trimmed to look as if a large red spider had just settled on his scalp. His ears were small and flat against his head; his eyes large with a small iris surrounded by white. People said of him that he was so energetic that an aura of heat could be felt eight inches from his body in all directions. Nimnestl told herself it was just imagination that warmed her hand as he passed.

Lord Arlmorin was from Braut, the only foreign ambassador at the court in Malbeth. Foreign representatives had made unofficial visits to the Palace Royal, but Braut was so far the only country to officially weigh Rossacotta's vile reputation against its vast wealth and come up with the more useful answer. It was Arlmorin's mission to lever some wealth, and possibly soldiery as well, free for Braut's ancient war against Dongor. Rossacotta had had no such request for fifteen hundred years, and the whole bureaucracy was aflutter over it.

Isanten and the rest of the Ministers were ecstatic. Braut was impoverished and embattled, but it was also ancient and reputable. Association with a country that had held out for centuries over a point of honor would be worth the price for the prestige it brought. Garanem, First Lord of the Treasury, wanted to know first what that price was likely to be. The other Lord Treasurers stood with him, more or less. The military was divided. General Kaigrol wanted to see one more resounding victory in combat. General Gensamar, and his brother Tollamar, thought victory was all well and good, but that the war would be chiefly useful for giving employment to idle armies. But Generals Torrix and Ferrapec were in total opposition: to go to war would be to leave the Palace Royal, and all the power they had amassed at court.

In the end, everyone knew, it would be the Regent's decision. And Kaftus, so far, was mum.

Which probably explained the box in the ambassador's hands. Arlmorin raised the lid and bowed again, displaying a set of pewter spoons bearing the royal crest of Braut. "A little token," he explained. "No doubt it will go unnoticed in all of today's gift-giving."

Kaftus lowered his head and shoulders, both in acceptance of the gift and so he could reach it. "The King was pleased with your box of lead soldiers," he noted. "Particularly the dragon."

"So I saw," the ambassador replied. "I was hoping it would not be construed as a hint."

"Perish forbid," replied the Regent, setting the box under a plaster model of a black rat sarcophagus. "It is, however, too early to tell."

Nimnestl restrained a yawn. Arlmorin glanced at her as if he'd heard it anyhow. "However," the ambassador went on, "it is on a less pleasant matter that I have presumed to consult you. A matter of theft, I'm sorry to say."

He paused for the proper exclamations of horror, but, hearing none, went on. "I am missing two silver pens, a teapot, and a small gilt mirror. They have been missing since late last night."

"I see," said the Regent, his face too solemn. "It is serious, of course, but not unprecedented. Were the objects of great value?"

"And there were a few papers of a purely personal nature," Arlmorin went on. "The person who took them probably couldn't even tell what they were. Also not unprecedented."

Kaftus smiled. Nimnestl listened a little more closely. The ambassador's tone was so careless that this was either a lie or a matter of vast importance.

"The papers are worthless," said the ambassador, "and it makes no difference to me if they are recovered or not. My chief fear is that someone may forge a letter to my detriment, shuffle it in with the others, and let the portfolio be found. But, as I say, my main interest lies in the valuables. The teapot was a family heirloom, given to my grandfather by King . . ."

Nimnestl disengaged her attention. The important feature was that Arlmorin had mentioned the papers and done his best to disassociate himself from the contents if they were found. That was interesting.

Kaftus had also had enough. "Yes, Lord Arlmorin," he said, breaking into a description of the pens. "We will investigate the matter, and if the items appear, you will certainly be notified. If you will excuse me, however, I must finish this . . ."

"Of course, of course," answered Arlmorin. "Thank you. I know that you would conjure up my belongings if you could, but since we must rely on mere mortals, I should not take up any more of your time. The best of the day to you, Your Excellency."

There were more bows, but Nimnestl was finally able to close the door behind the ambassador. "Could you have conjured up his belongings?" she inquired, returning to the table.

"No faster than he could, I'm sure," Kaftus replied, squeezing a blue goo from a tube. "It might be worth the trouble. Those missing papers might be of interest; more, even, than the missing banner."

"I'm going to talk to someone about the banner now," Nimnestl told him. "I'll have some of the men check the usual hiding places for the papers."

"Play nice," said the necromancer, stirring the material in the mortar. "Do keep Harliis's murder somewhere on the agenda, won't you?"

Halfway to the door, she turned back. "Do you think I should consider that first?"

"I do wish," Kaftus told her, as steam started to rise from the mortar, "that you could give up asking my opinion on matters when you have already made up your mind. It is inefficient, time-consuming, and . . ."

Nimnestl slammed the door on his last adjective and strode down the hall. Courtiers and servants dodged out of the way. This was a trick they had learned early on: the Bodyguard would pay them no serious attention so long as they did stay out of her way. They had learned to know her various walks: that dangerous casual stroll, the relaxed travelling pace, the attack speed. This was her "I am going somewhere now" gait: a long, steady drive that suggested irrepressible force. One could tell by looking that anyone who got into the path of those long, charging legs would be pushed away, knocked down, or walked over.

Rossacottans generally knew what to do when confronted with that much force. But one courtier did not step back. In fact, she put a hand out to the Bodyguard's belt. Nimnestl was aware of this immediately.

She saw the necklace first, a garland of golden threads mingled with pearls, and slowed to a stop. There was one necklace like that in the Palace Royal, a constant ornament to the dirty neck of its owner, setting off an equally expensive wardrobe. It belonged to Kirajen, Chief Assistant to the Third High Housekeeper.

Kirajen was a piece of human perfection for the eye to rest upon. Wherever one's gaze moved, from hairline to lace-laden hem, the result was satisfactory. A few purists might have objected to the frigidity in the eyes, and the fluid firmness at her mouth, indicating determination. Kirajen had long since decided that she was to be the next First Housekeeper. Everyone in the Palace Royal was a rung on her ladder.

"Yes?" Nimnestl demanded.

Kirajen had a right to be offended by this brusque form of address, but she chose not to be offended. "If I knew something no one else knew," she suggested, "what would it be worth?"

The woman's eyes glittered with the gold of her presumed price. "You are talking about what?" Nimnestl inquired, prepared to disbelieve, individually or in groups, every word the intrigante used.

The housekeeper released Nimnestl's belt, and stood back a ways. She seemed to find something of interest on the ceiling. "I know a fellow who wears brown robes in his spare time," she said, pronouncing "brown robes" as though it were the answer to all life's little problems. The Ykenai were sometimes known as the Brown Robes.

"And what does this have to do with what?" Nimnestl went on, giving her no assistance at all.

Kirajen's head came down, and she brushed a speck from one lace cuff. "I thought," she said, "that you'd be interested to know what this person was doing in the Treasury this morning. Or, really, what this person was going to do but what didn't work out the way he planned what."

Nimnestl did have more than a passing interest in knowing all these whats and whos. But she said only, "And in return, you wanted what?"

"Forokell's getting old, poor thing," Kirajen replied, jerking her head as the subject changed completely. "Did you notice that half the bread at dinner was undercooked? Fact. For her own good, I think she might be retired one of these days. Soon. And if . . ."

"I think," Nimnestl said, breaking into this reverie, "that you would like to tell me what you would like to tell me. For nothing."

Kirajen tossed her head. “I don’t see why I should do that.”

Nimnestl smiled. “I do.”

Kirajen’s upper lip drew back between her teeth, and little fists formed inside the lacy sleeves of her gown. Nimnestl’s remark was, in fact, a bluff: the Bodyguard knew nothing that would seriously hamper the little woman’s career. But Nimnestl had for years been cultivating an air of nonchalant omniscience, and Kirajen was the type who would always have something to hide.

“I can do my duty,” the housekeeper said at last, cheeks and chin stiff. “But not here. Lady Forokell wants to talk with me and the master baker, and I can’t spare the time. Later, after dark. We can meet on the King’s Beach.”

That was a long walk, but Nimnestl did not object. “Very well,” she said. “I’ll be . . . waiting for you.” Kirajen flounced away before the menace in her voice, a bundle of lace and fury.

II

ELDRED still lived in the barracks, away to the left and at an angle from the main body of the Palace Royal. Now, of course, he occupied a tiny apartment set apart from the narrow dormitory of men on active service. Jurly lived there with him, but she was not in evidence when Nimnestl pushed the door open.

In evidence, more tangibly even than the furniture, were the marks of occupancy by an habitual tobacco chewer. Nimnestl closed one eye as she entered the room, but made no other comment. She had brought tobacco along, as a bribe, but perhaps someone who lived in a room already so thoroughly decorated needed no further stock.

Eldred did not refuse it, though. "Good grade," he said, taking it from her hand and poking a finger into the container. "Now, you wanted to know about the fights in Malbeth, was that it?" He ran a hand from his forehead back to his neck, adjusting a frail wisp of white hair. He left the hand on his neck and leaned back.

Nimnestl found a nearly clean spot and sat down, prepared to waste some time. Eldred would lie, of course, but by now she knew the people in the Palace Royal and had listened to enough of them to have an idea how they lied. Before they got to anything useful, they would have to go through the tale of Eldred's faceoff with Gyrina (who had died on the eastern border and never saw Arnastobh's little corps at all) and probably the story of the fight in the sewers as well.

"We were all ready for a siege," Eldred began, "and we all crushed into the gatehouse." Nimnestl nodded, and went on nodding through his recollection of the exact moment he had that brainstorm about bouncing rocks off the slanted walls of the gatehouse up into the faces of the attackers, and Arnastobh's famous oration about death in battle being preferable to capture by a tired enemy at the end of a siege. Attempts to drag this monologue around to the Battle of Kairor would be futile, so she just thrust a small wedge in at the first opportunity, simply to nudge its direction a bit.

"There must have been some opposition, mustn't there?" she asked. "If everyone else was for sitting out a siege? I suppose he had enemies who wouldn't've liked it?"

Eldred spat, missing her by only a few feet. "Everybody has enemies. Arnastobh outlived his. Oc and Hombis, mainly. They looked to be friends at first, though I could say that about some others, too. Now, he had competition later on, as general, but back in that gatehouse . . ."

Nimnestl was tired of being confined to that gatehouse. "Where was Jintabh all this time?" she inquired. "At Southgate, or . . ."

His glare would have frozen an oven. "I know what you want me to say. You want me to say Jintabh killed him, slipped a little poison to him, don't you, morhane? Jintabh's all right."

"Oh, that's what I've heard," Nimnestl hastened to say, without bothering about making her tone sincere.

"I know better," snarled Eldred, sitting up and letting his hand drop. Finger signs indicated that he knew what part of a pig's anatomy that statement had come from, and he went on. "They say he was greedy. Okay, he was greedy. But let me tell you, he was ready to die. He wanted to be big, yeah, but he took risks the same as all of us. Jintabh was all right, all right. He just made the one mistake and maybe, if it'd been me made it, I wouldn't've come out so good, and Malbeth might be something else today."

"Well, that's all something else," Nimnestl told him, with a shrug. "The Battle of Kairor, now . . ."

"Southgate," muttered Eldred, leaning forward and resting his elbows on his knees. "I never grudged him his Southgate, see, because I knew what he paid for it. That's more than you can ever say. I had it from Arnastobh, the night I waited on him, and the others were all dead drunk."

"Probably drunk yourself, then," noted the Bodyguard, completely uninterested and buffing her right hand's nails on her left wrist guard. "I don't need any more stories like that, let me tell you."

"So so?" demanded the old soldier, sitting up again. He was breathing hard, and his eyes seemed to bulge more with each breath. "So so! In Reangle, I guess, all darks drink milk! Let me tell you, Bodyguard, and then you tell me. Jintabh was in with them, Oc and Hombis, during the battle. This was before we all went up to the gatehouse. Jintabh killed three Treasury guards—real guards, then, not the Regent fodder we've got today—and took the Pearl of Adriack. He figured if Oc and Hombis lost, they'd all pull back into the hills and bargain from there with the Pearl."

"Go on home," Nimnestl said, losing interest in her nails. "In a siege, they'd have had the Pearl in the gatehouse."

"Maybe so," Eldred informed her. "Maybe so. But Jintabh had it, all the same. And he knew what losing the Pearl would have meant. But in the retreat, they ran into trouble at Southgate. Jintabh could see enough to know when it's raining, and he knows what's coming to him if they catch him with the Pearl. So he runs to his brother and gives himself up. Arnastobh fixes it so everything looks like Jintabh came for help, and the Pearl wasn't ever stolen at all; they hid it for safekeeping in a little cell down in the larders. And that's that daring ride from Southgate, the way it was. They made Jintabh a hero for it, him so young. Took him out of service. It made him mad, you know, and he wasn't the same . . ."

"Supper!" called Jurly, pushing into the room. "There'll be . . ."

She saw the Bodyguard and backed out of the room with the tray. "I . . . I'm sorry, Milady," she said. "I . . . didn't . . ."

"She was just leaving," Eldred told her. "Story's getting so exciting, she'll wet her pants. I know the look. So tell me, was that just a drunkard's tale?"

"Probably," Nimnestl replied. She stood up. "But I'd hate to see Jintabh haul you up for judgement on it, so I'm not going to mention it to him. It's the least I can do for such an enterprising liar."

Her height, her color, and speculations on her sexual habits were blended in Eldred's reply, but she didn't spare any time for that. She was already moving out of the barracks. The story had been good enough, and if even partially true, it explained Jintabh's life a little better. It meant nothing to the investigation at hand, of course. She knew already Jintabh hated his brother; what she wanted to know was if he had killed Arnastobh because of it. But this was a tidy scrap of information to be added to her store for future use.

She opened the door to the courtyard just as a man tried to pull on it from the other side. "Aha!" exclaimed the man.

It was Ferrapec, and his wife with him. "Someone told me you were here, badgering Eldred," said the general. "Once again . . ."

Nimnestl shut the door and came forward, forcing the pair to retreat three steps. "Skim it, would you, General?" she requested. "I only have time for the cream."

"I informed you," Ferrapec replied, through teeth grinding to the left and right, "that my uncle's death was completely natural. Can't you get that into your head?"

"I can when I believe it," said the Bodyguard. Her voice was meek and filled with awed respect for the general's exalted position.

The general's teeth ground more loudly as he tried to compose a reply. "Oh, come away," said Raiprez. "I told you not to get into a debate with her. You'll never win because you're too civilized to strike a la . . . a woman."

Raiprez was cute. This was her profession. When she spoke, her big eyes rolled up and back, as if she was thinking of something else long ago and far away, somewhere, over her right shoulder. Her lips were large, and always on the verge of a pout or a merry insult. She was cute from head to toe. Further, she knew what she had and for how much it sold, which raised her head and shoulders above the only more experienced practitioner of cute in the Palace Royal: Harliis's sister, Hopoli.

"I want to talk to you," said that selfsame Hopoli, who had tripped daintily up behind Ferrapec and his wife.

Nimnestl ran her tongue across her teeth, but she could not stop Hopoli, who said, "I don't see why you should spend time on some old man when my brother was . . . was murdered."

Her lips trembled and great pools threatened behind her eyes.

Ferrapec and Raiprez had taken eight steps away, not sure they wanted to be seen with the sister of the favorite, once powerful but now dead and obviously out of the running. But now Ferrapec's choler prompted him forward to answer her. "Because she suspects me. Now, if you had murdered your brother, darling, you would be getting all the attention you could desire. But if it isn't a family murder, anyone from Reangle won't understand it."

He seemed to feel this was all that was needed for a dramatic exit, and ground gravel under his feet as he turned and marched away, his wife mincing along at his side telling him that had put some people in their place. Nimnestl did not watch them go. "That sound you heard," she confided, "was me howling in agony at the general's displeasure."

Hopoli was easily diverted, and smiled at this sally. But she put one dimpled white hand on Nimnestl's arm. The Bodyguard barely repressed an urge to knock it away, and went on. "The murder of Harliis is under investigation. On a crime of this importance, we would not move hastily. But informants have already begun to bring in useful clues."

Hopoli blinked naturally curly lashes. "Yes, but . . ."

A large black bird fluttered up, ignoring Hopoli's little shriek, and demanded, "Busy, Missy?"

Nimnestl replied by trying to roll her eyes as far up as Raiprez did. She failed. "Why?"

"Time for supper," said the bird. "Nurse looking for little king. Everyone tell her he with you. He 'long by Haeve."

"Go back to him," his master told him. "I'll be there soon." The bird sped up into the air.

Nimnestl lifted the little white hand with her thumb and forefinger, and removed it from her wrist. "We'll have to talk later, Hopoli."

"I know," whispered the little woman, her eyes now shining with mischief. "This is a race."

It was, too. Nimnestl started off across the yard at her best cover-ground gait. She couldn't run; rumor would have the King or the Regent dead in half an hour if someone saw her running. But she had to beat Nurse to the King.

What was he doing with Haeve on a holiday anyhow? Surely no one would have bothered with the Royal Tutor on a day when lessons were cancelled. Haeve was almost as unpopular in the Palace Royal as Nimnestl herself, feared and disdained because of his low, scholarly origins. Further, Haeve could smell a plot through a stone wall, and was not shy about mentioning it to the Regent if someone tried to influence him or what he taught the King. Politics in the present tense did not interest Haeve an ounce. He was wholly dedicated to the perpendicular pronoun, and sought to prove his intellectual superiority to the rest of the world by training up a mighty king.

Kaftus trusted him. By the Regent's orders, the King was accompanied at every second of the day by the Tutor, Kaftus, Nurse, Mardith, or Nimnestl. The arrangement suited everyone but Nurse. She had no confidence in Mardith at all (he pulled her hair) and loathed Haeve, apparently because he could read.

"This business of books has its uses, perhaps," she would admit, "but you can't trust a man who goes into it on purpose. I'd not trust him anywhere with the King, but sense is wasted on this court."

Despite the attempt in the Treasury, everyone feared less that someone would kill the King than that someone would kidnap him. There were no close heirs to the throne to lead a rebellion, and no one at court was strong enough to take the throne without at least a figurehead from the royal family. If the King were to die, the result would be chaos within the kingdom, and troops from lands to the east, west, and south riding in to divide long-denied loot.

Of course, this did not need to be obvious to everyone. There was no way to prevent some fool from thinking himself mighty enough to do without the King, as was apparent in the attempt in the Treasury. Unless the target had been the King's escort, she thought, with the King himself, and the Pearl, to be spirited away by the new government.

Nimnestl nearly collided with Elgona at the nearest entrance to the palace. "Excuse me, Milady," said the guard, turning pale. "I saw . . . I thought I saw a woman, all in black . . ."

"No one passed me," she told him. "Where's the Royal Tutor?"

"In the schoolroom," said Elgona. "Some of the Companions are with him. Did you not see . . ."

But Nimnestl was away. She hoped Haeve had been able to keep the Companions out of serious mischief, or Nurse would go on about it for the rest of the year.

Kaftus, Haeve, and Nimnestl had decided that the King would benefit from association with other children, which had set off a citywide competition that never ended. Anyone with a son or daughter within two decades of the King's age tried to get their darling into the glorified circle of the King's Companions. These children would run and wrestle and throw things and benefit from all the advantages of being instructed by the best experts in the land. And, from time to time, they could perhaps sigh a little about high taxes, or refer to Daddy's impoverished and threadbare estate.

In spite of screening, some of the Royal Playmates did occasionally introduce such propaganda into a quick game of goblin, and the personnel of the little group had to be altered to remove the contamination. But there was a core of regulars who had been with the King since before they rose to two feet. Chief and leader of the group was Merklin, Ipojn's youngest. By dint of status, the King always got to play Sir Simon St. Thomas in their mock battles, but despite this, it was Merklin who made plans, outlined strategies, and led charges, relegating the King to the role of sidekick. Ipojn might not have known it, but he and his son were getting a lot of attention in the midnight conferences of Tutor, Regent, and Bodyguard.

Merklin was not in the schoolroom just now, and the sounds of the game in progress were not grunts and yells of battle, but the ring of gold coins spinning on the floor. Haeve was kneeling among them, apparently showing them how to drop a coin so it would land on edge and roll to the wall.

"You can also set them on edge," said the lithe scholar. "Maybe." He went down to all fours and set up a coin. Each child imitated him with a gold coin of a different size. Rossacotta, with so many coins from other countries, not to mention counterfeits and restrikes, had never bothered to establish a standard currency of its own.

"It always seems," he went on, as his coin wobbled and dropped against his thumb, "that the harder you try, the harder it is to do." Now the coin fell back against his index finger.

"And then," he said, looking away, "a careless effort, when you aren't really paying attention, may have long-lasting results." He slipped his hand away, and the coin stood free.

The King applauded, and the coin clattered against the floor. The Tutor's mouth twisted to one side. "And yet a breath can ruin your efforts," he noted.

"Quite a little lesson in statecraft," said Nimnestl, stepping forward. She was gratified by their startled jerks. They hadn't heard her come up behind them.

"Yes," said Haeve, liking the appreciation but not the interruption.

"It's a good thing, though, that I got here before Nurse did, and saw you all on the floor," she went on. "Of course, mere children cannot be expected to understand what clothing costs nor how much trouble there is in the cleaning and repairing of it or. . . ."

Her imitation of Nurse's voice was good enough to draw a laugh. Haeve, nodding, stood up. "Many thanks for the warning," he said, with a bow. "Between the music in the hall and the ring of the coins, my ears were already suffering."

The King laughed again, as the others collected the gold coins and tossed them into a bag Haeve held. "Is it time to eat again already?" the monarch asked Nimnestl.

"Probably not for you," she told him. "Nurse will explain that your digestion is poor and that you will certainly have nightmares and no one ever asks her but all your food is far too highly seasoned and . . . But you are expected to put in an appearance at the singing contest."

The King sighed. He had no ear for music at all, and much preferred watching small men swallow live mice. "Well, let's go, then," he said.

"You go with Nurse," she told him. "I'll be along later. First I have to make a trip to the dungeons."

The King stamped a foot. "You never take me along!"

"Next time."

"Next time, like last time," he answered. "Foo."

Nurse entered just before the argument could start. Steel-grey eyes fastened on the King. "You," said Nurse, "have dust on your knees."

Nimnestl fled for the safety of the dungeons.

III

NIMNESTL did not ordinarily enjoy a trip to the dungeons. She had been locked up in similar ones and she didn't like it that she was responsible for other people being in these. Only fungus could thrive in the dungeons, particularly in the depths. Nimnestl had never been that far down; if you wanted someone from down there, you sent someone else.

Arual was not that far down. She was up where walls were polished, the floor firm and flat. In fact, her cell had been a royal bedchamber in the bad old days when captive royalty was bred for exhibition by the Council. It was still clean, watertight—for a cell.

Nimnestl unlocked the main door and stepped down into the dungeon corridor. One of the guards on duty handed her his torch when she nodded to him. She lit this from one of the wall sconces and stepped down into the shadows. Six guards generally stood duty during the day, when the upper dungeons were lit and people occasionally visited their relatives in confinement. By late afternoon, though, this became a guard of two, who did not patrol the dungeons but stood just beside the door. In an hour or two, they would leave as well. Guards didn't like to stay at night and, indeed, there was little need. No one had ever tried to escape once the last torches were extinguished. Something cried out in the darkness, they said: something left of long-gone kings and queens who stayed there when the locks were silver, and the bars gilt.

This time, Nimnestl didn't mind the trip. She would question Arual one more time. Barring a breakdown and confession, she would set the girl free. This had been her plan all day, and the multiplying complaints gave her the excuse she needed. Paru, the choirmaster, had made the biggest noise; he was premiering a new work in honor of the King by the children's choir, and Arual's voice was to have been featured. Then, during the confrontation in Arnastobh's room, Kodva had demanded her granddaughter's release. That hadn't been such a surprise as the similar demand made by Ferrapec when he entered the room. In fact, he had mentioned it several times, and would have done so again outside the barracks, no doubt, had Hopoli not intervened. This was the first time Nimnestl could recall being grateful for Hopoli's existence.

As she felt for the proper key on her belt, she speculated on Ferrapec's interest. Someone had suggested once that the general was shopping for a wife to replace the excruciatingly cute but highly expensive Raiprez, and was considering something in Arual's age group. Nimnestl thought it unlikely. The vice was not unknown in Malbeth (what vice was?), but this particular perversion had the dubious distinction of being forbidden not only by the Church, but by secular law as well. It was, in fact, included under the heading of treason, a remnant of the reforms that followed the age of king-breeding.

On the other hand, Ferrapec had never shown the slightest interest in his niece before. He might angle after Maitena's gratitude or support, but to what purpose?

Nimnestl reached the thick wooden door and raised her key ring. "Are you there, child?" she called through the bars. Hauling the door to one side, she stepped in.

Only Nimnestl was tall enough to have been thumped in the nose by the rump that dangled in front of her. Justifiably startled, she leaped back, her hammer free and raised for action.

The body was naked, a man's, hanging by one leg on a rope fastened to the hook in the ceiling. It swung away from Nimnestl, looking oddly off-center. She had to study it for a moment to realize that it had no head.

"Mira khirokhu!" she exclaimed. She ran one hand across her forehead.

When her own head was clearer, she inclined it forward. "Arual?" she called, turning the torch toward a long, narrow niche that served as a bed. The girl didn't seem to be around. All Nimnestl saw was an empty bowl there, and a shadowy lump off in a corner. That would be the missing head.

She stood back and studied the body. A long white scar dug across the right thigh, and a faded blue snake wrapped its permanent body around the skin of the right arm. Arms and legs were well muscled, but the rest of the body sagged. A merchant, perhaps, from those parts of the city where a good arm was the only available insurance. The head had been lopped off just above the shoulders: a neat cut, if a messy job.

"Milady?" called a guard, coming to the door. "We heard . . . Eru!"

"Exactly," said the Bodyguard. "Just go fetch the head, will you? This is trouble."

"Yes," the guard agreed. Nimnestl watched him wave his own torch back and forth until he sighted the missing part. Crossing the room, he got a handhold in the hair, and dragged it up. "The girl is gone, then?" he asked, bringing it to her.

"You're too swift for this kind of work," Nimnestl told him. "Too shrewd. Turn it so I can see the face, man."

The guard obeyed. Nimnestl felt a scream of irritation building up between her stomach and her lungs. The face was ordinary: a bit coarse, with thick black hair, narrow eyes, and an open mouth showing a variety of teeth in different stages of decay. The expression was nothing much; it looked a little sleepy.

Only two things made the face in any way worthy of notice. One was that it was on a severed head found in a cell occupied by someone else. The other was that it was a woman's face. It could have very little to do with the male body dangling from the ceiling.

Things would have been too simple the other way, thought Nimnestl, far too easy. Someone had made off with a prisoner and substituted a dead man under the noses of the guards? No, no: that had no romance, no style. It had to be a headless body and someone else's head. She felt the scream rising to her throat.

She didn't let it out. Instead, demanding "Is there no guard in this whole lintik palace who knows his job?" she let a hard, brown fist snap out into the guard's face. He dropped. The woman's head dropped with him.

It was too soon for Nimnestl to wish she hadn't done it; she turned to examine the cell door. She shouldered the heavy lump of metal and wood to where she could peer into the bolt hole. The bolt had been cut. Taking out her key, she inserted it and brought the bolt out for examination. It didn't even clear the door.

Cats were running out of bags all over the Palace Royal. Someone had to have opened the door with a key, and then cut the bolt to make it all tidy. It was either someone who knew nothing at all about locks—certainly a rarity in the Palace Royal—or someone who wanted it to be obvious that someone had gotten in with a key who wanted a non-keyholder to be suspected.

Maitena had a key. Or had Kaftus taken that one? Ferrapec could easily have gotten hold of a key, and made off with Arual to implicate his half-sister. Or someone else with a key could have whisked Arual away and left this to make it look as though Ferrapec was trying to implicate Maitena. Furthermore . . .

Nimnestl shook her head again. Most murders in Rossacotta came with far fewer possibilities, and less elaborate ornamentation. She knelt by the fallen guard to see how much damage she had done.

"What is all this?" demanded a voice at the door. Nimnestl rose to find Lady Jilligan and a new pair of dungeon guards.

As Fourth Chief Housekeeper, Jilligan had authority over, among other things, the dungeons and dungeon-keepers. That is, she did until one hour past sunset, when, according to custom, that responsibility switched to the Treasury Department.

"Someone came visiting and left gifts," Nimnestl replied, reaching down one hand to help the groggy guard sit up. "Beyond that, nothing is very clear. Have your men remove these bodies while I report to the Regent."

"Where is Arual?" the woman demanded. "If anything has happened to her . . ."

"Later," said Nimnestl. "See that no one knows about the bodies until the Regent sends orders. I would suggest . . ."

"I am in command here," Jilligan reminded her, breathing loudly through flared nostrils. "I need none of your suggestions until I have been told precisely what occurred here. It is my right . . ."

Nimnestl straightened and drew herself to her full height. "If you wish to speak of rights, we can do so before the Regent and Mitar."

It was a low blow, but it silenced the opposition. "Now, have these bodies taken away, quietly. You need no reminder to help you realize that being in command here leaves you responsible for the well-being of Lady Arual. If she is not found, it may bring you more trouble than my suggestions can turn away."

The housekeeper's bodice rose and fell furiously. Jilligan was set up with Tusenga, a colonel of the city guard. Ancient law forbade younger sons to marry during their father's lifetime, so Jilligan and Tusenga were waiting for Praimal to die. Until they were married, Jilligan, according to the letter of the law, had no rights. High Housekeeper she might be, with all the power that position entailed. As common-law wife of a reputable officer in Malbeth, she had influence in other quarters as well. But before the cold eyes of Mitar, the Court Lawciter, she was an unmarried women. And Rossacottan law dealt unmarried women about the same status as trees: a useful resource, but too plentiful to bother about as individuals.

"More trouble," growled the housekeeper.

Nimnestl was actually as sorry as she had been about hitting the guard, but her primary concern was seeing that her orders were carried out. "Everything will be reported to you in time," she said, by way of palliation. "For now, get these bodies away from here and have two of your men—I won't call them guards—look for signs of the girl in the lower levels."

"Yes, Milady," answered Jilligan, with a smile and a curtsy. Nimnestl let her, but pushed out of the cell before she was tempted to any further displays.

IV

THE courtyard had less than the population of Malbeth in it. Nimnestl pushed through the mob, one hand on Meriere's harness, leading the horse past a knot of people watching sword-swallowers, and a small enclosure where two men were offering to attack each other with maces if sufficient copper was dropped into a broken jug at their feet. Nearer the gatehouse, a pair of husky men, each missing an ear, held a rousing game of Mumble-the-Sparrow as onlookers laid bets. The sparrow was winning, as usual. The crowd roared approval as one man dropped back, a hand clapped over his wounded eye.

A constant parade of servants moved back in the other direction, trying to get loads from the bakery and brewery to the palace kitchens without losing too much to the crowd en route. Four armed guards walked with each delivery, but at this hour they were as much threat as they were protection.

Nimnestl would miss the meal, but she didn't think this would hurt much. She doubted any of the contestants at the singing competition would have songs to dedicate to her, either. If they did, these would probably be songs easier to perform in her absence.

She paused in an open space near the V.I.P. gallery to mount, first chasing off scavengers plundering the platform for the remaining scraps of gilt cloth, or the nails. She did this just to make room; they would be back as soon as she left. Loss of anything exposed to the crowd was figured into the budget, and would be made back from the merchants who bribed the Regent for a seat near the head table.

One hand was on her hammer as she rode for the gate, particularly through the dark passageway of the gatehouse. Not everyone came to the courtyard to watch wandering players jig for pennyetkes or wrestle for a prize.

Istena was on duty at the gate, and saluted as she passed. "Another hour until we close!" he shouted.

"Good luck!" she answered. It would take more than an hour just to clear the courtyards.

Meriere and Nimnestl were alone on the bridge. Hurbis raised the gate for her on the far side. "A fair night, Milady," he remarked. "I feared weather like yesterday's."

"No profit in that," she replied. He nodded. Theoretically, passage through the gate cost nothing, but no one in Malbeth could live on theory. Guests figured the standard gifts into their plans before coming to the Palace Royal. Nimnestl had gotten Hurbis the job at this gate in compensation for the thankless work he did when there were no festivals, keeping city residents from using the dry moat as a garbage dump.

The road ahead and the bridge behind were bare as she urged Meriere forward. She was not being followed. Vague suspicions proved false; neither sound nor shadow pursued her. This was annoying, some: guessing right was part of her job.

No one approached her as she passed down into the city. At Kneath Square she nearly ran into a riot of color and music, a little carnival for those without the price or inclination to dare the palace courtyards and their pleasures. She skirted the celebration, hoping this meant the Blue Bottle would be empty. It did. Nimnestl stepped in for a quiet word with the proprietor. Meriere was taken to the inn's stable, and Nimnestl left the place on foot, hammer in hand. She moved west, taking the long way around to the King's Beach in case she was observed by anyone still sober enough to be curious.

Long strides took her far to the west, where men wore felt boots, and the outdoor carnivals included little wooden shrines for burning incense to the King. It was an exotic and perilous land, the Swamp, more so now that the sun was set and human wolves prowled for unwary prey. Nimnestl did not see any of these. Either they were harrying the herds at the carnivals, picking off stragglers, or they recognized a larger beast of prey, and left her alone.

Following the river, she passed through the Swamp and came at length to the King's Beach. Feeling under her heavy purple travelling cloak for keys, she put one hand on the gate.

"Halt!" ordered a voice from the sentry box.

Nimnestl whirled, considerably surprised. Biandi had been assigned guard duty at the beach over a little matter of one of Laisida's daughters. For six months of the year, this was the dullest guardpost in the country. The King's private piece of shoreline was closed for the season, and a watch was posted chiefly to scare away squatters who might find it a quiet place to spend the winter. Hardly anyone performed the duty without a jug, if not two, between the ankles. This being a holiday, Nimnestl hadn't expected anybody to show up for duty at all.

"Be off, there!" ordered Biandi, coming out of the sentry box. "This is His Majesty's Beach!"

"I knew it," replied Nimnestl. "Be off, yourself."

Biandi came at her sword-first, but not so fast that he couldn't recognize her when she swept off her hood. "I . . . I beg your pardon," he said, sheathing the sword. "I was not expecting you."

"Indeed?" she replied. "For all that, you seem to be very diligent. I'll remember it. But I have a reason for being here, and I will stand your watch tonight."

"If you say so," Biandi replied, hesitating lest this turn out to be some kind of test.

"I order so," she replied. "If I were you, I'd pick up a little something for Aperiole on your way. She's sitting at the contest: alone, so far."

The guard saluted her and hurried off into the darkness to locate his horse. Presently, she heard him ride away. Nimnestl worried about Biandi. Anyone else in Malbeth would have lingered, to find out what she was up to. She shrugged. What could be expected of someone who showed up for beach duty on a cold night in Nelvère?

She waited at the gate, listening for sounds of his return to prove she had underestimated him. She heard none; perhaps mentioning Aperiole had overcome all his natural suspicions.

Unlocking the gate, she stepped out onto the beach. Biandi had, at least, not bothered about patrolling the beach; no footprints in the dank sand showed that he had stepped beyond the little guardhouse, where the wind couldn't hit him. If she hadn't bothered about the gate, he would never have known she was there.

The windswept stretch of sand and pebbles was desolate, and dead silent except for the occasional lap of waves out beyond the breakwater. Nimnestl strolled down to the waterline, taking a deep breath when the wind whipped around her. A few splinters of early ice crackled as she stepped among rotted driftwood and sodden plant life that had long since ceased to be plant life.

Kirajen was nowhere in view. Nimnestl kicked at a broken oar. "After dark" was a loose appointment. Forokell might be keeping an eye on the little schemer; Kirajen wouldn't escape that quickly. Perhaps Kirajen had duties at supper. And perhaps the housekeeper knew nothing useful, really, and wouldn't come. Nimnestl swung her foot into a frozen blot of humus, dislodging a few twigs.

She expelled a long breath and watched the cloud spread, stretch, and vanish. Nimnestl had lived in mountain caves on the border for two years, in colder winds than these, with nothing but Torsun and two blankets to keep her warm. Some nights she did without the blankets.

Torsun was a long time ago and far away. She remembered, with a light, nostalgic sense of loss, his rippling muscles under smooth, satiny skin, and his hard, thick hands. Not that he had ever been worth a nail for anything else. If the King of Reangle's army hadn't finished him in that last battle, he would undoubtedly have succumbed to terminal sloth in the end.

Nimnestl kicked at another lump of leaves. She was enjoying this rare solitude, and found that she was in no real hurry to have the little housekeeper appear with dark, dire news that would call for action.

The lump of leaves rolled, exposing a splotch of white. Nimnestl set free a soft, whispered string of blasphemy.

If the little housekeeper had known anything of value once, she knew nothing now.

V

THE body was earth-still on the sand, its long hair abetting its resemblance to beach flotsam. Nimnestl studied the sand to be sure none of the other lumps were human, and then knelt to check the body.

Kirajen had been strangled; the necklace of pearls and gold had been replaced by a ring of bruised flesh. Nimnestl rolled the body up to see if the garland had fallen underneath. A knife rolled from the little woman's right hand: her eating knife, a dainty piece with pearls set in the handle. More useful knives showed in the housekeeper's sleeves; she must not have had a chance to go for those.

There was no necklace. Nimnestl would have liked to see the necklace. If it was gone, the murder could have been the work of a passing thief. But a thief would have taken that pretty knife, and the rings, too. Nimnestl could think of only one reason for a nonthief to take the necklace, and it meant future trouble.

She shook the fragile lace at the woman's collar. Nothing fell out but a little sand. The ruffles weren't even torn, as they would have been had the necklace fallen among them and snagged.

It just wasn't there. Nimnestl ran a hand through cold, wet hair, for stray pearls or golden threads. She found a bump on the back of Kirajen's head, but that didn't mean much. Forokell was wont to swing things when she was upset. Nimnestl set the body down and looked it over. The necklace could have broken in back and slid down the bodice. She slipped one hand in behind the fabric.

"Ooh!" gasped a tiny voice.

Nimnestl had her hammer ready before she stood up, and had stood up before the lace could settle back against the cold white throat. She could have saved the trouble; she saw no targets. The wind wasn't strong enough just now to make that sound in the trees, even if there had been any trees. The lap-lap of the water was the only sound. Nimnestl held her hammer at the ready and turned in a slow circle to check again. Three sets of footprints led to the body. One stopped at Kirajen's body; another would start again when Nimnestl moved away. The third, belonging to someone with boots wrapped in muffling cloth, came and went. The killer was long gone.

"Quiet, isn't it?" said the same voice.

It was coming from above her. Nimnestl looked up. Ten feet away, a foot above Nimnestl's normal range of vision, was a naked child perhaps four inches tall. It, or, rather, she, was suspended in the air by a pair of translucent wings almost as long as her body.

She flew in closer. "You just go ahead with what you were doing," she said, nodding her head in encouragement. "It looks like fun. I'll just watch."

Nimnestl reslung her hammer. She might be able to hit the pixy from here, but she doubted it, and didn't know what good it would do anyhow. "How long have you been here?" she demanded.

"Long enough," said the pixy. "Was she beautiful, when she was living?"

"Some said so," Nimnestl replied. "What does 'long enough' mean? Was she alive when you got here?"

"Oh, no," said the pixy. "My name's Chicken-and-Dumplings. What's yours?"

"Was someone else here before I came?"

The pixy fluttered back as Nimnestl stepped forward. "Did you ever have a red dress?" she inquired.

Nimnestl licked her lips. She had no experience of pixies (they were not known to stray this far north) but she knew from stories that it did no good at all to lose one's temper. "Um, no," she said.

"I didn't think so," said Chicken-and-Dumplings, with obvious satisfaction. "Do you mean that guy with the brown robes?"

"Yes," hissed Nimnestl.

"I haven't seen him," the pixy replied, with a giggle. She had a long, high giggle. If it was meant to be infuriating, it worked.

Nimnestl just breathed quietly for a few seconds, cleared her throat, and then said, "I was supposed to meet him here."

"Ooooh!" breathed the pixy, flying down next to her face. "What were you going to do?"

Nimnestl repressed a desire to snatch the little being and strike its head on a nearby rock. There were no nearby rocks. "I missed the last meeting of the Brown Robes," she explained. "They were talking about changing the meeting place. He was going to take me there, if it was changed."

"Oh, no," Chicken-and-Dumplings told her. "He went to the same old place."

Nimnestl scratched her upper lip. "You don't even know where that is," she said. "We can hide it from, huh, pixies."

"What?" shrieked Chicken-and-Dumplings, flying a furious figure-eight. "Sump sump sump! You don't know, either! You aren't any member because you don't have your brown robes on!"

"My robe is at the meeting place," Nimnestl retorted. "They took it away from me. That's why I missed that meeting. They were going to decide if I could still be a member. They caught me, see, doing something a little, er, nasty."

This had exactly the effect she had expected. With another "Ooh!" the pixy swooped in and settled her small, moist posterior on one of Nimnestl's thick shoulders. "Tell me, tell me, tell me!"

"Well, let's make that our bet, then," said Nimnestl, twisting her head around toward the pixy. "If you can really show me where the meeting place is, I'll tell you . . . after the meeting. I'm late now."

"Let's go," cried Chicken-and-Dumplings. She jumped up into the air, zipped twenty feet to the west, halted, and flew back to Nimnestl.

"What if I can't show you?" she inquired demurely. "What do I lose?"

This had not occurred to Nimnestl. What could one threaten to do that a perverse pixy would be certain not to enjoy? "Oh, er, I'll think of something just dreadful," she promised.

"You have to tell me what you thought of if I show you the place," said the pixy. She reached out and gave Nimnestl's left earlobe an affectionate tug. "Maybe we'll do it anyway. I bet you have a really dirty mind."

"Let's go, can we?" said Nimnestl, accepting the compliment but contemplating pixicide. The little creature squealed and sped away.

Nimnestl recalled from stories that pixies tended to live in marshes. It was not a detail she had had reason to contemplate before, but as she followed Chicken-and-Dumplings through all of the filthiest back alleys of Malbeth, she wondered if the delicate creatures actually preferred the miasma of insects and potent odors, or whether she was just drawing too much from the behavior of one demented member of the species.

"Do you know every dunghill in the city?" she demanded, pausing to knock her boots against a wall.

The pixy giggled and said, "We're getting close now."

Nimnestl's hammer was already up. They were back in the Swamp, where you carried your life in your weapon hand. Chicken-and-Dumplings darted among the shadows and stopped before a rough wooden door that was indistinguishable from the last hundred rough wooden doors.

"Here we are," she trilled. "Recognize it?"

Nimnestl knocked. A tall man, his head hidden in a brown cowl, swung the door open as if he'd been expecting her. Nimnestl planted a boot against it in case he changed his mind.

"I am coming in," she told him.

"Of course you are," the man replied, looking up into her eyes. He threw back his hood. "The Ykenai have no secrets from the King's Bodyguard."

Nimnestl stepped forward and leaned her whole body against the door. The man looked friendly, but she could make out two faces: one that showed in his eyes and teeth and the welcoming one superimposed on the real one.

"What is it, Brother?" inquired another man, stepping in from the next room. Nimnestl recognized Trioafmar. "No, I see. To what do we owe the pleasure of this visit, Milady?"

"I'm looking for a murderer," she told him.

"A murderer!" said the first man, raising his hands, palm out.

Trioafmar shook his head. "We never allow anyone to enter our meeting rooms but Ykenai."

"That's what I thought," she told him. She did not, however, back out of the room.

They stared at her. "One of us?" demanded the first man. "But the Ykenai never kill anyone, except spies. There are so many more civilized ways to settle affairs."

"True," said Nimnestl, giving her hammer a practice swing. "But a murderer is what I said. Do I get to look at that next room?"

Trioafmar's mouth barely budged under its black foliage. "Of course, Milady," he said. "At last the court realizes our full potential."

He turned to the door he'd entered through and pushed it open. "We knew we could attract more attention by seeming to be a threat than by proclaiming our loyalty to the crown. No one trusts friendship at court. Slorvick, a cup of spiced wine for our guest."

The first man pushed past Trioafmar into the next room. Trioafmar turned back toward Nimnestl and pushed out his right hand. "We are proud to have you among us," he announced. "This is the beginning of a new age for the Ykenai."

Nimnestl stepped forward. Trioafmar knelt and took her free hand in both of his, gazing up at her in pure joy. But she saw a vacant quality in his eyes, as if he weren't quite seeing what his eyes were aimed at. His chin jerked down.

Nimnestl whirled, her hammer up, but couldn't do it fast enough while Trioafmar hauled on her arm.

CHAPTER FIVE
Polijn

I

POLIJN let the door swing shut behind her and started for the Great Dining Hall again. These benches with holes in them were new to her, and, to judge by the condition of the floor, to most of the rest of the court. She wasn't sure she approved of them.

The maze of halls and corridors was beginning to make some sense, so she decided to try what she thought would be a shortcut. Halfway down the hall, though, a knot of excited people blocked her passage, so she couldn't find out. Most of them seemed to be pointing at a massive scarred door.

Of course Iúnartar was among them. "Oh, come here!" she cried, on seeing Polijn. "There are a dozen bodies in the dungeon, and a dozen heads, and they don't fit!"

Polijn tried to make sense out of this. "Oh, don't make owl eyes at me!" said the smaller girl. "Look, here they come!"

The crowd contracted toward the door. Polijn didn't push forward. Dead bodies were no novelty to someone from the Swamp, not unless they had something special about them, like Kronja. Polijn shuddered; she hadn't thought about Kronja lately.

There seemed to be something special about what was on the stretcher carried by two guards from the dark door. Iúnartar's mother strode behind them, with her assembled retinue. "Just told me to clean up after her, polite as you please, and everything to be explained later. There's some little behind this, and the Council must certainly . . ."

The crowd was more interested in the body than in the housekeeper's rage. Murmurs of "Witchcraft!" and "Horror!" filtered back to Polijn. She touched Iúnartar and asked, "What is it?"

The girl did not give up trying to force herself through the wall of people. "Twenty people are gone from their cells, and dead bodies without heads were put in," she said, not even glancing back.

"You got that all wrong," sneered a courtier. "The Bodyguard came in and carried Arual away to her office, knocking the heads off two guards who tried to save her."

"You don't know any more than a lumpuck," a woman informed him. "The Bodyguard found the bodies. Two men and three women, and nobody knows who."

"It could have been two guards, then," argued the man, shaking three fingers in her face. "And likely there's more bodies to be brought out."

The stretcher-bearers had to shoulder a path forward. To Iúnartar's delight, the easiest route passed within a foot of her position. But some spoilsport had thrown a blanket over the stretcher; nothing showed but one arm. "Looks like there's just one body on there," she said, in disgust. "The head's right there, too."

A courtier who was strategically placed accidentally thrust his eating knife forward, somehow catching the blanket. With an exaggerated gesture and a cry of disgust, he pulled back and yanked the cover away. It and a woman's head hit the floor, to the screams and bellows of the crowd.

"Rooogosh!" exclaimed Iúnartar. "I can't look! Tell me what happens!" She did not turn away or even shift her eyes until the blanket had been retrieved and replaced.

"Isn't it spooky?" she asked Polijn, when the stretcher moved on.

Polijn wasn't there. One look at the head had sent her scurrying around the crowd, headed for the Great Dining Hall. She stood at that door now, peering across the room at the head table.

"Out of the way, brat!" ordered a brightly clad young courtier escorting a lady from the room. "Come on, Aperiole. I hear there's nineteen bodies and twenty heads."

Polijn stepped aside and scanned the crowd. The Head Bodyguard wasn't there; some soldier Polijn did not know sat in the Bodyguard's seat, angled well away from the great black bird watching him with gleaming eyes.

Now what? She had no desire at all to talk to the Regent, still less to try to reach the head table with all the officials and guards between it and the door. Ynygyn was busy eating and judging contestants, and, she imagined, wouldn't be overly interested anyhow. Aesernius might be able to do something, but she couldn't spot him in the assembly.

Perhaps it was just as well. In view of the whispers of witchcraft and the apparently mysterious circumstances surrounding the discovery of the body, the affable magician might be involved somehow himself. Polijn didn't think Aesernius was the murdering type, but she knew too well not to trust offhand impressions.

Her fists were clenched, and started to quiver. Somebody had to be told. She didn't know why somebody had to be told, but she knew she had to tell someone. The Vielfrass had sent her to report on anything she found. And as far as she could find, she was the only one in the Palace Royal who had recognized that head.

It belonged to Menapri, who operated a pawnshop in the eastern end of the Swamp. Trustworthy, as pawnbrokers in that section of town went, she made a reasonable profit, though not an overscrupulously legal one, on items servants and minor courtiers sneaked out of the Palace Royal. She had protected her investment by marrying a large, muscular ex-soldier named Calongir. Calongir had a purple snake tattooed on one arm, like the one on the exposed arm of the corpse hauled out of the dungeon.

As Polijn pondered her next move, the features of Menapri and Calongir merged and melted in her mind. Was Calongir's tattoo on the right arm, or the left? Was the snake purple, or blue? Didn't Menapri always wear a wig? Maybe it was someone else. What could a couple of pawnbrokers from the Swamp be doing in a cell in the royal dungeons?

It just might be safer to keep quiet for now. First, she thought, she could make sure Menapri and Calongir weren't working the store as usual at the sign of the Grey Bear. The evening was young; she could reach the Swamp and be back before anyone missed her. The singing competition would go on for hours.

Having made up her mind, she turned to go. She walked face-first into a wall of stained, starched muslin.

"Three's the charm, girl," said Maitena, looking down the wall at her. "Now you go to work."

Both the housekeeper's hands were clamped on Polijn's shoulders. She knew she couldn't break out of the grip, and didn't try. "Milady! I . . . I have a message to take to . . . to the Bodyguard!"

"That excuse won't serve," snapped the housekeeper, spinning her captive around to face front. "You are in the Palace Royal to work, not to carry tales. If your owner can't keep you busy, I can find something to occupy you in the kitchen. Unproductive persons can be dispensed with."

"But . . . the Bodyguard, the Chief Bodyguard . . ." Polijn stammered, trying to brace her feet on the stones of the floor as she was forced forward.

"If I see her, I will tell her you are doing something useful," Maitena replied, giving her a good shove forward. "I shall tell her where you are, and be assured that I shall tell her what you are. Keep moving, or I'll call someone who can move you."

Contradicting herself, Maitena reached down to grab an ankle without calling for assistance. "A moment, Maitena," called a soft voice.

Maitena turned her head to look, sniffed, and then bent over Polijn again. She had both her captive's wrists and one ankle clamped in one hand before the owner of the voice reached them.

"I am going to see the Bodyguard now," said the slow, languorous woman, who wore a sumptuous gown designed for slow, languorous investigation. "If the girl really has a message for that woman, she may come with me."

"She doesn't," snapped Maitena, trying to gather in the last limb without losing the other three. Polijn tried to dance it out of her reach. Half a dozen idlers near the door of the hall came to offer advice. "She's lying. A lazier . . ."

"I think she should come with me," the woman insisted, leaning back from the sheer weariness of it all, and blocking the advance of a courtier who had flicked out a long, thin sword. "In fact, I am reclined to desist."

The man sidestepped her and inserted his sword, but was either too drunk to aim or undecided whom to help, for he poked both Polijn and Maitena with it. The Housekeeper batted the sword from his hand, and swung to face the woman, whirling Polijn around with her.

"Milady Feetintheair may recline or incline, whichever she likes better, all evening," she said. "I have work to do. And people to do it." Then she darted in and caught hold of Polijn's free ankle. A few members of the audience cheered.

"I think," said Hopoli with dignity, "that I should go ask Kaftus. If she really has some commendication for the Bodyguard, he would know." She tipped her head back to study the ceiling as she thought about this.

"Your brother is dead!" spat Maitena. "You have no influence with the Regent now!"

"Yes," Hopoli decided, still studying the ceiling, "I think I have to ask Kaftus. He'd know if the message was general or fake, and he'd know who was in fluids, too."

The housekeeper's reply was a mixture of splutters. Then she threw Polijn to the floor at Hopoli's feet. "You can have her! It doesn't surprise me that you've become procuress for that black oddity. I hope you have as much joy from that position as you do from all the others."

Maitena stormed away. One or two audience members followed her to offer consolation and advise on revenge. Two or three lingered to congratulate Hopoli. The rest melted back into the Great Dining Hall to spread the story.

Hopoli ignored her admirers and helped Polijn to her feet. "She didn't hurt you, did she?" the woman asked, pulling her aside into a window. "Sit down."

"No," said Polijn. "That is, she really didn't, Milady. I . . . I wasn't really . . ."

Hopoli giggled, startling Polijn considerably. "Oh, I knew that all the time. It was just a device. I'm not going there, either. But I used to work in that kitchen, and I wouldn't be one of her scholarly maids for whirls. She's just a petty tirade; she picks on people. The old toad. You go off and have fun. I hope he's cute."

"I . . ." Polijn began. "I don't . . ."

Hopoli rose, and then bent to pat her cheek. "You don't have to thank me. But if he's really cute, you might tell me his name sometime. I never have enough beaus to my string." She giggled again and ambled down the hall, bouncing cheerfully with each step.

Polijn watched her go, fascinated. Then, with a shrug, she walked away herself, trying not to imitate that infectious gait.

II

POLIJN could understand now why the Vielfrass had said it was better not to go on foot through certain parts of Malbeth. Lights burned at patrolboxes along the clean streets, and patrollers, big muscular sentries with tiny eyes, stopped anyone they caught walking. Nobody in these neighborhoods walked unless they couldn't afford to ride. And if they couldn't afford to ride, they didn't belong in these neighborhoods.

Fortunately, it was the King's Birthday. Little carnivals had broken out all over the city, and festival-hoppers wandered from one to another. Polijn figured out quickly that the best answer to a strong hand on the arm was "On my way to the next fair." You generally got a shove, but no worse.

By the eighth time this happened, she had nearly reached the darker, more familiar alleys of the Swamp. "Just on my way to the next fair," she said, without looking up.

"I know," said a voice with an accent subtly exotic. "But if you stop a moment, you may see something fairer."

Polijn suspected what it was, but she was in a hurry and couldn't spare the time. She tried to pull free. The hand did not release her, and its partner came down to catch her arm and turn her around. She was looking up into a face she knew she ought to recognize.

"My Lord Arlmorin," she said, remembering.

The man's mouth spread long under his fierce mustache. "You know me, eh? Well, I know you as well, little one.

You're Ynygyn's slavey, not?"

"Yes, my lord," said Polijn, watching that one hand as it pulled away from her arm.

"Ah," said the Brautian. The hand slid back to a low stone fence, making sure it wasn't boobytrapped. Then he sat down, pulling Polijn along with him. He trapped his captive between his knees, so as to have both hands free.

"Now, Ynygyn is a friend of mine." One hand slid inside his cloak. "I don't like to bother him with trifles. It's politer, not? And he is a man who does not care for little things, outside the line of business. But I think I left some papers of mine in his room. Can you keep an eye, or both eyes, open for them? They will have this seal on them." He took a piece of paper from inside his cloak and spread it out on his thigh so that she could see the wax impression of a large eagle perched on a brick wall.

"Yes, My Lord," Polijn replied, not mentioning the chink she could spy between what the man had said and what he had not. If the papers were trifles, why stop someone down in the city and ask her to look for them?

"I am from Braut," he told her, sliding his paper away. "You might like Braut. The climate is rather like this, but we build our houses tighter, warmer. When I go back, I might have some use for a servant who had already proven herself useful to me. And, in Braut, where nobody knows her, she might be anybody, not? If I were to call her a Rossacottan countess, there would be none to contradict me."

He released Polijn. She pulled back as he stood up and shook out wrinkles in his cloak. "The papers," he said, patting her on the back, "if you can remember such trifles. Good-night, Countess."

He turned back in the direction of the Palace Royal. Polijn watched until he disappeared in the shadows between patrolboxes. The papers were not trifles, then, and the man knew she knew so. What would it be like to live as a countess? She wondered if Ynygyn had stolen the papers. Then she wondered what she would do if she actually did find them.

Then she decided to finish what she'd been doing in the first place.

For several blocks, she recognized nothing, and wondered if she'd taken the wrong turn at the last alley. But at the next open square a bonfire shot light across a crowd of celebrants, and she saw Thyrik throwing in a cat. So this must be Breakneck Square, or the next one east. Jelono was there, too, with a new black eye. Polijn wondered if Humbian had given her that, or her husband. Farther along, on the far side of the fire, she saw Giriona offering incense at the King's Shrine. Hiptus was being hauled off by a matched pair of patrollers, demanding as he was dragged, "Whatcha doon, boy? Ima persnl frennada genrl!"

But she didn't realize how close she was to home until she saw Gloraida and Hylarith on a small platform, singing "I want to be a porcupine's concubine" while Fikemun played pipes in the background. She looked nervously around for Karlikartis.

A blade seemed to lodge in her throat, from the inside. She was jerked deeper into the shadows, and a hoarse voice whispered, "Devening, my darling, my dove."

Torat, Karlikartis's consort, was a man of consequence in the Swamp. His hand with the garotte was widely known, and he carried his wire openly, using it sometimes to attract the attention of passersby. It worked.

"I like your new dress," he whispered. An accident with a rival some years before made it impossible for him to speak any other way. "They told us you'd met easy day, up at the palace."

"Yes," croaked Polijn. She should have thought to change the shift before she left.

The wire pulled tighter. Polijn tried not to struggle. "Do you see the Regent?" whispered Torat. "Is it true he drinks blood? What does the King look like, up close? Or is it true the one we see is just a doll? Is Harliis as . . ."

The wire was convincing Polijn that breathing was sinful, unnatural, an imposition on the good nature of creation. But she pulled her head back, exposing more of her throat, pulled in one gasp of air before the loop tightened again, and expelled, "Harliis is dead!"

The wire forgave her. "What?"

"Dead," she gasped, as the wire slackened. "Someone hit him on the head."

"Harliis is dead?" Torat whispered. He put a knee between her legs and forced her forward. "Say it again."

"Harliis is dead," she said. "Someone hit him on the head while . . ."

The knee lifted, propelling her out into the light of the

bonfire. A few more sober merrymakers turned to look. "Shout it," whispered the man with the wire.

Her throat hurt. But Polijn sucked in a lungful of air and bellowed, "Harliis is dead! They hit him on the head!"

The crowd turned to stare. Her mother was the first to recover. "Harliis is dead!" shouted Gloraida, and her partner joined her on "They hit him on the head!"

It was good news, true or not, and kind of catchy besides. It spread from mouth to ear, and soon the whole crowd was chanting "Harliis is dead! They hit him on the head!" Gloraida and Hylarith fell backward into leafless bushes as six men hauled on the platform and pulled it across the bonfire. Flames darkened and then caught at the wooden platform, leaping into the air.

"Harliis is dead!" roared the crowd, pulling back from the increasing heat. "They hit him on the head!"

Torat pushed to one side and ran to help six others who were ripping down the badges Harliis had ordered displayed on stores which had paid their tithe to him. Polijn stumbled away, but didn't get far before she hit a thick, heavy holiday dress. Looking up into the face of Karlikartis, Polijn dove and rolled before the whip. It snapped in the air above her and Polijn zigged to the left to avoid a second shot.

She wasn't fast enough. To her shock and utter horror, she found herself wrapped in long arms, lifted, and kissed four times. Then the woman dropped her and ran to join the jumping crowd, laughing like the dying jester.

This was too much all at once for Polijn. She scrambled away on all fours, away from the light to a safe, dark alley. Crouched against a gritty wall, she caught her breath and spat the taste of Karlikartis out of her mouth.

Once she felt healthy enough to move again, she slipped along the alley to find Menapri's place. It stood next to the All-the-Way, which in spite of its name presented a pretty boring show. The pawnshop was dark, but Polijn knew it must be open. This was the King's Birthday, and celebrants would be in and out all night, hoping to prolong festivities by pawning belongings, theirs and those they happened to pick up in the course of the evening. Polijn stepped up to the door and pushed it open.

III

THE only light to be seen came from two flickering dips, their smoky light hardly strong enough to reflect in the blades of weapons displayed well behind the front counter. Clothing, most of it torn and much of it dusty, lay in untidy heaps on boards or in bins. Polijn could see nothing of the proprietors.

"Something?" inquired a voice. A pile of rags moved and was revealed as Lintrosn, Menapri's sister-in-law. She limped up to the counter. The limp was a souvenir of her run-in with Chordasp. The hands she spread on the rough counter lacked three fingers where she had tried to deflect his knife.

"Oh, er," Polijn answered. She cleared her throat. "I was just, er, looking for Menapri."

"She's at the bonfire, enjoying herself," spat the woman. "Haven't seen her all night. You want something with her, or is that just talk?" Idle conversation was simply an excuse to come by and try to snatch something for resale. Lintrosn had an unnerving and accusing stare, partly the result of a suspicious nature and partly because she was nearsighted. That Chordasp had cut off her eyelids hadn't improved matters.

Polijn tried to think of an excuse. Harliis's death wouldn't do; it had to be something that could be of specific importance to the pawnbroker. "Well, it wasn't much," she said. "The Banner of Kairor is missing, and they're looking for it up at the palace. I thought I'd warn her, you know, that if anyone brought it here there might be trouble. But I guess . . ."

She was turning away by this time, but Lintrosn stuck out a hand. "Hold it, there," said the maimed woman, her voice lifted in urgency. "The Banner of Kairor, you say? Red, isn't it? Law and lifting, a woman came in today with a banner, and she set good store by it. Menapri bit her down, but if it's from the palace, you've got that right: it's trouble."

Lintrosn pushed the counter to one side and beckoned. "It's here in back. We figured she'd come get it later, she was so set on a good price. Take a look and tell me what you think."

Polijn had no idea what the Banner of Kairor looked like, beyond its proverbial redness. But she stepped behind the counter; it would be a good excuse to wait around and see if Menapri or Calongir stepped in to disprove her theory about the bodies. And, too, if it did turn out to be the Banner, bringing it in would be a decided triumph. Menapri could have any monetary reward; the gratitude would be enough for Polijn.

The back room was darker, dustier, and even more cluttered than the front. "I'll get it," said Lintrosn, kicking a stool over to Polijn. "Sit down while I check where she put it." She reached up for a couple of the long, greasy candles she sold, and stuck them into broken holders. Polijn glanced back at the front room and the still open door of the shop, waiting to see if either proprietor stepped through.

While her eyes were fixed on the front door, a pair of strong arms took hold of her. Polijn looked up and pulled away, but the man folded her forearms together and held them. It was Lintrosn's hulking husband, Ostapavo.

"Got her," he said.

Polijn looked to Lintrosn to tell him it was all right; this guest was an invited one. Lintrosn did not do this. She jerked her thumb toward the ceiling. Ostapavo kept hold of Polijn's arms with one hand, and used the other to yank her shift up to the waist, bending her backward a little. Lintrosn set one of her candles on the stool and lit it from a dip.

"Ever played Burning Shame?" she inquired.

That was a game Polijn had never thought much of. Everyone knew at the outset who was going to lose.

"Why?" inquired Ostapavo.

"It's Polijn," his wife told him. "Gloraida's wiper who went up to the palace. She comes in, asks about Menapri, and then goes on about this lintik banner. There's someone behind it all: the Bodyguard, or the Regent himself, maybe."

She pushed the stool a few inches forward with her foot. "Right?"

"That's right," Polijn said immediately, her eyes on the candle flame. "He sent me. The Regent sent me. And if I'm not back by . . . dawn, he knows where to come look."

"He does, does he?" said Lintrosn, easing the stool forward an entire foot. Polijn imagined she could feel the heat, faintly, on one thigh. "By dawn, eh?"

"Yes," said Polijn. This lie better be as big as possible. "I told him just where I'd be. He might only send the Bodyguard, but with the Banner business, he might come himself."

"Could be," suggested Ostapavo. But he didn't squeeze her arms any the less for it.

"Why, maybe I believe that," said Lintrosn. "Heh. I'll flip a coin and see."

She took a small coin from her pocket, let it shine in the candlelight for a second and then, crying "Heads!", sent it flipping up over her head.

They all watched it come down. Lintrosn snatched it from its fall and peered at the uppermost side. "Heads," she announced. "I believe it." She shoved the coin out of sight and waved her hands at Ostapavo.

Polijn was swallowing with relief when Ostapavo pulled back on her arms, nearly wresting them from their sockets. Bracing himself against a bin, he used his knees to spread her legs farther apart.

"But by dawn," said Lintrosn, hunching her shoulders and lowering her head to stare into Polijn's eyes, "we will have sold the thing and be out of the city. We have ways through the country that even he can't find, and he can track the Banner first, if it's so precious to him. We'll be gone, be long gone. We even have time for some bonfire fun of our own." She put a foot on the stool and pushed it forward.

Polijn tried to pull to the left, preparing a scream. To her surprise, Ostapavo came with her, well nigh throwing her against the wall as he straightened and turned.

Lintrosn was as startled as she was. "What are you doing, you . . ."

Her husband jerked his head toward the door. A squarish figure had stepped up into the shop. His heavy-booted footsteps indicated ready money and his cheerful whistle a willingness to do business.

"The Banner," whispered Ostapavo.

Lintrosn motioned to a corner out of sight from the door. "Keep her quiet. Time enough for her to make noise once we're shut of the goods." She took a metal cap and extinguished the candle, but smiled at Polijn to let the captive know it could be relit.

Ostapavo dragged Polijn to the corner indicated, the hand that had been holding her shift now covering her mouth. Polijn considered biting it, but decided to wait until the time was right.

Lintrosn hurried out to meet her customer.

IV

POLIJN could see through a crack in the door, and frowned as the man strolled in, his arms folded behind his back in reckless carelessness, his head turning from side to side in amiable curiosity. There was something familiar in that silhouette, something she recognized in its jaunty step. Nonetheless, it was a shock to hear the shadowy figure call, "Good evening to you, my good Lintrosn!"

Now was the time for action. She bit down hard on Ostapavo's hand. He probably wouldn't yell; she doubted his vocabulary was that extensive. But if his hand would move just enough for her to get one word out, surely the Vielfrass would recognize her voice as she had recognized his.

Ostapavo tightened his grip on her arms and drove his knee into her back. The hand that closed her mouth did move, but just enough to allow the thumb and one finger to close off her nose as well.

"Good evening, Master," said Lintrosn, out front. "We have it here."

"The Banner of Kairor?" replied the Vielfrass, setting his elbows on the counter.

"Sssh, sssh!" hissed the pawnbroker, her head snapping around to check the door to the street. "The walls have ears, Master!"

"And ears often have walls," answered the sorcerer. "What

is the going price for Banners of Kairor tonight?"

"Sixty," Lintrosn breathed. "In gold."

"You obviously skipped over my warning back there," said the sorcerer, standing up straight and removing his elbows from the countertop. "I didn't hear any of those words well at all. The only thing I made out was the part about 'six.' "

"There is only one Banner of Kairor," Lintrosn reminded him.

The Vielfrass spread both hands out in the air, one finger on each pointing at the pawnbroker, the other fingers toward the ceiling. "My good, my very good woman, by the time the news reaches the Swamp that the Banner of Kairor is missing, there will be ten. By the end of the week, there will be two hundred, and once this month comes to its frigid end, every child in the Swamp will have a Banner of Kairor to sell. In spring, Lintrosn, the ratbirds will be nesting in Banners of Kairor. I offer you ten."

"Sixty, sixty, sixty," said Lintrosn, slapping the larger of her hands on the countertop.

"Six, six, six," answered the Vielfrass, copying the gesture. "Adding up to eighteen, and I haven't even seen it yet."

The woman drew a roll of cloth from under the counter, but did not set it down. "Now you've seen it."

In the back room, Ostapavo let Polijn's nostrils open for one quick breath and then shut them again.

"For a whole glimpse of it, I raise my bid to twenty," said the sorcerer. "But for that, I'll want the Banner and the contents of that blue sack in the back."

"Blue sack?" demanded the woman. "I don't . . ."

"It contains a Polijn. The value of Polijns is negligible, and I make the purchase strictly on sentimental grounds." Ostapavo released Polijn's nose again and left it alone. Her head hurt, and she wasn't sure she had heard correctly.

"I don't know what you mean, Master," said Lintrosn, slipping her bundle back under the counter. "There is no Polijn here, and I do not believe this is really the Banner of Kairor after all."

"Oh," said the Vielfrass, sounding let down. "And I was so sure. Perhaps I should call in an expert appraiser, someone familiar with the provenance and points of Banners and Polijns. Whom should I call? Shall I go to the Regent, for example?"

He leaned on the counter to gaze up into the woman's eyes. "You can go to the devil, if you haven't been there already!" she declared. She snatched up a long dagger from a rack behind the counter, and thrust it into the countertop. Polijn couldn't tell, in this dark, but it hadn't sounded as though the blade had hit wood, and the only thing on the countertop besides the knife was the Vielfrass's arm.

The sorcerer, knife or no, did not move that arm. "Lintrosn," he said, "yours has been a hard life. I am a meek and tender man of mercy. So I will warn you, once, that you have one foot in the grave and the other on a banana peel. This is your last chance: give me the Banner and the girl."

Lintrosn had a good arsenal at hand, and plunged another dagger next to the first one. This time Polijn was sure it had gone through flesh.

"You've scared plenty of people in your time," Lintrosn declared, "but you don't scare me! That's what I'll give you, and there's plenty more of that for free, if you like it!"

"Lintrosn." The Vielfrass's voice was low, and gentle, as it had been when he explained to Polijn about bunnies. "There are many last chances in the world. There are 'last chance' taverns and 'last chance' inns and 'last chance to snatch a doughnut before we get up from the table.' But not many are really your last chance. Real last chances are rare, and seldom bear labels."

His voice rose as he went on. "The way to tell a last chance is genuine is to discover that it was final. You had your last chance before you got this far."

He plucked the daggers from his arm. Lintrosn reached back for a battleaxe, but stared as the blades began to glow. From their bloodless points rose four hideous faces, with no bodies save those formed by their long, flowing hair. Fangs glowed like knives on each face, and their mouths opened in mute laughter as they grew and surrounded the pawnbroker.

The woman screamed, a high, harrowing sound completely unlike her usual voice. Throwing Polijn to the floor, Ostapavo rushed for the door. It was blocked by a naked, incandescent man-thing that stood eight feet tall, with claws for hands and not much in the way of face but teeth. One arm, clotted with muscles, reached out for the big man, pulled his wrists together over his head, and lifted him off the floor. With its free hand, it then divided Ostapavo into three equal sections, which were bounced into different corners of the front shop.

Torn by the hair-creatures, Lintrosn sprawled on the floor. The grisly heads spun into four whirling spheres of red light. Finding herself still alive, the pawnbroker began to crawl for the door, using her arms, mainly. Little jets of flame were shooting around her hips and legs.

The glowing green monster, sweeping bits of Ostapavo off its claws, turned and watched with mild, if hostile, interest, like a man waiting for the fly to light where it could be squashed. Lintrosn had one hand on the threshold when it stooped and caught her up, one claw at her neck and the other between her legs. Polijn dove for cover under a pile of pledged cloaks.

She didn't move, through all the ugly sounds that followed. It must have lasted only seconds, but to Polijn it seemed she curled there for hours, her hands smashed over her ears. At length things seemed to settle. She pulled her hands down. The silence went unbroken. She chewed her upper lip for a moment, and then pushed one rag aside to peek out.

Her eyes met the tiny, glittering eyes of the shining monster. The steaming fangs parted to inquire, "You okay?"

Polijn gathered a great lungful of air and expelled it in a long, chest-opening shriek.

"Oh, good," said the creature, and thereupon turned back into the Vielfrass.

V

WITH the gesture of one who is quite used to it and not really showing off at all, the Vielfrass banished the glowing spheres from the front room, leaving only the flickering dips to light the shop.

"That was," he said, not looking back at Polijn, "I fear, not very nice."

Polijn felt she could agree with that. "But even the most superb examples of humanity can lose their tempers," he went on.

Frowning, Polijn stared at the floor. Clothes still lay in untidy heaps, and dust still covered much of the room. Of the bodies, there was no trace.

"And I never could abide a price-gouger," the Vielfrass went on, straightening a pair of bent candlesticks. "First they get Menapri killed, then they price up things to ruin her business. That's adding something to something else, as the poet should have written."

Polijn remembered why she had come down this far in the first place. "Killed? Were they the ones in the cell up at the palace, then?"

"I suppose so," said the sorcerer, picking up a few small objects, looking them over, and dropping them into an inner pocket. "They had to die. They turned out, rather to their surprise, to be more honest than was good for them. They were going to return the Banner and claim a reward. That would have been very awkward for those who left it here."

"Who?" breathed Polijn, rising to her knees in the tumble of rags.

"La, child," he remonstrated. "Do you expect omniscience?"

"Yes!" she snapped, and sat down again, glaring at him. She hated being toyed with, hated it. She had seen now what kind of power the man possessed. He had the power to know everything, obviously, so he must know: that was what power was for. He just wanted to be mysterious, to keep people and events confused so as to display his talents the better.

The possibility that snapping at a man with such power, indeed, one who had just saved her from a very unpleasant evening, might not be wise occurred to her a second later. But the Vielfrass didn't even glance in her direction.

"Foo," he said, looking around for anything else he could use. "There are things I know and things I don't know, and, what's more, I know I know what I know and I know I don't know what I don't know. Not everyone can say that. Half of those who can can't even understand it."

"You're a sorcerer," Polijn pointed out, in case he had forgotten. "You can read things in a crystal ball or get answers from the stars or . . ."

"Crystal ball?" he demanded, much offended. "Stars? What do you think I am: magic? Now, generally, when I wish to read signs and omens and such, I resort to thyromancy, but it hardly seems worthwhile without a sleazy sidekick nearby to wrinkle her nose in disgust. All the other spells I know for that kind of viewing require the assistance of a virgin, and, naturally, there is no oversupply of those in this district."

"Um," said Polijn.

"Ask me something else and I'll tell you that," he said, raising one majestic hand. "Ask me how many eleven-year-old nephews the King of Braut has. And no peeking."

"Um," said Polijn again, bringing her knees up and putting her arms around them. "What does the, er, virgin have to do?"

The Vielfrass inclined his head down a little. "You don't mean to say so."

Well, there was something he didn't know, at least. "Um," she said, for the third time.

"No, no, I forgot, I forgot," he said, fluttering fingers through the air. "Ronar will have been saving up for the auction. Yes, I see it now. Well, if you really want to learn something, stand up and hold this."

A hand dipped in behind his vest and brought out an oval mirror. Polijn rose and came over to him. He folded her hands around it. "Hold it just there," he commanded.

"I can't see it," she noted.

"That's the way it works," he told her. "The virgin gets no fun out of it at all. Been like that since the willow, first tree of the forest, sprang in the first spring. Just hold that pose."

He raised his hands and small dots of light sparkled on the floor of the shop. "Ab kadef," said the Vielfrass.

The specks streamed together to form an oval, which slid soundlessly across the dusty boards. The Vielfrass, standing between the light and Polijn, stepped to one side.

"I . . ." Polijn began.

"Sssh," said the man of shadows.

The oval halted an inch from her toes and began to swing back and forth, edging a little forward at each stroke. It brushed the fourth toe on her left foot and jerked back, as if startled. For a moment, it held its position: thinking, perhaps. Then it plunged forward, easing up Polijn's body in silent invasion. Her heartbeat quickened as it rose, but the Vielfrass was behind her now, and she couldn't step back from it.

For a third time the oval halted, having reached her chest. It paused there for but a second, and then moved along her raised arm. It found the mirror, and moved from her view.

"Well, well," said the Vielfrass, looking down over her shoulder. "Twelve fortune cookies sitting in a row: six say yes and six say no."

"What do you see?" whispered Polijn.

"Tings," he replied. "Oh, so many games are afoot that I barely know where to sic my dogs. You can put it down now."

The mirror was dark. Polijn set it gently on a handy shelf. "Did you see who stole the Banner?"

"Ah, the Banner," said the sorcerer. "I was forgetting." He pulled a bag from the accumulation near the back door and moved out to the front room. Using a dagger from the display rack, he caught at the roll of cloth and pushed it into this container.

"Note how carefully I avoid touching it," he instructed. "The pain and hatred of the losers are in it, and everyone who has ever touched it is dead as of five minutes ago. Most of them died of old age, yet it's best not to take chances."

"What about the killers?" Polijn demanded, glad that she didn't have the carrying of it.

Instead of answering, the Vielfrass turned toward the front door. A bat fluttered inside, almost as if called. It was a funny kind of bat. It was waving its hands and swooping back and forth, crying, "Helphelphelphelphelp!"

"Have no fear," said the sorcerer. He raised one hand, and a glove of light sprang from it into the air. Rays from the fingers revealed a small woman with wings and very long black hair. Polijn gaped.

"Oh, good!" sighed the creature, throwing an arm across its pale forehead. "This is all too much for one pixy to handle. You wave your hands and swoop, and I'll cry 'Helphelphelphelphelp.' "

"You got to cry 'Helphelphelphelphelp' last time," pouted the Vielfrass. "It's my turn."

"The last time you did it," said the pixy sternly, "you forgot your line and started crying, 'Cockles and mussels, alive, alive-oh!' "

Polijn stepped slowly into the front room. "Is that your . . . I mean . . . that isn't . . ."

"The seditious sidekick?" inquired the sorcerer, raising an eyebrow. "Land, no. Though I suspect a relationship somewhere. You never can tell about pixies. That's why they're pixies."

The little woman fluttered down to study Polijn's face. "I bet I'm going to like you," she said. "You must know some positively vile stuff. Let's let her yell 'Helphelphelphelphelp,' huh? I'll swoop and you can wave."

"Oh, I suppose," sighed the Vielfrass. "Never let it be said that I stood in the way of budding talent. Come along, oh child with a vile and tired mind." He set a hand on her shoulder and guided her past the counter.

"Where are we going?" she demanded.

He shrugged. "To the rescue."

CHAPTER SIX

Nimnestl

I

A VOICE far away was complaining, "But if Brown Robes don't kill anybody but spies, why would they kill Harliis? Besides the reasons that anyone would kill Harliis. I bet the pixy did it. She strangled him with a red dress."

A second voice answered, "Unless Harliis had been snooping and knew something he shouldn't have known. Hard to imagine Harliis knowing anything."

"Shut up, both of you!" ordered a third voice. "You're talking crazy!"

Nimnestl recognized all three voices. They were hers. She rolled to her left side and moaned. How long had she been dead?

What should have been an hallucination fluttered before her half-opened eyes. "And you told me you were a member!" it scolded, shaking both hands at her. "A deliberate falsehood! You ought to be ashamed!"

Nimnestl's eyes and mind focussed. If that was really Chicken-and-Dumplings, then she probably wasn't dead after all. She should have been dead. She had been snooping, and the Brown Robes killed snoopers.

"Why didn't they kill me?" she wondered aloud.

"You got away," said a new voice.

Nimnestl rolled slowly onto her back and then to her right. A thin white face pulled back from hers. She thought she recognized it. She knew she ought to. It wore a "maybe-you-recognize-me-because-we've-met-before-but-if-you-don't-it's-all-right-because-you-probably-have-more-important-faces-to-remember" expression.

But it was the Bodyguard's job to remember faces. "Polijn," she murmured.

Satisfied that she had kept her place, she rolled onto her back again and closed her eyes. "I got away?"

"Somebody said something to that effect, yes," answered the voice that had said so.

The voice was too rich and amused to be coming from that thin white child. Nimnestl opened her eyes and looked up into a swirling mop of black hair that surrounded a perverse pale face with glittering black eyes. She knew she had met this face before. Meeting it again was the cap to an enchanted evening.

"Yon flutterling led them astray while we dragged you in here," the sorcerer informed her. "You could stand to lose about thirty, you know that? Or maybe it was the hammer."

Nimnestl put a hand down to her belt. "Here," said Polijn. The girl took the handle in both hands and dragged the hammer to the side of the bed.

"Do you make anything with that?" demanded Chicken-and-Dumplings.

"Angels," said Nimnestl. She wound one hand around the polished wooden shaft and thought. Having assimilated the fact that she was alive, she had to deal with the question of what to do about it.

She took a long breath. "I want back inside that building," she announced. "The sooner, the better."

She looked up at the Vielfrass. "You could break in the back way," she told him, "and make enough noise to distract them while I go in the front."

The Vielfrass looked very bored. "There is something in what you say, but that something is not sense. You'd still be outnumbered and, I must remind you, when I break into something, I don't make noise."

"Just do it," she told him, taking another deep breath before trying to sit up.

"She's so bossy," whined the Vielfrass, turning to the girl and the pixy. "One day we will stand before the Throne of

Judgement and I shall be called to testify in the case of Nimnestl, Late Bodyguard. I intend to use a voice delicately tinged with bitter wrongs, mingled with monumental patience and a touch of . . ."

"I want inside before they can hide things," she told him. "Let's talk about it on the way over."

It was too bad; she was going to have to move. She slid around on the pallet and let long legs drop over the edge. Gripping her hammer, gritting her teeth, she hauled herself upright.

Her legs and arms sent pleas for pity to a swollen brain. Her stomach tried to register equal disapproval, but she kept both fingers and teeth clenched. Sweat beaded across her forehead.

"Are you all right?" asked the pixy.

Nimnestl shook her head. She wiped away that part of her forehead that was trying to run down into her eyes. Then, gritting her jaws almost hard enough to crush the teeth between them, she took a staggering step up and forward. Polijn ran to help, though what the girl could do if she fell, Nimnestl didn't know.

"Yay!" cried Chicken-and-Dumplings, as the Bodyguard held her balance. "Hooray for our side! I knew you could do it. Bend over; I'll kiss you on both cheeks."

The group broke no speed records returning to the shack, taking long detours to avoid hunting parties of Ykenai. Nimnestl placed her feet very carefully, gently sidestepping uneven or missing cobblestones. If she stumbled, she would fall, and if she fell, the urge to remain horizontal, even on cold stones, would keep her from ever aspiring to the vertical again.

The delay gave them time to argue details into the plan. On her previous visit, Nimnestl had noticed the cracked wall of the building next to the Ykenai headquarters. The crack was large enough to hold a spy, but danger had come from an entirely different direction. Now, stepping away from her partners, she took up a stand herself inside the crack, and waited for the little drama to begin.

Much of the basic storyline had been suggested by the girl, after the Vielfrass had turned down most of Nimnestl's suggestions. The pixy and the sorcerer had embellished the plot a bit, but the basic premise, which Nimnestl hoped would seem as plausible to the Brown Robes as it did to her, was Polijn's. The girl had her uses.

In moments, the gentle shriek of Chicken-and-Dumplings split the air, demanding to know what the thief was up to and wasn't he ashamed of himself and was he after anything really, really good. Seconds later, Polijn's voice, now resonant as a brass bell, asked what he intended to do with the money. The Vielfrass shushed them profanely and with great originality.

The conversation grew louder and more heated, gradually accumulating shouts and laughter from spectators. These spectators, Nimnestl hoped, were primarily the Ykenai. They had to be; who else was still sober enough by this time?

"Well, maybe you'll have some money from somewhere else!" cried Polijn.

That was the signal. Nimnestl strode from her hiding place. The door of the little building was locked. Good. It was a thick, heavy door, difficult to break down. This was also good. Nimnestl tapped at it with her hammer and bits of it fell away, along with some of the Bodyguard's frustration.

Only the doorman, Slorvick, was behind it. He did not look happy. Nimnestl made no attempt to cheer him up. She concealed neither the presence nor the purpose of the weapon in her hands. The head of it pressed against the chest of the doorman and thrust him backward into the room.

She tipped her head. An axe flashed past it, knocking the door shut. A second axe, following the first, fell to the floor, its haft broken. A great deal was broken over the next few minutes. New breaks were announced by loud cracks, last sighs, and dull thuds. Breaking seemed to be the order of the day. It was as if the Brown Robes had decided to go into the breakage business full-time.

A sound of running feet, suddenly cut off, concluded the concert. Soon the only sound in the grand meeting room was that of one set of lungs expanding and contracting with great force. Nimnestl looked around the room, counting bodies. Several showed little sign of violence beyond a few puncture wounds. A hand waved at her through a window with a broken shutter, and then withdrew.

Having seen all she needed to of the dead, Nimnestl studied the merely inanimate. The Ykenai claimed to be the most civilized religious group in the nation, apparently with reason. Book presses stood in each corner of the room. They must have had extensive contacts to keep such expensive items safe in the heart of the Swamp.

One book stood open on a broad, massive stand. Nimnestl stepped over the bodies to check it; someone had been in the process of adding something to a page headed "Snoop List" when chaos broke loose.

She snapped around when the back door creaked, but shrugged as the pixy flew inside. Polijn and the Vielfrass followed, the latter singing, at the height of his voice, "All de sorghum am a-weeping; molasses in the cold, cold ground."

The snoop list was enlightening, listing a number of courtiers who had succumbed unexpectedly to unexplained illnesses. These names had lines drawn through them. At the end of the list, several names were uncrossed. The first was "Nimnestl"; she had expected it. A pen line went halfway through it and ended in a blot. After that came other names: Kirasov, Ipojn, Elgona. That made sense. If Elgona had found out that Trioafmar was an Ykena, there was no reason Trioafmar could not have learned that Elgona was prying. Trioafmar was also a suitor of Einoel's, which might explain the mutual investigation.

"And I helped her kill them all," said Chicken-and-Dumplings, making a celebratory swoop around the room. "I am quietly proud, do you hear me, quietly proud."

Kirajen's name came next. That was the name she'd wanted to find. The line through it made her very happy. The Ykenai already knew, then, that the little housekeeper was dead. Very nice, but they gave no credit to the slayer.

"The other one was good, too," the pixy went on, "I like her, don't you? She's so little and slinky."

Arnastobh's name was not on the list, though; she supposed that was too much to hope. She flipped back through the book to see what other treats waited. On a hunch, she checked the first pages and found the roster of current members. Oh, this was a book worth adding to the Regent's library. Some of the courtiers had never even been suspected: Tolyn, Nellys, Flact, Trevardis, Palompec . . . One name had a big, blotted line scratched through it. Apparently even the Ykenai died, occasionally. It was "Har" something. She bent closer to the page.

"Harliis."

II

THE Bodyguard had been quiet before, but now she became perfectly silent, and everyone in the room noticed. Even Chicken-and-Dumplings came to rest, sitting on a book press to study her. The pixy leaped up into the air when Nimnestl slammed the heavy book shut and turned around with it pressed to her chest.

"You look like somebody who could use a drink," said the Vielfrass, wiping some blood off his boots with a hand that was not his own. "Don't you think she looks like somebody who could use a drink?"

"Oh, I do, I do," answered Chicken-and-Dumplings. "But hardly anybody around here serves pixies."

"Flutter along, oh, rancid butterfly," said the sorcerer. "We'll find some place where they aren't so finikin. Come, children."

Nimnestl was hardly paying attention, and followed automatically, one arm around the book, the other down against her hammer. When she did think about it, out in the street again, she decided she could use a drink. It had been a strenuous evening.

She would have preferred to do her drinking at the Blue Bottle, which was much farther east. The Swamp had a whispered reputation in the Palace Royal. Nimnestl had visited the area, naturally, but with distaste and profound distrust. She knew she was going to die; anyone who pursued her line of work with any sincerity would. Why go out of her way to make sure of it?

The Swamp was a land where any sin you wanted to sample could be procured within a beagle's howl. If you didn't want to waste time hunting for your specialty, you had only to find someone smaller than you. Back lots were filled with forgotten graves and their untidy contents. Gensamar kept suggesting that everyone in the Swamp be rounded up annually for a general trial. Nimnestl wondered if that was such a bad idea.

Before she could mention any of this to her tour guides, however, the sorcerer and the pixy had selected a watering hole. Yarvin's Liquid Vault was exactly what Nimnestl would have expected them to choose. Most bars in the Swamp were bare rooms with broken tables and a board across two kegs for a bar. Yarvin did not aspire to that level of sophistication. A bin of clay mugs sat by the door. Customers took a mug off the top and, for a pennyetke, could fill it at any keg that lined the back wall. They then took a seat on any of the benches tumbled about the establishment.

"They aren't so choosy about their custom here," the Vielfrass explained, pushing into the room first.

Nimnestl saw no reason to contradict that, smelling the crowd long before she was close enough to the door to see it. She pulled out a mug that looked reasonably dry and joined the others at the kegs, expertly dodging hands that reached for cloak, hammer, book, or anything else that might be worth a grab. Not a novice at this, she bypassed the kegs ostentatiously branded with the marks of the more famous breweries. These were certainly forged, and the kegs might contain anything remotely resembling beer.

The crowd parted before the Vielfrass as he aimed for one of the corners of the room, where elderly tables were provided for high-class customers. When the sorcerer indicated to nine burly men, all earless, that he wished the use of their table, the thugs rose, said it was quite all right with them, they were going back to the fair anyway, and melted into the crowd. They knew when they were outclassed.

"Here," said the Vielfrass, once they were seated on the less splintered parts of the benches pulled up here. He brought out a large bag. "A gift for our guest of honor. A woman is said to have pawned this. Your underfed sidenudge there can tell you stories about it that will uncurl your hair."

Opening the bag, Nimnestl saw nothing but red cloth. She reached in, but was arrested by the sight of a delicate white hand on her arm.

The Bodyguard looked down at the girl. Polijn jerked her hand back, and seemed to blush. "He . . . he says something happens to people who touch the Banner of Kairor," she said, pointing at the Vielfrass.

Nimnestl looked across at the sorcerer. "Foo!" exclaimed Chicken-and-Dumplings, reclining against her mug. "How do they get it up to hang on the wall, then?"

The Vielfrass set his elbows on the table, absentmindedly bumping the mug so that the pixy fell off backward in a splash of dark ale. "Why is it," he mused, "that people pooh-pooh curses simply because they haven't been killed yet?" He folded his hands. "Such people should be stepped on."

"Fine!" shouted a furious, ale-soaked pixy, beer spraying from her wings as she rose into the air. "Fine. You can be like that. Be like that and, the next time you get a chance, don't hesitate to drop dead!" With a flip of her fanny, she fluttered away, taking note of those customers who laughed, and knocking their own mugs onto the dirt floor.

"Hi-de-ho-de-hum," sighed the sorcerer. "I'd better tag along, to make sure she does no expensive damage to the fabric of our fair city. Some folk are so flighty, they'd never notice. Ta." With the tip of a hat he wasn't wearing, the Vielfrass strode away.

Nimnestl attended to this with a fraction of her mind. The rest was far away, hearing Kirajen offer to tell her about an Ykena whose plan had not worked out. Had she meant Harliis and his ceremony? Had there been something tucked into the ceremony to make trouble for the government? But how would that have paid Kirajen? The knowledge of Harliis's membership in the Ykenai was a coup, but worth little once he was dead. Maybe Kirajen had been trying to salvage what she could, expecting payments for hints.

In that case, though, there would be no reason to kill her. They could have safely let her live, if all she had known was that a certain dead man had been a Brown Robe, at least until some later date when she could be killed without attracting much attention.

Kirajen had a key to the Treasury. What if she killed Harliis and meant to confess, using his membership in the Ykenai as an excuse? Nimnestl shook her head. Kirajen would not have put herself in anyone's power with such a confession, least of all the Head Bodyguard's power.

So the little woman must have known something else about the Ykenai, something about a plan, and the Treasury, and probably Harliis. How much must she have known to prompt her murder before she could talk to the Bodyguard?

And now there was the Banner of Kairor. A woman had pawned it, according to something the Vielfrass had heard. Kirajen? Maitena? Raiprez? But any of them would have known to return the Banner for a reward. More likely, some servant had found it and tried to realize a quick profit on it, not knowing what it was.

She bounced one fist lightly on the table. Anyone in the Palace Royal would have known the Banner was missing, and tried for the reward.

She turned to Polijn. "Tell me something to uncurl my hair."

The girl opened her mouth, but her mind was obviously as elsewhere as Nimnestl's. The pupils of her eyes jerked to the right. Nimnestl turned, reaching for her hammer, just as a heavy body crashed into her left shoulder.

"Watch it!" snarled the body.

Once the Vielfrass was gone, his guests were fair game. No one in the Liquid Vault would have identified the tall, cloaked woman as the Head Bodyguard, even if they had been sober and Yarvin allowed enough light for anyone to see she was from Reangle. Everyone knew the Bodyguard was nine feet tall and never moved more than two feet from the King, except when she sent her spirit flying forth by night to crush men and drink their blood. The woman at the table was just another inhabitant of the Swamp and, to judge by the book and heavy bag she carried, returning from a successful expedition.

The man who had decided to make the first move was very large and very drunk, but not too drunk to see the profit in making trouble. "Who you shoving?" he demanded, each hand suddenly full of knife.

Nimnestl looked up the vast body slowly, estimating distances. "Did you come here to drink or to fight?" she demanded.

"To fight," answered the man, moving his knives around, a forefinger on each blade. "Come on." To these four syllables of invitation he added a few more, just by way of provocation.

Nimnestl declined the bait. "I came here to drink," she said, turning away.

The man swore and stuck one of his knives in the table, just to free a hand. With that hand, he took Nimnestl's shoulder and pulled it up, necessarily bringing the rest of Nimnestl with it. "Well, you're going to fight," he said, bringing his other knife forward.

"Maybe," said Nimnestl. One large fist mingled with the man's features. The knife went wide, and he dropped to the floor like a bag of green bacon.

"But you won't," she added.

Yarvin's bouncers, who had been sitting forward, sat back. They were not paid to interfere in the private affairs of customers, just to make sure no one damaged the room in the process. A woman who had been creeping up on the bag of booty screamed and scuttled away. Other customers found other things to do, at tables farther away. Two of them unobtrusively jerked the fallen man along the floor, either to revive the body or loot it.

Nimnestl turned and saw that Polijn was staring, her mouth agape. "Something?"

"That was Chordasp," whispered the girl.

"Who?" Nimnestl inquired. The girl shook her head.

III

"ALL right," said Nimnestl. "Then tell me about the Banner."

The girl took a long breath, making her shoulders spread out. Then, after one more look at the unconscious bully boy being towed off, she poured out a tale that began with a snake tattoo on a dead body and ended with a perverse pixy crying "Helphelphelphelphelp!" She told the tale without much ornamental detail, but without missing any pertinent facts. Horror slipped through here and there in her voice, but so quickly it could easily have been missed.

The part about the pixy was the most surprising part of the tale—Nimnestl hadn't expected any rescue to come via that miniscule monster—but the matter of the pawn brokers was more immediately useful. That was why the Banner of Kairor had travelled to the Swamp: so someone from the Palace Royal could follow it and find out that "a woman" had pawned it. Menapri and Calongir nearly spoiled it all by deciding to return the Banner much too soon, before all the plans for incrimination were in readiness. They had to be lured off to their deaths.

What Nimnestl did not know was which woman the plotters had wanted her to suspect. If it was Ferrapec's plan, she would be expected to accuse Maitena or one of the daughters. If Maitena had planned it, though, Raiprez or Kodva would be the proper target. The plan was a little subtle for Maitena;

it was something the Ykenai could have concocted. In fact, Ferrapec loathed the Ykenai; sitting and writing all day was suspect, in his mind. It might all have been one coherent plot: the Ykenai killing Arnastobh and stealing the Banner, setting up the general to be blamed for both.

She tried to recall whether Ferrapec was mentioned anywhere in this book of lists. After a quick look to be sure no one was close enough to see what she was about, she lifted the book and began to riffle the pages. A loose sheet snapped up in the shuffle, caught for a second between two pages, and then dropped to the floor.

Polijn bent to get it for the Bodyguard, but did not hand it over, staring instead at a gray blob on the back. Nimnestl plucked the page from the girl's hand and checked the blob herself. It was the national seal of Braut: "the bird on the bricks," Kaftus called it. Beneath it was scribbled, "How did Aesernius come by this? Genuine?"

She flipped the paper over and, angling so as to get the best light available in this dismal corner, ran through the text, her eyes picking out proper names. The page was directed to Arlmorin and was signed, "Your friend, if I have cause, Ondihiuch." That was the name of the First Minister of Braut.

The text was nothing to steal, forge, or deny. It dealt with the possibility of a marriage between the King of Rossacotta and one of the royal nieces in Braut. Ondihiuch admitted he knew nothing of Rossacotta beyond rumors. If King Conan had a sister, one of the royal nephews could be spared for a match there as well.

It might certainly irk Arlmorin to have this information leak to the court, since this marriage alliance had not even been mentioned yet officially. Such a revelation might throw off his timing, which had its advantages, but that was nothing such a low-level schemer as Aesernius could use. But perhaps there were other papers Aesernius had collected that the Ykenai didn't get.

She ran through the text one more time, to see if she'd missed something. In the long paragraph of ceremonial greeting and compliment at the top of the letter, skipped on first reading, she found her prize. She set the letter back into the book and said, "Let's go back, girl."

Arlmorin was a merchant, a trader. The salutation of the letter made it clear that he had volunteered his services to the ministry in Braut, and that Ondihiuch had gladly accepted these. But factions at the Brautian court had opposed any connection with Rossacotta. So Arlmorin, despite the laud and honor piled on him when he arrived at the Palace Royal, was actually no official ambassador at all. The Brautian court had accorded him no actual official status. He could act for the Brautian government, but was not empowered to enact any final agreements. The Brautian government could pull back from any promise he made to the regency in Rossacotta.

That was the sort of paper Arlmorin would want back. The little squib of information could have given Aesernius or the Ykenai enough leverage to tip the red-headed envoy any direction they liked.

Polijn, rising from the table, jumped to one side as a dozen rats skittled past, fleeing a corner of the room where the majority of the crowd, having witnessed Chordasp's catastrophe, had gathered. There were more lights in that corner of the room, and a good deal more noise as well.

"Let's see the color of your money!" bellowed a thickened voice.

"You will be disappointed, good son," answered a calmer one. "It is the same color as everyone's money."

"If I don't see that money, I'll see the inside of your belly!" roared the first speaker.

"That's a different color," admitted the second.

Nimnestl set the book into her bag and rose. She hesitated, glancing at the door. That second voice was surely familiar, though the confidence in it was not. Shrugging, she pushed through the crowd. It wasn't necessary to push very far, as she was a head taller than most of the onlookers, and most of those were more than willing to give her room.

"The stakes go on the table!" declared the first man, a huge bale of muscle. He thumped the table for emphasis, and both cards and coins shifted position. "You have to put the money down! The stakes go on the table! No money, no play! That's my rule!"

The smaller, thinner man across the table gathered the cards together. He didn't touch the coins heaped before him, but he did wave the deck of cards over them. "I have money now."

"It's mine!" bellowed the first man. "You can't play in here without money, so you shouldn't've sat in, and you cheated besides!"

The player under siege was indeed the hopeless jester Arberth, but he was more composed than he ever was on stage. He was calm. He set his hands out flat on the tabletop so everyone could see how calm he was. "Money has no name," he pointed out. "It isn't your money now, so you're out."

"This money's got my name on it!" roared the burly gambler, standing up before the jester could. He had a knife in his hand. The crowd pulled back to give him room. Nimnestl slid a hand to her hammer, but that was all. It was her policy not to give unsolicited help.

Arberth stayed where he was, his hands flat on either side of the cards. "Clam yourself, clam yourself," he said. "We can do without all this noise. Sit down and we'll strike a deal."

The loser stood where he was, a nostril cocking up into a sneer. "What kind of deal? I'm not even listening, only I hate to kill people in my place on the King's Birthday."

A long, thin hand rose and swooped across the table. "I have all the money. You've got no money. But you've got a knife. Now, besides the knife and the money, we've got a deck of cards. Let's play one more hand, all this money against your knife."

The first man scratched his chin absentmindedly with the point. "Yeah. There's that." He looked down at the money.

"You're due to win a hand." Arberth leaned forward and pushed the coins to the center of the table. Then he plopped the cards on the far side of the heap. "And you deal: just to keep me honest."

The big man chuckled and sat down. "All right," he said, reaching for the cards.

"Hold it," said the jester, raising one hand. "Your rule, remember? All stakes go on the table."

"Oh," the man said. "Right." He tossed his knife onto the heap of coins and picked up the cards.

He dropped the cards when someone in the crowd hooted, but this was way too late. Arberth had grabbed the knife by the blade and flipped it into his other hand.

"Yarvin," he said, "you could still leave the table a winner."

The big man stared at the knife pointed at him and let his fist fall again, breaking off a corner of the table. "That's my money, lintik blast you!"

"Come take it," Arberth replied, raising the knife point toward Yarvin's throat. "The wall between you is neither too high to climb nor too low to tunnel under."

Yarvin looked inclined to take a chance. Nimnestl felt the game was over. She elbowed her way forward and tapped the big man's shoulder. "Go away," she suggested.

Yarvin glared at her. "She took out Chordasp," someone whispered.

The bar owner's fingers unrolled as he considered his alternatives: go away, or go away. He went away.

Nimnestl took his seat, and turned it a little so the lights would show her the crowd. "Just out of curiosity," she said, "were you cheating?"

The jester shrugged. "Only fools rely on luck. Did you really floor Chordasp? He knocked off an Uruch-tai trader who crowded him once. They say he propped the body in that corner and left it for two weeks, just so people would get the idea."

"I didn't expect to see you going Swamping," she told him. "Not alone." There were courtiers who enjoyed the coarser amusements to be found in the Swamp. They generally went Swamping in groups of four or five, though.

Arberth picked up the cards and passed them from one hand to the other. "I never expected to see you, either. I thought you'd be at Lord Flact's party."

The way he said it, it held a hint of sedition. But this was no place to venture on explanations. She sneered at him. "I'm more interested in that money you borrowed."

The jester's eyes widened, and he smiled. "Your memory is fading with age, Amorcho. I paid that—you must remember—the last time the King went forth to bless the waters. You wouldn't have let me go, otherwise."

"Last time the King blessed the waters!" she snorted. "Last blue moon, maybe. I'll have that money now, Choung, as long as it's so handy."

Arberth pulled his winnings toward him. "I would love to stay and chat, my dear, but I must—I simply must—go talk to Flact. He wanted some music for his little affair."

There it was again. Nimnestl jerked her head toward the door. "Outside," she snarled. "I don't want anyone else picking up my money after I beat it out of you."

The jester threw back his head and released a high giggle. "I love it when you try to be so tough," he said. "Come away to the stables and I shall ride off with you across my saddle!"

He jumped and strode from the room. Nimnestl followed as quickly as she could, pausing here and there to glower at bystanders who seemed inclined to come along. Only Polijn was behind her when they stepped into the street.

Arberth was waiting some yards away. After a glance to be sure no one had come to the door to watch the fight, he whispered, "I don't suppose you'd really care to be carried off across my saddle? I can go buy a saddle."

Nimnestl just fastened her eyes on his face. "Very well," he sighed. "Our overworked Minister of State has been leaving his window open at night several days this week. It's the wrong time of year, and very dangerous for his health, particularly with that rope hanging out."

"A rope," said Nimnestl, taking his elbow and ushering him a bit farther along the street. "For what?"

Arberth shrugged. "Ask me something I know and kill me if I lie. But I can't see him being that tricky if it's only a matter of someone else's wife."

"Tricky?" Nimnestl demanded. "On a festival night? Anybody could have seen that rope."

"It's tricky for Flact," said the jester.

Another large celebration was slowly dying in the square ahead of them. Couples and threesomes were peeling off into the alleys. "Are you going back to the Palace from here?" Nimnestl asked.

"I can," said the jester. "Why?"

"Take a chair," Nimnestl said. "And take this with you." She gave Polijn a little push toward him. "Ynygyn will want her working in the morning. I have to fetch Meriere."

She turned away, but looked back. "And, Arberth, if your information does us any good, you will be paid. You know that?"

The jester's mouth crooked up. "Probably not what I want, though, eh?"

Nimnestl stalked away to the alley, heading for the Blue Bottle, and her horse. That was all the company she wanted on her ride back.

IV

COUNTING windows from the now-deserted parade ground, Nimnestl came to the one that should be Flact's. Sure enough, when she came up to the wall, she could see the slender rope, nearly invisible against grey stone. She tested it with a gentle tug.

On the way up, she rehearsed what she intended to tell Kaftus—again—about these new windows. The foreign architects who were supposed to bring such a civilizing touch weakened security with each improvement.

What was Flact up to? An alarming number of his subordinates had listings in the book of the Ykenai. Their infiltration had been so quiet that Nimnestl had no idea what Brown Robes thought about trade, the army, or foreign policy. Trying to pick out their influences from among the hundreds of plots and counterschemes in the Ministry of State would be agony, even leaving out diplomatic complications with foreign envoys.

Something brushed her shoulder. Looking back, she saw only dark air. Her cloak flapped at the breeze. She pulled herself higher.

Reaching the sill, she closed her eyes to slits, so that she could see without being seen by the light reflecting off her eyes. She could have saved the trouble; the room, when she was far enough to see it, was dark and silent. A hard push opened the sash. Inside, she pushed it shut again and turned around to find she was in the wrong room.

The lack of a tapestry over the window should have told her. This was a workroom, filled with little tables. A second look, and she could make out the inkstands that identified them as writing tables. The ink itself had probably been removed for the night; it was getting to be the season when ink left here overnight would freeze. For the same reason, none of the clerks who slaved here were sleeping on the floor tonight.

There was only one exit. A crack of light showed under the door, and men's voices came through it.

"Yu'd be'er have 'at cer'ain i'em or a hull lo'a people gonna know wha' i' was."

Nimnestl frowned. That was the accent of the Divided People of Turin. And it was a strong one; the speaker had not been away from home long. As far as Nimnestl knew, no one in the Palace Royal fit that description. And she was supposed to know.

"Look," said the other voice, Flact's voice, "there's been complications. A murder . . ."

"Load it," ordered the Turinese. "Tha' was a lo'a money ta me. If y'think these pre'ies'll do i', forge' i'. Necklace is broke, too."

Nimnestl suddenly wanted very badly to be on the other side of the door. She eased among the writing tables, holding her hammer steady to keep from knocking into anything. One hand went out to feel for the door. When she found wood in front of her, she slid that hand down to the knob.

"You want this, don't you?" demanded a little creature, flying past her face with a key.

She turned to snatch at Chicken-and-Dumplings but got the key instead. Boots moved on the floor in the next room, and she returned to her previous pose.

"Oh, that was the wind," said Flact. "Listen to me, can't you?"

Nimnestl's hammer was up in her hands. She didn't look for a hiding place. In the light from the next room, the man from Turin would see her whether she was standing by the door or wedged under a little desk. This way, she might get one clear swing at him before he realized she was swinging.

"This is going to be fun!" squealed Chicken-and-Dumplings.

The head of an axe pushed the door open in a slow, gentle swing. The owner of the axe had time to get one wide-eyed look at the tall dark woman before her hammer swung down. He dodged, raised a gray, featureless shield. Hammer rang against steel and the axe whipped around at one muscled leg.

Nimnestl knocked the blade back. She was being gentle. He had to be alive to answer questions. By the same token, however, she had to be alive to ask the questions.

The axe moved in at her again. Chicken-and-Dumplings shouted "Whoopee!" The lights in the next room were extinguished. What followed was a dark medley of clamor and hammering as the opponents aimed their weapons by guess and a tiny sliver of light that seeped in from the corridor outside Flact's chamber.

"Death!" hissed the Turinese.

"If it's here," Nimnestl panted, "it's here for you."

"Yes," agreed her opponent, and now she could hear the life hissing from his body in and around the word.

Someone lit a candle. Minister of State Flact, breathless, rushed into the room with it. "Thank you," he gasped. "Oh, thank you. He's a spy, a thief from the south. Silmarièn, I think. He was . . ."

"Turinese," Nimnestl corrected. She wasn't much interested in Flact's story; he would think of a better one later. She knelt to probe the body.

"She does that a lot," Chicken-and-Dumplings confided to Flact. "She gets a whee out of it."

Flact stared at the little creature, speechless. Nimnestl added that to the pixy's tiny list of uses. The thief was dead, all right. Nimnestl was sure she wasn't responsible. She had been careful to swing at nonlethal spots, and nothing vital seemed to have been crushed.

"Eru!" croaked Flact, tearing his gaze from the pixy's shimmering skin. "There!"

Nimnestl glanced down to the spot he indicated with his candle. The thief was wearing a belt pouch. Torn open, it had leaked onto the floor. A broken necklace, wrapped in linen, dangled from the opening. A pearl dropped from the strands as Nimnestl lifted them.

"Lady Kirajen's necklace!" Flact exclaimed, in case she hadn't recognized it. "And broken! I hope he didn't have to resort to violence to get it!"

Nimnestl sighed and unwrapped the jewelry. The handkerchief was an expensive one, so laced with gold thread that it was useless as a handkerchief. Nimnestl was only moderately surprised to see Maitena's name picked out in gold dots in the center.

"Maitena!" gasped the Minister of State, clutching his free hand to his heart. "And look!"

Nimnestl looked. The thief was done up in Rossacottan armor, and a large iron fist was bolted to the front of his helmet. That was the insignia of a dungeon guard, and, of course, dungeon guards were part of the housekeeping staff.

"This . . . this is amazing!" said Flact. "Do you suppose . . ."

"You know we must be discreet about this," Nimnestl told him in an imposing whisper as she checked the wounds on the thief's neck. "Maitena may escape if we are not careful. We will need to lay a trap."

"Yes," said Flact. "Ah, yes." He smiled and rose, setting the candle on the nearest desk. "I know I can leave this in your capable hands. But you will allow me to know . . ."

"You will be informed," Nimnestl promised. "And the Regent shall hear about the assistance you rendered me, Lord Flact. I will send someone for the body."

She bowed lightly, and left the room by the door. Chicken-and-Dumplings followed, asking if Nimnestl required a new corpse every night or whether she saved up and had an orgy like this once a month.

V

WITH the minor exception of the pixy's presence, Nimnestl thought the conversation had been a model of palace etiquette. She had not mentioned what she had overheard, and the Minister of State had not remarked upon her appearance in a room that could have been entered only through his chambers or the window. All had been polite and reasonable.

That Flact was responsible for the death of Kirajen she was now certain. But that didn't help much. How was it connected to the death of Harliis? Unless the result threatened the King, she didn't care whether Flact killed Kirajen or Kirajen killed Flact. She couldn't follow up on every murder in the Palace Royal.

She was pondering all the possible links this latest development could have to the other people and events surrounding the death of the unlamented favorite as she turned into the corridor that would lead her to the King's Apartments. Heavily used during the day, it was hung with costly tapestries and bright lights at all hours. But now the hall was dark, lit only by what illumination slipped in from side corridors.

It seemed to be empty, which was natural at this hour. But Nimnestl moved forward cautiously, one hand on her hammer, watching with both eyes. She froze as a shadow moved; then she took a step back. A tapestry, sagging, was pulling loose of the wall. Nimnestl saw no reason for a tapestry to loosen itself the same night the torches were inexplicably dark.

She backed away, around a corner. Availing herself of the first torch that came to hand, she returned to the hall to study embroidery.

A heavy object pinned to the cloth was what had torn it loose from some of its fasteners. Nimnestl knew it was a girl only because what was left of the face was Arual's. But this was perhaps the least damaged part of the body. From waist to knee, little was left but torn flesh and hanging splinters of bone. An awl or some other pointed shaft had been used to force a hole through the skin at each rib. And something, or, rather, everything about Arual's face indicated that much of this had been done while the girl was alive to notice.

"Darlin'," said Chicken-and-Dumplings, fluttering up for a closer look, "this is plumb excessive."

Nimnestl pondered the possibility of getting both the culprit and the pixy into a slow oven and baking both.

Beneath the tapestry, among a thick pool of ugly blood, was a linen handkerchief laden with gold thread. Nimnestl was almost more nauseated by this sight than by the rest. Maitena's hankies were going wholesale tonight. She lifted the cloth by a clean corner folded it gingerly, and tucked it away in her pouch. No sense just leaving it here as a clue for anyone who happened by.

There was always the possibility that Maitena had gone berserk. Yet she was the quick-fury, knife-in-the-chest, skewer-to-the-stomach kind of killer. When she broke into violence, she didn't hide it. She would hardly have strangled Kirajen quietly on the beach, or slowly mutilated her own daughter in some secret hiding place, much less have done both on the same night.

Footsteps made Nimnestl turn. They belonged to the girl, Polijn, who had apparently been dropped off by Arberth and picked up by Aesernius.

"What's . . ." the sorcerer began to say. Then he saw Arual and went pale. Nimnestl thought he trembled a little. He was squeamish, for a sorcerer.

Turning to face the bodyguard, he declared, "Whoever did that is so low he could sit on a sheet of paper and swing his legs over the edge."

Polijn didn't look well, either. Her mouth moved soundlessly until the sorcerer swept his cloak around her. "Don't look at it, child," he said. "Come away, quickly." He hurried the girl down the hall and out of sight.

Once they were gone, Nimnestl unhooked her hammer and reached it up to knock away the supports still bearing all that weight. Some came out; others snapped the cords they held. Nimnestl eased the body of Arual to the floor. She studied the face for a second.

Then she let Arual down into the cloth of the tapestry and folded the ends over her, securing the bundle with the loops that had held it to the wall. Snatching up her torch from the sconce where she had set it, she strode up the corridor.

"You!" she called to the first guard she spied around the next turn. "Get two of your mates and run back there for a bundle of tapestry. There's a body inside, so be careful with it. Get torches and watch you don't slip in the blood. Take the tapestry to my office; this will admit you." She handed him a silver pine-branch token. "Anyone who looks inside the bundle will be handed over to the Regent. Move."

She stood against the wall at his post as the three men went out, and stayed there until they returned with their gruesome bundle. She waited there a while longer after they had gone. Weariness dragged on every muscle.

Nimnestl was not quite thirty. She felt sixty. When confronted with a mirror unexpectedly, she thought she looked like her mother, at a poorly preserved thirty-nine. Each day, of course, death was as close to her as it was to Jintabh, at seventy-odd.

Gauging the amount of time it would take the men to carry the body up and then return, Nimnestl took a long breath and heaved herself away from the wall. She reslung her hammer, put her hands over her eyes for a moment, and then marched away, a tower of untouchable, indomitable strength to awe the guards as they passed, returning to their stations.

Another corner, and she was in the King's Corridor. She saluted the guards on duty at the door of the Royal Bedchamber, unlocked the door, closed it behind her, and stumbled toward bed. This had been too long a night on an empty stomach. She wanted to throw off her armor and rest, to lie down and put her hammer where it couldn't weary her arm.

In the semidarkness, she located the low mattress she shared with Nurse. By now, of course, the older woman would have all the covers. The King liked to sleep with his windows open, too, with only a mystic screen of rowan twigs and small bones that filtered out unwanted visitors but did not interfere with ventilation.

Working her way to her own side of the pallet, Nimnestl's foot caught under a small, crumpled form. For two silent seconds, she closed her eyes and recited a prayer without moving her lips. Then she crouched and gently let her hands slide up and down the shadow. It was only one of the furs from the King's Bed, kicked away or thrown off.

At this point, Nimnestl would gladly have curled up on the floor, with the fur over one shoulder. Instead, she slipped across to the King's Bed and reached in under the draperies, to set the fur among the others.

Despite her care, the King sat bolt upright. Had he not instantly recognized Nimnestl, he would have screamed. As it was, he grabbed at her arm, pulling her close enough to see tears streaming along his nose.

"It was a nightmare," he said, sobbing and whispering both. "There was this big wind, and clouds, and a tornado, and everybody was smashed flat against walls. Just flat. And then they turned to dust. And when I ran to get you, you were flat, too, and there was dust running out of your clothes."

Nimnestl felt like turning to dust. Flat sounded peaceful, too. But she said, "It was just a dream, you know. Does that arm feel flat? Or dusty? I put it up to you, Your Majesty."

"Don't go," he whispered, the tears running into his mouth. "I want you to stay by me. I . . . I order you to stay."

Nimnestl's muscles howled objections, and her eyelids sagged like the tapestry. She blinked, smiled, and said, "Well, if you order it." She climbed up onto the bed, armor and all, spreading her long body across the furs.

"There," she said. "I'm with you. Better? Go to sleep immediately now, or I'll wake up Nurse."

The King wanted none of Nurse's fussy attention. He pulled the furs up over his shoulder and planted his head on Nimnestl's right shoulder. Somehow he found this position comfortable and settled against her arm, his right hand on her chest. He did not notice, or at least did not protest, that his royal command somehow carried less weight than Nimnestl's threat.

With her free hand, Nimnestl tugged at her hammer and let it slide down to rest against the side of the bed, handy but out of the way. She tried to turn her long legs in some comfortable direction. It couldn't be done. It didn't really matter. She had been hoarding exhaustion all evening. Now she let it go.

CHAPTER SEVEN
Polijn

I

POLIJN was relieved to see the bulk of the Palace Royal rising in the darkness. Walking with Arberth through the city had been a silent, uncomfortable journey, and this was somehow all her fault.

"We might as well try out a few jokes as we go," the gambler turned jester had said. "I was going to use this one at the tournament tomorrow. If a ratification is a large rat, why isn't a fortification a large fort?"

Polijn had heard neither of these words before, but could see her cue. "I don't know," she said. "Why not?"

Arberth didn't say another word until they reached the castle gate. And then he spoke only to the guards who were hauling the last of the stragglers out of the courtyard. The guards recognized the jester, and, after a suitable tip, let him pass.

"Good night," said the jester, and shambled off into the shadows. Polijn shrugged and started for her own tower.

"Ah, there you are." Aesernius appeared out of a different set of shadows. "Are you returning to Ynygyn, then? Come, I'll escort you."

"Oh, you don't have to," she told him. "I know the way now."

"But you don't know all the shortcuts," the sorcerer told her. "This way, child." He put a hand on her shoulder and guided her firmly in what she thought was the wrong direction.

"I hope you enjoyed the festivals," he went on. "I see you went down to have a look at those in the city. Where did you happen to run into our Arberth? I've always wondered what he does at night, creeping outside."

Polijn wondered why he wondered. She shrugged. "I just met him on the road, outside," she said. "I thought it would be easier to get past the gates if I was with somebody the guards knew. And it was!"

Aesernius stepped up onto a flight of stairs and turned back to look at her. His eyes narrowed for a moment, but then he shrugged. "They'll soon learn to know your face. Things will be easier, then. I heard you had problems with Maitena tonight. Ynygyn was worried. But that'll all stop as people become more familiar with you. Here, child, up this way. They're jumpy. Some woman . . ."

They stepped up off the staircase into a small corridor and then up a very narrow flight of stairs without many lights. "Watch your step. I don't know what they're thinking of, but perhaps no one's on duty tonight."

The hall at the top of the stairs was dark. Light from a far corner showed them a solitary figure studying the wall, a torch in one hand. It appeared to be the Chief Bodyguard.

"Evening!" called Aesernius. "What's . . ."

Then both he and Polijn saw, beyond her, the sagging tapestry, and what made it sag. A series of thin knives held the body of the girl against the cloth. Her chest was punctured with a double row of round red wounds. Parts of her legs had been shaved to the bone. The face was a mask of agony.

Polijn could barely crack her mouth open. "That looks like . . ."

"Whoever did this," Aesernius declared, "is so low he could sit on a sheet of paper and swing his legs over the edge."

Polijn looked up at the sorcerer. His eyebrows were drawn down toward his nose and his face was whiter than the paper he had invoked. He was shaking with rage, and Polijn stepped back, afraid he would call down lightning to blast the culprit there and then.

When he didn't, she licked her lips and began again. "That looks . . ."

But the man swung his cape in front of her. "Don't look, child," he ordered. "Come away. She can take care of it." A hand descended to her shoulder again and pushed her ahead of him.

Polijn could see the face of Kronja before her, hanging on a wall in the Swamp. The nose was snubber and the freckles less pronounced, but the expression was the same. When Aesernius finally slowed down, well clear of the corridor and its hanging inhabitant, she whispered, "Who was that?"

Aesernius checked his retreat. "The body, child? That was little Arual."

"Oh!" said Polijn. "The girl who . . ."

"Yes?"

"The girl who was in the cell," said Polijn. "The one they thought poisoned Arnastobh." Aesernius nodded.

Polijn didn't see him nod. She was remembering the Banner of Kairor, and the Vielfrass's remark that all who had handled it "were dead as of five minutes ago." Had he seen that in his mirror?

She looked up; he was still looking at her. Her head felt hot. There was no need for that; she'd just tell him. "There was a . . . girl," she said. "A girl down in the Swamp, named Kronja. She . . ."

"I wonder who did it," Aesernius broke in.

She shook her head. "We never found out. But . . ." The heat slipped from her head and she raised it so she could look into the sorcerer's face. "But, sir, couldn't you, er, find out? Through magic, I mean?" She wanted to go on and mention the mirror, but felt it was presumptuous of her to tell him his business.

The sorcerer shrugged and half-turned away. "A needle's sharp at only one end, child," he said. "I can't . . ."

He paused. "Or can I?" He came back around and looked her up and down. "Come here, child. We can try, at least, can't we? We can be like the little boy who decided he'd never know whether he could fly or not if he never tried." He put that hand back on her shoulder. "Do you know what a mirror is?"

"Oh, yes," she told him, shivering a little in anticipation.

He bent his head toward hers. "There is a . . . magic mirror," he confided, "Up in my room. It has three large . . . skulls at the top of the frame. It is just about the size of your hand."

"Yes," she said, nodding: just the size of the mirror in the pawnshop.

"It will be on a table near the door. And next to it, you will find a silver bowl. Bring these to me in Ynygyn's rooms; we'll be safe enough there, and he won't lose his temper at your being out so late. Do you understand all that?"

"Yes, sir," she said. "A mirror with three skulls on it, by the door, and a silver bowl. Bring them to Ynygyn's rooms."

"Correct. No, don't run off that way. Take the long route, or you'll have to pass the body again." Polijn shuddered and he laughed. "That's right. And it would look suspicious to our noble bodyguard. She's the type to believe a murderer always returns to the scene. Off, now!"

Polijn hurried back down the narrow stairs, around, and out into the courtyard. Seeing Maitena march across the open space, she kept to the shadows and dashed to the tower she had been making for originally.

II

POLIJN charged up the tower stairs, wishing her legs were longer or the stairs shallower. She stayed to the middle of the stairway, to be clear of anyone stepping in on a landing and equally clear of that railing that separated the stairs from the sheer drop down the stairwell.

What an amazing development, after all these years, to learn that there was another market for virginity. Maybe she could make a career out of holding mirrors for soothsayers. Helping them see the future would relieve a few of her worries about her own. Someone who observed carefully might pick up some of the techniques of reading the future herself. She could be a power on her own, controlling situations with the lift of an eyebrow, giving orders in a cool, mocking voice. Sorcerers were never terrified in dark corners at night.

Or were they? Aesernius had looked a bit sick at the sight of Arual on the tapestry. Polijn slowed a bit at the thought of Arual, or, actually, the thought of Kronja. Had she heard about this new murder two weeks ago, she would have felt it proved the Swamp story that the Regent or the Bodyguard, or both, were behind the torture slayings. Everyone already knew the two held orgies of blood and death in secret rooms at pale hours of the morning; these public atrocities were part of some new scheme.

The Bodyguard didn't look like that, up close. The Regent did, yes, but not Nimnestl. Polijn wasn't sure what she thought of Nimnestl, beyond the respect and fear she automatically accorded to anyone that big. It was a grim, hard woman, with a rather shapeless face and an unattractive nose. Once or twice, though, when caught in a smile, the face had dropped decades, cheekbones appearing and lips slipping up. These smiles hadn't lasted long enough for Polijn to tell, but she thought she had even seen a trace of dimples. This was a positively treasonous thought.

Something brushed her cheek. Polijn put up a hand to swat away an insect and instead slapped a small naked person, who was airborne. It was the pixy that had called the Vielfrass to Nimnestl's aid earlier.

"Hi," it said, taking no offense at the swat. "My name's Chicken-and-Dumplings. What's yours?"

"Polijn," said Polijn, resuming speed.

The pixy kept abreast of her without seeming to hurry. "Short," she said. "Short and sweet. Like you. I like it."

Chicken-and-Dumplings turned around, flying backward so she could look Polijn in the face. "Polijn," she went on, "what do you suppose he's going to do to you?"

They had reached a landing. Polijn pulled up sharp. "Who?"

With a sharp crack, all the torches that hung along the stairwell went out. "Him," said Chicken-and-Dumplings, now invisible in the dark.

Long hands took hold of Polijn's neck. Trying to remember how far she was from the railing, she twisted down and around, pulling free of one hand while the other caught at her shift. She bit down on the wrist of that, at the same time reaching back one hand, down below his waist. Her hand swept against thick, coarse fabric, but found nothing to take hold of.

A fist landed along the left side of her jaw. Polijn rolled with it, but hit the railing. Had she been taller, she might have fallen across and over, but she braced herself and held on. The metal was cold, very cold.

Polijn heard the man coming in at her and tried to duck. Her arms stuck fast to the metal, as if frozen, like her tongue the time Mokono dared her to lick the backside of the big statue of Birulph on his horse, in winter. She jerked her head down against her chest and prepared to kick.

But the man stayed out of reach. Something whistled through the air as he brought it down, but it landed nowhere near Polijn. There was a clang, and the whole railing shook under her. Something cracked.

The great shaft of the stairwell was designed for quick movement of materiel in time of war. Naturally, things could be moved with more efficiency if there was no need to lift them over a railing. So this protective rail had been built so that it could be quickly broken away by a couple of men in an emergency.

Suddenly Polijn could not recall how many floors she had climbed. But even from the first floor it would have been a serious drop to the stone floor at the bottom level, down below the kitchens.

Polijn had learned early in life how and when to scream. As the railing trembled under a second blow, she let a wild shriek cut loose.

"Oooh, good one!" exclaimed the pixy. "I bet that fetches someone!"

The railing shook again, this time behind the soft thud of a body as someone else joined the brawl. Two bodies bounced back and hit the floor, twisting and pummelling.

"I simply must see this," said Chicken-and-Dumplings. "Be right back."

Polijn couldn't see her leave, but saw her come back, dangling some bright burning material between her legs. She dropped this into one of the dead torches and it flared into life. Then she dodged under the torch bracket thrown up at her from the floor.

"Oh, I hope you're struck toothless!" she told the thrower, with a variety of obscene hand signals.

Polijn looked down to the floor, where Aesernius seemed to be locked in mortal combat with a bundle of brown satin. The sorcerer managed to rise on one knee and force a fist down into the bundle. Something grunted and Aesernius pulled free.

He didn't waste any time. "Tuostrid nisedit!" he cried, with a long, complex wave of the hand.

The bolt of cloth rose, resolving itself into a man in brown robes. Polijn read violent contempt on his long, thin face. Then she gasped. Frost was growing up the man's brown sleeve.

Observing this, the man raised his arm. He said nothing, but just shook his hands forward. The frost snapped away from the cloth, forming blades of ice in the air. These slashed into Aesernius's sleeves and hood, though the sorcerer was able to ward them away from his face.

Polijn leaned forward, and found that the railing behind her was warmer. The fight must have broken her assailant's spell. She pulled free of the metal.

"Oh, gittim, gittim, gittim!" shouted Chicken-and-Dumplings.

Polijn felt inclined to second the sentiment, but said nothing. "Tuostrid nisedit!" Aesernius cried, more forcefully this time.

Ice swarmed out of the floor at the Brown Robe's feet, and flowed up the cloth. The evil sorcerer watched with some interest, and then lowered both hands. The ice, which had reached halfway to his waist, stopped moving. Then it shifted and grew toward a central point between his hands. In a second, it had formed a solid sphere. Then the Brown Robe threw his hands up.

With a cry, Aesernius fell back. Either the yell was nonmagical or he didn't have time to finish the spell, for the iceball hit him square in the chest. He hit the railing hard and a section cracked away. Metal rang against the stairwell and clattered against stone with a faraway echo.

The Brown Robe gave his back and ran to the corridor. Polijn jumped forward and got one hand in Aesernius's belt. They stood there, balanced between life and death, for what seemed to be about forty-seven years. Polijn couldn't reach out far enough to grasp the nearest piece of railing, and wasn't sure it wouldn't break, too.

Chicken-and-Dumplings fluttered past their heads to study the stairwell. "Ooh, that's a long ways down! We can't have that!" She swooped in to tug at Polijn's left ear.

Whether that was enough weight to break the impasse or whether it would have come out that way without the pixy's assistance, Aesernius and Polijn rolled back onto the landing in a heap. "Don't thank me or anything," said Chicken-and-Dumplings, buzzing by overhead. "I do it all the time. Oh, what would the world do without me?"

When no one replied, she fluttered away up the stairwell. Polijn, who had had the easier part of the skirmish, recovered first.

"Who . . . was he?" she panted. "Did you recognize him?"

The sorcerer rose, white-faced, shaking. "No. He was . . . nobody I knew. I . . . thought he was . . . some acquaintance of yours."

"No," she told him. "What did he want?"

The sorcerer didn't answer. "How did he do that?" he asked himself. "And why?"

Polijn remembered her original errand. "Maybe he's the one who . . . did all the killing. You can find out in the mirror."

The sorcerer groaned. "No, no. Not tonight. The battle has . . . weakened me. I won't be good for any more tonight. Let's go see Ynygyn, child."

He tried to take a step and stumbled. Polijn was instantly at his elbow, helping him along. He didn't look at all well. Was it just terror at the narrow escape, or was it as he had said, that the battle with the other sorcerer had weakened his powers?

The two limped along the stairs until they reached the minstrel's floor. Polijn knocked when they reached the door. "Come in, sorcerer," called Ynygyn, his voice as bored as ever.

The door was opened by Imidis, and they staggered inside. The minstrel stood facing his chair, but turned as the door closed. One eyebrow rose into an interested arch. "What's this? Has she been flitting about like a pixy?"

Aesernius shook his head and dropped onto a low stool. "I feel as if I have three broken legs."

Ynygyn leaned against the back of his massive chair and smiled. "Poor Aesernius," he said, with mock sympathy. "You were not meant for this role."

The sorcerer snorted. "It isn't easy to be a judge, either, I see." He pointed to a bandage on the minstrel's neck. "What happened, minstrel? Did one of the losers bite you?"

Ynygyn waved a limp hand in the direction of the other room. "You have duties in the morning, do you not, Polijn? Best to sleep now, I think."

Polijn started to go, but then turned to face them. Clumsily, she curtsied, not an easy job with a shift so short. "Thank you,

My Lords," she said. She had more to say but couldn't think how it could be said. "Thank you both very much."

She went to her cabinet, climbed inside, and shut the door. Then she tried to convince her heart to stop beating so hard and let her sleep.

III

A FEW paces, and Polijn stood by the cabinet again. She shrugged. This morning's tasks were done, and she had taken a quick tour, looking for something else in the rooms to occupy her time. Knowing as little as she did, however, about the routine of the place—what was what and went where—she had found nothing.

Then it was probably safe to practice some more. She knelt to open her sleeping cabinet, and reached in for the flute. Her back complained, and she arched it to get some of the kinks out.

A sound like a soft sigh made her jump back. A quick look showed her she was still alone. A trick of the wind, perhaps; just the same, she straightened up and pulled her dress down farther.

Why was she alone, anyway? Where was Imidis? If he was a servant, why wasn't he busy serving? Of course, she didn't know what his duties might be. But while Ynygyn was out, might his servant not be slipping through the palace, knife in hand?

That was just nerves. Everyone was nervous this morning. Dashing around in the confusion at breakfast, Iúnartar told her Hopoli Feetintheair had been found dead in the night. Coming so soon after the death of Harliis, this was bound to cause commotion. Polijn had not mentioned Arual; she had a feeling

Iúnartar was the type to find out everything, sooner or later.

There would be more than enough opportunity for Iúnartar to run around and pry information loose during the tournament. Everybody who was somebody would be in attendance. Polijn was not particularly somebody. This meant, she realized, that she would very likely be alone up here most of the day. She could close herself into her little hidden room and play without interruption, if she liked, for hours.

She bent forward for the instruments again, but this time was alerted by a heavy footfall. There was just time for her to slide the cabinet door shut and straighten up before Ynygyn pushed into the suite.

The minstrel strode back to the study without apparently noticing Polijn standing next to the cabinet. He sat at a writing table, his eyes on the shelves. With his left hand, he drew a walnut from a bowl on the table and cracked the shell. His right hand toyed with a scrap of paper. He looked as lazy and disinterested as ever he did, but Polijn wondered if anyone could possibly look so bored unless he was working at it.

"Those shelves," he said, his voice oozing into her reverie, "are filthy."

Polijn shivered herself awake. "Yes, sir. I'm sorry, sir." Imidis had not yet gotten around to that promised lesson on cleaning shelves. She hoped she could fake it.

The minstrel's hand waved her back. His left cracked another walnut open. "You were in service to the Paryice, I believe you said. What did you do there?"

His head turned slowly until the pale, cold eyes were full on her. What did he want to know? Did he think she'd been lying, that anyone who worked for the Paryice would know how to clean shelves? But he didn't sound angry.

"It was with his mother, sir," she said. "I . . . we . . . she'd had an accident, and she wasn't right in the head any more. He wanted us to play checkers with her, or read to her. . . ."

"You read?" demanded the minstrel.

"Just a very little, sir," she told him. "Mokono did most of that, my sister. And we helped her around, when she went places, because she couldn't remember where things were. We slept in her room, nights, to be sure she didn't try to leave. And we tried to keep her room clean and . . ."

That hand waved at her again. "Enough," he said. "All this activity is exhausting me. I think I see a story there, and I would like to hear it some other time. So you read, a little, and play checkers, and have any number of unnamed talents. Yes, I think something might be made of you, if we apply ourselves. But . . ."

There was a knock at the front door. "Come in, Aesernius," sighed the minstrel.

The door opened and the sorcerer limped in. He stopped for a moment to study Polijn, without comment or salutation.

Polijn wanted to ask about the mirror, but looked to Ynygyn for permission first. Instead, the all-commanding hand waved toward the door Aesernius had left open. "Leave us here to talk, Polijn," he said. "For sorcerers are arcane creatures and must discuss everything in secret. There will be music at the tournament. Go and listen to it. Study and remember. Watch the trumpeters, if you come near them; it is not a difficult instrument."

She was turning to go, but caught sight of that hand rising again. She waited to see what it would do. The index finger was raised to mark a sentence. "This will not be the normal routine of your days. These are merely the last rays of light before night falls. Through the long, hard winter days there will be no contests or tournaments, and you will spend all your waking hours working or . . ." He raised an eyebrow. "Playing."

This was Polijn's cue to giggle, so she did. "And you will be hard put," he went on, shaking the finger twice, "to decide which is the harder. Go frolic, Polijn."

She obeyed. As she closed the door behind her, she missed the words of a fierce whisper from Aesernius. "No," she heard Ynygyn reply. "No, I think we would do well to save that one for the King."

Polijn shrugged and hurried to the stairs. It was nearly time for the games to begin, and the halls of the Palace Royal were nearly empty. There was no one on the stairs at all. Just the same, Polijn stayed next to the inner wall all the way down.

Relief flooded through her as she reached the courtyard level and left the stairs. This did not last long.

"You! Girl! Come here!"

It was the command of someone who expected immediate compliance. Polijn feared for a moment that it would be Maitena again, but turned to see a tall, thin, balding man.

She knew the face; Iúnartar had pointed it out to her. His name, she recalled after a moment's effort, was Kercia, and he was an unofficial agent of the King of Dongor. But he reminded her of someone else, too. As she came up to him in the arched doorway, a ray of light from beyond the door hit his bald spot, and she remembered. He looked like Pterish, the bouncer at the Little Lost Duckling. In fact, come to think of it, Pterish came from Dongor, exiled from that embattled nation deep in the lands known as the Northern Quilt. Pterish was an easy and frequent killer. He had throttled one big bull of a man for saying that all people from the Northern Quilt were good for was target practice, and he had finished off dozens more for mentioning his lack of hair.

Kercia had the same sort of look about him, and not just because he was balding. "You're the minstrel's slavey," he snapped, like an accusation. "He or his sorcerer friend have a paper I want. It will look like this."

He eased the edge of a letter from under his cloak. It bore the same seal that Arlmorin had shown her, and had been on the paper the Bodyguard held. He slid the letter away.

"Find it," he ordered. "You people see everything in the rooms. Bring it to me. You need not fear your master. I can take you far from here, if need be, to Dongor. No one knows you there, and you have a saleable face. If I say you are a noblewoman from Rossacotta, our warriors will vie for your hand. All it requires is that you bring me the paper."

Polijn would not have brought him a glass of water. He looked as if he'd slit her throat for doing it.

"Take the paper to anyone else," the man went on, "to Arlmorin, to Ferrapec, to the Regent, and you'll get it just where the chicken got the axe. Now, go."

He obeyed his own command, charging out toward the courtyard. Polijn waited until he was gone, a little frightened and a little angry. This was unreasonable: the second person in two days who easily assumed she wanted to go west and would rummage through Ynygyn's and Aesernius's private things to bribe someone to take her. Was every day like this in the Palace Royal?

She did not intend to rummage; she hoped she never saw that blob of wax again. Maybe the Bodyguard had the right paper. Anyway, besides the obvious danger if she was caught prying, if she did find the paper she'd offend whoever didn't get it. And she had no desire at all to see the Northern Quilt. Would she be safe just doing nothing, taking it to no one, knowing nothing about it? She hoped so, but the way things worked, she couldn't be sure.

The tournament was not yet in progress; she could hardly run afoul of any documents if she went to see it. She stepped forward, only to see another tall figure emerge from the shadows, not more than a yard from where Kercia had stood. Polijn gasped.

Imidis must have heard every word. He stopped in the center of the passage as though seeing Polijn for the first time, but she knew better. "I wouldn't . . ." she started to say, but had to swallow. "I wouldn't do anything like that."

Imidis inclined his head politely. "I wouldn't, either," he said. He took a knife from his belt and leaned against the wall, cleaning his nails.

Polijn took a long breath and then walked on past him; no use trying to run. She expected to feel the knife at every step, but when she reached the exit and looked back, the valet was gone.

IV

IMIDIS was not out in the courtyard, but it seemed he was the only inhabitant of Malbeth who was not. People jostled and pushed and shoved through the big open field, not because even this mass of people could fill the huge yard, but because it was a festival day, and people expected to jostle and be jostled. It was a traditional part of any festival.

Bright streamers and gay bunting hung around the courtyard wherever it had been attached too firmly for industrious merchants to tear it down for resale. Dozens of torches burned and hundreds more waited to be lit, for clouds were increasing and festivities were expected to stretch long into the night. Tents and booths stood around the yard, selling beer, bread, cheese, and fruit. Even the kitchen help was allowed some time out of that smoky pit, as no cooking would be necessary for hours to come.

Merchants, soldiers, and thieves crowded around the stands, spending bright, shining coins. It was a demonstration of one's financial successes to spend one's newest money first, and a mark of high standing to show numbers of worn, elderly coins still in the purse. The older one's coins, the more obvious it was to viewers that one's family had not had to stoop to trade (or burglary) in recent generations.

Even in the surge of the crowd, social order of a sort was observed. Booths lined both the western side of the yard and the eastern. Visitors from the city ate and jostled on the "Malbeth" side, on the west, while courtiers stayed on the east, or "Palace," side. Both sets of booths sold the same wares, and in each crowd Polijn could see the same rich brocades, the same poor rags, the same mixture of exotic hats and torn hoods, and she could smell the same perfumes, exotic and homely.

And in both crowds, she saw the same pickpockets and the same dark-browed, scarred men who whispered that if you would just step into the shady sections between or behind booths, you could see something very interesting. Polijn stayed well away from the shade; she had no pockets to be picked, but she had three things that could yet be stolen.

Farther back in the shadows, on both sides of the yard, crept similar scavengers, checking the dead and disabled for anything the original assailant had left. It was dangerous work, for there were others who specialized in being dead bodies, to spring up and prey on the scavengers.

Excitement was available without going back to the shade. Before the games began, there were other tables and booths to visit, where one could lose shiny new coins or respectable old ones in games of dice or chess or backgammon. Wrestlers and archers showed off their skill and accepted the challenges of self-proclaimed champions. If that palled, jesters and lesser minstrels had taken up stations here and there about the yard to fill in dull spots. Polijn thought she could hear Arberth asking someone about fortifications and ratifications.

She tried to push through to find out what the proper answer was, but between her and the jester came a pack of apothecaries and leeches, talking shop and walking slowly. Like the rest of the crowd, they were here not only for entertainment but possible profit as well. They knew they'd all be needed. Rossacotta had imported the civilized spectacle of the tournament, but was not yet sophisticated enough to understand the use of blunted weapons or padded barriers. To set two men on to kill each other and then try to keep them from getting hurt made no sense to a Rossacottan at all.

Polijn had been to one tournament, long ago. She remembered feeling sorry for the horses.

Until the time came for the battles, she simply drifted through the crowd, catching at this sight and that scene and storing them up for the promised long, cold winter days. She had no money to spend or wager, and didn't know which spectacle she wanted to stand and study, with so many others going on. So she wandered, just soaking it all in.

Where she moved, she saw not just the pickpockets and spendthrifts, but also the tight, worried knots of people passing the latest theories and rumors about the death of Hopoli. Combined with the death of Harliis and the attempt on the King in the Treasury, had he but been there instead of Harliis, this was proof positive of a plot. They speculated on who was behind it, which way it was moving, and where they should go to jump out of its path.

On everyone's lips was the story of the bloody afternoon two years earlier, when a strange, wild woman ran into Malbeth shouting, "They've killed the King!" Forty people died in the ensuing riot, with a fire killing two hundred more. Later, ten men had died on the platform for setting her to it.

"And this will be worse," one young woman told another. "Two murders weigh more than four words."

Polijn did not know the woman, but Iúnartar had identified her companion as Maiaciara, Ferrapec's legitimate daughter, and one of the most civilized people in Rossacotta. She wore underwear, an innovation so new it was still denounced by the religious clergy. Polijn watched her closely. She didn't seem to walk any differently.

Frowys pushed past the women to a fruit stand. She wore a dazzling dress that was sheer gauze down to gold ruffles below the bust. From there it was red silk to the waist, with a red and gold skirt, and at least seven underskirts of alternating red and gold. It must have been exceedingly expensive, Polijn thought, but even she could see this was not the dress for Frowys. The dress itself was all right, if a bit light for this weather, but all it showed off on Frowys were muscular arms and a number of old scars.

Jilligan, dressed more sumptuously and further bolstered by a beautiful, heavy cloak, strode up next to Frowys as she paid for an apple. "Very nice," said the older woman, fingering a black band of silk on Frowys's left arm.

Mourning was very, very civilized. In the old Rossacotta, one death more or less was seldom worthy of comment. It still wasn't remarkable, but civilized to pretend that it was. Frowys could (but seldom did) claim distant kinship to Arnastobh. A few dozen people with similar relationships also sported the armbands.

Maitena wore several, as Arnastobh's daughter. In fact, her whole attire, garment upon garment, was black, hat and cloak and shoes, save for one or two ivory ornaments. All that clashed were the yellow apron and red face.

"Look at this!" she bellowed at Frowys and Jilligan, waving an arm at the booths on the Palace side of the courtyard.

Frowys took a bite of her apple. "Look at this!" Maitena ordered again.

"I'm looking at it," replied her assistant, through a mouthful of apple. "I don't see anything new."

Maitena waved both hands toward the booths. "You've let them build too close to the balconies!" she shouted. "You remember the last one! They were climbing in and out all through the night! The Regent ordered . . ."

"He will be upset, won't he," said Frowys, with a loud crunch. "It certainly doesn't seem to be your day."

Maitena's chin came up as she realized the problem was not ignorance but calculated insolence. Her shoulders rose as well. "I am still Third Chief Housekeeper. What I order still goes."

"Goes as far as you can push it," Frowys told her. Frowys considered the apple for a second and then, with one thrust, pushed her right forefinger straight through the center. Two wrestlers who had been grappling left their exhibition to gawk.

"Hey!" A hand tugged at Polijn's shift. She turned and saw Iúnartar.

"Have you seen . . ." the little girl began, but then looked beyond her. "There she is! I haven't seen my mother all day!" She wiped her forehead, which was dry, and released a long sigh. "Isn't it mad? I had to run all over the place. First they couldn't find Hopoli and then they find out she's dead and now they can't find Kirajen! Mother's been wild all morning, with all this fuss and bother to . . ."

By the fruit stand, Maitena had just about reached the point of pulling a knife, while Frowys and a large crowd waited for her to do so. But now a greater disturbance was working through the crowd, and spectators fell away to watch that one.

Iúnartar's eyes and ears seemed to catch at everything. "Let's go," she said, hauling on Polijn's sleeve. "Iranen got into the kennels again."

Seven men and three women pushed toward the palace, half-carrying and half-dragging the hysterical housekeeper. Blood ran from her face and arms, soaking into her bodice. Fur stuck to her up and down her clothes. Her lace was in shreds, and ribbons seemed to flow back from all parts of her body. Her dress was torn far enough to reveal brass kneecap guards decorated with spikes. Polijn paid more attention to her shoes. Polijn hadn't seen many shoes.

Iranen barked and growled as they hauled her through the crowd, her head thrown back and her mouth open to reveal unnaturally long canine teeth. But though she snapped and bit at her captors, there was no chance of her escaping. Four or five could have handled her. The others, judging by the positions of their hands, had merely come along for what they could get out of it.

"The kennel keepers usually watch for her," Iúnartar explained, "and her sister does, too. I wonder where Kirajen is, anyhow. Maybe she's with Ullofar, up in the Red Tower. He's . . ."

Polijn let the girl chatter on and turned back to look over the crowd. Frowys and Jilligan had vanished in the excitement. Maitena, seeing them gone, strode on, mouthing imprecations. The wrestlers had been pushed off their platform for a zerok, a little satirical skit. This one concerned theories about the death of Harliis, mingling considerable ingenuity with inevitable coarse humor. The crowd approved the jokes, but the laughter was forced. Unless that thief who had been carried out of Flact's rooms was indeed the culprit, the murderer of Harliis and Hopoli was still at large. A normal murderer would not have disturbed them; a possible regicide represented too large a threat.

The actors saw that they had struck the wrong note, and the skit was changed in mid-line. A small, squarish woman brought out an effigy of the Head Bodyguard, minimally clad and anatomically exaggerated. The lead singer propped his ficdual against his chest and sang,

"Little black Nimnestl-girl sat upon the green
Washing of her candlesticks, which weren't very clean;
Her cupboard was that musty, her table was that dusty,
And little black Nimnestl-girl, she was not very lusty."

Iúnartar crowed as the small, squarish woman moved the jointed limbs of the statue to illustrate the lyrics, and the other players offered not very subtle contributions in ensuing verses. This was just the prologue; they were preparing to move into the main body of the zerok when trumpets blared.

Up on the main balcony, members of the Royal Bodyguard stepped out to announce the arrival of the King. The performers of the zerok took off so fast that they simply disappeared, leaving the obscene effigy behind them.

"Oh, good!" exclaimed Iúnartar. "Now we'll have some excitement!"

V

THE Regent appeared on the balcony as trumpets blared again. The horns did more than herald his arrival: they drowned out the remarks of the crowd. The King would have a glorious reign, Polijn thought, if he lived. Everyone did hate the Regent so much.

The chubby little monarch appeared next and this time Polijn could not even hear the trumpets as the crowd bellowed approval. Behind the King came other bodyguards. A large black bird flapped over their heads, and then disappeared back into the palace.

"There's the black bird," said someone behind Iúnartar. "Where's the black dog?" But Nimnestl did not appear.

The King was required to make a few opening remarks while the soldiers below pushed away some platforms that blocked his view, and set up barricades to keep the audience out of the fight. "Come on," said Iúnartar, while he spoke. "Let's get up where we can see."

Iúnartar had the magic touch, and was able to pull Polijn along behind her to the very rail of a barricade. They took up positions in front of Akoyn, the Head Laundress, who was going cross-eyed from the effort of trying to keep one loyal eye on the King and the other turned north toward the approaching parade.

The parade did not, however, actually begin its approach

until the King had finished and given the signal. Then a column of dancers and musicians bounced down the marked-off lane, beating drums, flashing and clashing great cymbals, and making what noise was needed to fill the space with trumpets. The dancers, economically clad, rolled and tumbled among the players, flicking long scarves of all colors at the spectators, who grabbed at them, generally a second too late. Behind all this rode Seuvain, Master of Parades, a figure of disdain and dignity.

"He hates this," Iúnartar confided to Polijn. "He wants to be Minister of State, and he says all this entertainment work keeps him down."

"Down!" shouted Akoyn. "That's all that keeps him up!"

After him came a band of soldiers on horseback, most of them from Ferrapec's retinue and each sporting an ostentatious black chestband in honor of their commander's uncle. Several large floats followed them. Each drew cries of amazement, but the favorite was a big shelled elephant, a replica of what was believed to be a real animal down in Gorgalle. Its trunk and tusks waved ominously as the huge spiral shell rattled. Iúnartar, as usual, knew all about it.

"Marndell paid for that," she told Polijn. "He sells cloth down in the city. But you'd know that. There's his wife, Bersba, snipping that piece off Aleia's sleeve over there. She'll take it . . ."

Six ranks of drummers were barely enough to drown her out. Behind these came soldiers who finished enclosing the miniature battlefield. Spectators took this opportunity to dash back for more beer and bread. Several bought apples to hurl during combat, but most were willing to make do with rocks, which were free. A Brown Robe with a clay mug of beer passed, the silken sleeve of his robe brushing Polijn's cheek. She shrank back to Akoyn's left.

A thin hand gripped her shoulder and spun her around. She stared up into the face of Einoel. With an oath, the tall girl pushed her away, adding, "Keep away from me! I thought you were a ghost!"

The tall girl pushed back through the crowd and stumbled over a booted foot. She would have fallen if there'd been room, but instead hit the arm of a huge bearded man, spilling most of his beer across the bosom of her gown. The man, who had apparently been working at the beer all day, roared with amusement and stuffed a handful of bread down after the spilth, saying this would sop it up. He laughed again, and just about everyone within reach joined him.

"You know," said Iúnartar, running a critical eye over Polijn, "you do look a little like her sister, the one in the cell. She's still missing. It's the dark . . . Oh!"

The trumpets had called again. Small boys in livery cried out from opposite ends of the field that the first contestants would be Anrichar, son of Kirasov, and Nactuimn, son of Pammel, son of Kaigrol. The crowd roared and pushed forward. Kaigrol was the oldest general still active in the army, while Kirasov was commander of the Treasury Guard. This ensured a bloody, fiercely fought match. In fact, fierce battles were breaking out among audience members discussing it.

Nactuimn rode to the south end of the field on a truly massive brown horse. His armor was mail, but so well polished that it was brilliant even under cloudy skies. On his head rode a glorious winged helmet, with brass studs.

Anrichar was a little less magnificently decked out, but his horse's saddle was trimmed in silver, and the sword he carried was generations old, a family heirloom. Admittedly, it had not been an heirloom of his family before his father bought it from a bankrupt count, but it was still a storied weapon.

Assistants hoisted heavy lances up to the men. These were socketed, the signal was given, and the men urged their horses forward at attack speed. Polijn noted with approval that they had their lances aimed at one another, not at the horses. She expected a mighty crash, but when the moment came, she couldn't tell. The crowd was bellowing.

Nactuimn's helmet was broken, on the ground. One great wing sailed across the field and hit Frowys, who went over in a flurry of skirts. Her friends near her tried to help her up but perhaps did not notice they were lifting her by the ankles instead of the wrists.

Back at the main spectacle, Anrichar threw his lance from him. It had broken off three feet from the point, and he had elected to replace it with a pike. The crowd argued the merits of this as the men prepared for another pass.

This time Nactuimn had the advantage of the longer weapon, and the impact threw Anrichar from the saddle. The crowd flinched in horror, except for those who had bet on the army. Anrichar was related to half the court; if anything happened to him, they would all have to spend money for those mourning bands.

Nactuimn was not taking this into consideration as he wheeled his horse and came back for the kill. Now Polijn flinched as Anrichar drove in his sword. Nactuimn was able to throw himself free of the falling horse, and came to a jarring landing on his feet and one elbow. His sword came out. Anrichar flung away his cloak and charged forward with the heirloom. Assistants ran in with shields, but Anrichar waved his away. Nactuimn took this distraction as an opportunity to attack, nearly slashing Anrichar's shield-bearer in the process. The crowd cheered, finally deciding it could afford the mourning expenses if it got to see a little blood first.

Anrichar pushed his assistant out of the way, stepped on the broken-off point of his lance, and went rolling. Twisting to stay out of Nactuimn's reach, he landed hard on his chest. Nactuimn planted a foot on either side of his opponent and raised hands and sword above his head for a death blow.

Kicking out with one foot, Anrichar found a post of the barricade. One hand hit his discarded cloak. The kick sent him clear of Nactuimn's first stroke. Getting his knees under him, he hauled hard on the cloak, which was under one of Nactuimn's firmly planted boots.

Nactuimn flailed backward. Trying to cover himself in case Anrichar had a weapon ready, he inadvertently turned his sword in toward his own stomach. Akoyn shrieked and turned away as he fell. Iúnartar shouted something Polijn could barely hear, but which sounded like "Wow!"

He hit the ground, the sword point in his mail jacket, the hilt buried in the damp earth. Thus braced, it tore a small strip loose from the armor, spraying the crowd with broken rings.

"Ah, I knew it was cheap stuff!" shouted a connoisseur next to Akoyn.

Now it was Anrichar who stood with feet spread. Nactuimn tried to pull free, but couldn't figure out how he was pinned. Spectators shouted conflicting advice as he thrashed around, kicking up mud and tugging at his dagger.

The volume rose to new heights, but over it all came a cry of "Enough!"

It came from the Regent, of course. No one without mystic reinforcement could have been heard in the turmoil. The crowd turned to look up at him.

Both his hands were raised in the traditional gesture that ended the match. "The combatants have fought well," he declared. "They shall both be allowed to live."

The crowd growled disapproval. Anrichar's mouth was shut tight. He laid down his heirloom sword next to his fallen opponent, and turned to go. Then, with a single swoop, he snatched up his discarded pike, brought it over his head, and plunged it into Nactuimn. It flew apart, the head buried in earth deep beneath his opponent's chest, the butt in his hands, and fragments of the shaft flying into the crowd.

One section slashed across Frowys's shoulders. Another flew as high as the V.I.P. gallery on the town side of the crowd, where it was caught by the daughter of a wine merchant. The largest piece wobbled end for end through the air until it struck the chest of the dark wooden effigy of the Head Bodyguard. The jointed statue wobbled and fell across the platform. The head snapped off and bounced along the ground to rest at Polijn's feet.

The crowd, which had been cheering, fell silent.

CHAPTER EIGHT
Nimnestl

I

THE finding of Hopoli, quickly dead with a slit throat, upset Nimnestl less than it might have. The murder had been a simple affair: one slash. Nimnestl was not going to miss the plump little pigeon, but was glad the murder had been swift.

The fact that someone had been able to sneak the body into her office and trade it for that of Arual mattered a bit more. But the pine-branch pass was not impossible to steal, and it was a hopeful note. The killers, like Chicken-and-Dumplings, realized that things were getting to be excessive. If they hoped the substitution would go unnoticed in the festival excitement, they must be nearing panic levels. That was good: if events were moving too fast for the conspirators, there was hope for the investigators.

Nimnestl questioned the guards whose duty took them past her door, and servants who might have gone that way. She knew she would get no answers, but felt inclined to try. Those questioned, of course, denied knowing which rooms were Nimnestl's, denied knowing anyone had died, denied knowing who Hopoli was. They would have denied the sun existed if they suspected Nimnestl was blaming them for it.

Once the Bodyguard was finished with them, though, they knew plenty and were quick to spread it to their masters and coworkers. By breakfast, the news of Hopoli's murder in the Head Bodyguard's apartments was all over the court. That bit of gossip, with the fact that Chicken-and-Dumplings, feeling neglected, had appeared at the head table, dancing on a tambourine, made the morning meal even madder and less organized than was usual for the King's Birthday festivals.

This could all be to the good; Nimnestl hoped it would throw the plotters still further off their game. She tried to keep an eye on all her suspects in the confusion, to see how it struck them. Maitena, probably fussing down in the kitchen, was nowhere to be seen. Ferrapec, though, who had been known to enjoy Hopoli's favors, was in evidence, with his father and Kodva. They, however, were just busying themselves discussing tactics with Kaigrol and his grandson Nactuimn, in preparation for the coming tournament.

She decided there was no point trying to check on all the men who had shared Hopoli's sleeping space. A quick run-through of her suspect list indicated that all of them had, with the possible exception of Flact, the one verifiable murderer in the bunch. And she wasn't even sure about excluding him.

After breakfast, she picked a half-dozen of her more discreet subordinates and sent them down to the King's Beach. They brought back a bundle in a box, unobserved by the revellers in the courtyard as she admitted them to the Palace Royal.

Jurly bustled by in time to see them smuggling it into the main keep through one of the less travelled secret gates. "What's in that?" she whispered to one of the bodyguards.

They had been primed. "Surprise from a merchant in the city," he whispered back. "You'll find out later. For now it goes straight to the Treasury."

Jurly sped off to spread word that security was being tightened, and that all the King's presents were being transferred to the Treasury, for fear that the rebels would seize them. Her listeners nodded sagely. They had seen it all coming.

Nimnestl and her procession met another procession moving in the opposite direction. In the center of this second crowd were Kaftus and the King.

"What's in there, Nimnestl?" demanded the King, pointing to the box. "More new presents?"

"Actually an old trick," Nimnestl told him. "I'll explain later." She whistled, and a black bird flew down from a torch bracket.

"Mardith," she said, "you go along with His Majesty while Kaftus and I chat. You men, take that box up to the Treasury and wait there. Answer no further questions asked by anyone; refer them to me."

The two knots of bodyguards separated, going their opposite ways. The Regent and the Bodyguard were left alone.

"Did the pawnbrokers have anything to say?" she asked.

"When have I had time, woman?" demanded the necromancer, with some asperity. "Getting a corpse to make small talk takes time, even if one has all the parts."

"Oh, I am sorry," Nimnestl told him. "We mortals sometimes forget and make unreasonable demands on you mere magicians."

The Regent furled his brows at her. "But you were correct about the book," he said. "Once I picked it up, I couldn't put it down. I shall return your bookmark." He handed her a folded page with the seal of Braut on one side. "How much truth is there to the rumors I hear of Flact's visitor last night?"

"A bit," she said. "I'll tell you the whole story later." She checked over the letter to Arlmorin, to be sure it was the same one she had seen before. "You will let me play this one?"

"I won't have time to do it," Kaftus replied. "As we discussed?"

Nimnestl nodded. "Do I know about it?" the Regent went on.

Nimnestl slipped the paper into her armor. "Not yet," she said. "And I think it would be best if you knew nothing at all about Kirajen and Arual for a while."

"I shall be as shocked as you like when I hear about them," he said. "The rest I leave to you. This will take managing, and I have to attend all these lintik ceremonies. By the way, Liaouvan has disappeared again; he'll be in Hacude by now."

Nimnestl nodded. During every palace crisis, there were those who rushed out into the country to inform the noblemen who had placed them in the Palace Royal for just that purpose. If the crisis proved lasting, these nobles could then rush into the city to "save" the populace from the confusion of an interregnum. The crown of Rossacotta would never fall to the ground for lack of heads willing to wear it.

"I promised the King we could slip out and go riding later," she said. "Would they consider it sinister if he were absent a while?"

"Those of us on the balcony would welcome the relief," Kaftus replied. "Nurse has been warning us alternately to keep him out of the sunlight if it gets too hot and out of the wind if it gets too cold. I have no reason to expect she will be less insistent once there. And that idiot of a Maitena let them build the booths too far in again, so there'll be that for her to complain of, as well."

"He may be bored by that time," said Nimnestl. "Don't come down on Maitena. Frowys and Jilligan have been plotting a coup ever since you took her keys. Kirajen was after her job, too; once they learn she's gone, they may decide they have a clear shot. Keep an eye on them."

"Them and a thousand others," said Kaftus. "But it will be more interesting than seeing two piles of weapons ride at each other. Where are you off to?"

"To lay a trap," she told him.

He raised his eyebrows. "Play nice."

She snorted and turned toward the Treasury. Before she reached the end of the corridor, a large shadow had settled on her shoulder. "Why didn't you stay and watch the slaughter?" she inquired.

"More trouble in here," Mardith replied. "You need someone guard you back, Missy."

"Old crow," she said, putting a hand up to ruffle his plumage. They moved on down to the Treasury, where they found the bodyguards standing at the door, the box still sitting on their shoulders. Facing them were the Treasury guards on duty, Troan and Hani.

"I thought I ordered that box inside," she said, showing she had no doubts about it whatsoever.

"They won't let us in without your order," answered Culghi.

"That isn't what we said," Troan objected, with a glance at the Bodyguard. "We said we had to be careful."

"Commendable," said Nimnestl, bringing out her key. When she stepped forward, Hani brought out his sword.

"You am better to put that down," suggested Mardith.

"No one is to be admitted without Lord Garanem's approval," said Hani. "The last time you were in here, someone got killed."

Two of the bodyguards who could spare a hand for it drew weapons of their own. Troan brought out his sword. "Ever you is heared of dungeons, master man?" demanded Mardith. "They wind ever down and down. You go there to bottom, I know!" Troan, looking uncomfortable, took half a step away from the door. Hani glared at him.

Nimnestl stood where she was, studying Hani. Usually, the guards had better sense when facing an official who outranked them so far, even one from a rival faction. They knew that an offended superior would be hampered by no considerations of moderation or justice. But let an officer show weakness and they would begin to close in, wolves around a wounded sheepdog.

Her men waited to see what she wanted done. Troan looked to Hani.

"Guard," said Nimnestl, softly and a little slurred so Troan would not know whether she'd said "guard" or "guards." "Does the Regent know your name?"

Hani snorted. "No. I'm not pretty enough."

Nimnestl smiled. "Would you like him to?"

Hani frowned and tried to read between the lines in her expression. Nimnestl smoothed them out, looking thoughtful. "Such loyal and watchful service merits recognition. Someone with your talents shouldn't be wasting his life standing here. We can have you working with a broom in the mews by this afternoon. Or perhaps the Regent could suggest an indoor job, in which the wearing of such cumbersome armor would be unnecessary."

Mardith cackled. "You can for sure do that job, master man."

Troan now took four steps away from the door. Hani sheathed his sword, his hands shaking a bit.

"Of course, Lord Garanem's order was not applicable to those officials with keys," he murmured, as Nimnestl stepped forward to unlock the door. She ignored him.

The lights were lit inside the Treasury again, and she stepped inside. "Over there, along the wall," she ordered. "Yes, and keep your hands in full sight, or our diligent guards may decide to massacre us where we stand." She stepped back to make room for them to pass.

The blood had been washed from the spot where Harliis fell. The room looked much as it always had. One more murder or one less murder meant little in a chamber filled with bloody plunder.

A large sack sat alone in the aisle. Nimnestl stooped to give it a shove. It was full of pennyetkes, and there was blood on it. She raised the sack and hefted it, frowning. This was the bag she had found near Harliis's body. Nothing so common as a pennyetke was kept in the Treasury. She hoped those other sacks, presumably filled with gold, had not been replaced with similar bags of cheaper coins.

There didn't seem to be any other signs of disturbance. Lord Garanem would have to answer for this. Perhaps he already had. This bag had been next to Harliis's body; was it possible Harliis had been about to do something useful, announcing this discovery?

She glanced back toward the loyal guards at the door. The Great Iron Horn of Drawziw, which had hung for centuries next to the door of the Treasury, now dangled from one hook. The other hook was in place; the Iron Horn had simply slipped loose, for some reason, after sitting in place through a thousand lives of kings.

Behind her, the box containing Kirajen's body thumped to the floor. She tossed the bag of pennyetkes onto a stack of crystalline skulls, and smiled.

II

SHE regained her frown for the benefit of Hani and Troan when she left the Treasury. After supervising the closing of the door, she sent her men to the balcony and moved off in the opposite direction herself.

Once away from the corridor, she said, "Is Arlmorin in the gallery at the tournament, or on the balcony?"

The bird shifted on her shoulder. "No, Missy. Messenger come for him."

"Messenger?" she demanded. "What messenger?"

"Not knowing, Missy," Mardith replied. "Up in room."

Messengers were supposed to check in with some official of the Regency before delivering a message anywhere, particularly to a foreign envoy. She moved to the stairs. Arlmorin had been assigned a suite low enough in the complex to confer a certain status on him as sole ambassador at the court (low rooms were closer to the King's Chambers, as well as being down out of the wind) but high enough so that, should another ambassador arrive someday, a comparable suite would be available.

They passed Aleia on the stairs. Her usually well-kept hair was tousled beneath a hat that looked like a straw bucket. She turned her face away as they passed.

"She wasn't the messenger?" Nimnestl asked.

"No, Missy," said Mardith.

At the door to Arlmorin's suite, Nimnestl paused. "Go to the King," she ordered.

The bird flapped its wings in dismay. "What name, for sake of love, Missy, you go in alone?" he demanded. "It be very trouble."

"You're always a help to me, Mardith," she told him. "One of my best aides. But you talk too lintik much."

"I be quiet, Missy," the bird promised. He hunched down on her shoulder. "I sit here, look wicked."

Nimnestl liked the idea. Mardith could look positively infernal when he really worked at it. "Very well," she said. "But not a word, or I pluck feathers."

"Foo," said Mardith.

The Bodyguard nodded to the single guard on duty at the door and pushed through to the front room. The ambassador had his back to the door, apparently studying a fan that rested on a red lacquer chest while three of his aides watched a servant shining the ambassador's boots. They all looked up as Nimnestl marched in.

"You can go," she told them. "I'll talk to the ambassador alone."

They looked to Arlmorin. The ambassador took his eyes off the fan and turned to regard the intruder. He frowned, saw the paper she was bringing from under her armor, and smiled. He waved toward the door, and the Brautians departed. Then he nodded to a large chair that had obviously been sat in, and reached for a bottle of wine on the table at his elbow.

Nimnestl walked over to the chair, but preferred to stand. She said nothing, surveying the ambassador's face. Mardith opened and closed his beak.

"Something, Milady?" inquired Arlmorin, finding a second glass to fill, and then refilling his own. "You have news for me, perhaps?"

"Perhaps," she said. "I'll want something from you first."

He smiled, studying the level of wine in each glass. Then he slid one glass toward his guest. "What is it?"

"Information," she told him.

His smile broadened. "Well, that's the coin we both deal in, not? Ask away." He handed the glass up toward her in case she hadn't noticed it.

The smile was genuine. Arlmorin was happy to hear questions at any time. Questions kept him current on what other people wanted to know.

She raised the glass of wine for Mardith to sniff. The bird grumbled something noncommittal. Nimnestl set the wine down without tasting it, and raised the paper.

"This says you are no ambassador at all," she said. "Is this news to you?"

"Ah, now we are moving along," said Arlmorin, padding his hands together silently. "We are not progressing, no, but we are moving along. Progress may come after. Yes, Milady Bodyguard, it is news to me, but hardly a surprise."

"No?" she inquired politely.

He shrugged. "I warned you that forged papers bearing my name might turn up."

Nimnestl inclined her head. "You did," she said. "I knew you would want to be informed that one had been found, before I took it to the Regent."

Arlmorin sipped his wine. "And why bother him with such a poor forgery?"

"He has lived in Rossacotta a long time. No doubt he can recognize the forger's technique if he studies the paper. In fact, it might be best if we took it to him now, and clear the matter up at once."

"Such a rush!" protested Arlmorin. "On a holiday? He'll not want to be bothered."

Nimnestl took one step toward the door. "I should have checked with him before I brought this to you at all. It is you who have been bothered, to no purpose. Better that the Regent and I should have sought out the culprit first and sent him to the dungeons for your questioning. Or perhaps the Regent could send some spell to strike down the writer of this, without knowing the exact identity." She took another step.

Arlmorin sat back. "Well, if you feel you must annoy him," he said, reaching for a folded sheet of paper on the table, "take him this as well." He handed the paper up to her.

Dated two months ago (but four months after the other letter), it was a brightly decorated certificate from the King of Braut, naming one Arlmorin, "hitherto agent of our majesty in Rossacotta" an official ambassador to King Conan III. It bore the royal seal. Nimnestl compared the two documents, and could see no reason to doubt the authenticity of either.

She supposed he had known this was coming, and had wanted her to find the previous paper from the moment he had information that the messenger was in Malbeth. This would alter the play of the game a bit.

She handed the newer notice back to Arlmorin. "I think it will not be necessary," she told him. "Do take good care of that, My Lord. It would be tragic for anything to happen to it before the Regent sees it."

Arlmorin honored her with a nod of the head, and put out a hand for the second letter.

She raised it out of reach. "Because it has been a busy week. The Regent is always easily irritated during holiday periods, even when unattended by treason or murder. If he saw this letter first, he might still be upset enough to take rash action."

"He can hardly see it if it is in my possession," Arlmorin pointed out. "Not?"

"Not," echoed Nimnestl. "But it is not in your possession and is unlikely to be until I get my information."

"My lady," said the ambassador, "I would not trade my worst vice for your best virtue. You are a stubborn repository of all the inelegant features available to a human being. In short: a credit to our profession. What would you like to know?"

What business he had being so cheerful, for one thing. Nimnestl frowned down on him and demanded, "What do you know about Harliis?"

"He died," said the ambassador. "Men do that."

Mardith let a small chuckle escape. "Do you know of any connection between him and Kirajen?" Nimnestl went on.

A faint flicker of what might have been genuine surprise passed across the ambassador's face. "No. That might explain why she's nowhere in evidence this morning."

Nimnestl made exasperated noises. "Is she missing, too?"

Arlmorin leaned on one arm of the chair. "It must have slipped past you in all the excitement. Lady Iranen ran amok this morning and had to be locked away; I am told this would not have happened had Kirajen been on the job. Someone let her into the kennels."

"Ah," said Nimnestl, nodding. "Perhaps Kirajen knows, or knew, something about Harliis's death."

The ambassador shrugged. "I can't help you there."

Nimnestl believed him. She had hoped he would know something, even if he wasn't involved, since he seemed to get news so quickly. She had not, in fact, heard about Iranen yet. But Kirajen was a lone plotter, which helped her keep her secrets.

"Back to business," she said, rattling the letter she held. "Had Aesernius any interest in your doings? What did he want from you?"

The ambassador shrugged again. "Probably the answers to a number of impudent questions. Ask him yourself, unless you had to damage him to get that piece of paper."

"Aesernius didn't have it when it was found," she informed the ambassador. "A religious cult had taken it from him."

Another tic of surprise bounced through the ambassador's expression. Again it looked genuine. If he'd been acting, surely, he would have made it more obvious.

"The Brown Robes," he said, stroking his mustache. "We may have a common enemy there. But I am sure I know less about them than you do. I've never paid them more than passing attention."

But he had guessed which sect she meant. "At the moment," she said, "I'm more interested in Aesernius. He is practically the least useful of the sorcerers in the Palace Royal. How was he able to take this from an experienced, ever-vigilant diplomat?"

Arlmorin raised an index finger. "Unfair. We have not allowed that it is genuine, or that I have ever seen it before now."

Nimnestl looked down her nose at him. "A courtier must be something of a minstrel, quick at song and story. You did not compete yesterday, ambassador, but I'll give you a private audition. Why don't you tell me how it might have happened, if, by some rearrangement of fate, this paper had been genuine?"

The ambassador shook his head. "Why, it could have been mere carelessness. I might have carried it with me while visiting a woman and set my clothes too close to a window."

"And staged the rest of the robbery later in your rooms so you could mention the document without raising too much suspicion," Nimnestl finished for him.

"It could have happened that way," said Arlmorin. "Remind me not to have it conjecturally happen that way again, since it probably wouldn't work."

"Why not mention this woman as a suspect while you were at it?" Nimnestl demanded. "Were you so sure she hadn't taken it herself, or was it just wounded pride at being taken in by one of the older tricks of the trade?"

Arlmorin shook his head. "I was sure she had not done it, and a woman's name was at stake. Now that I know she didn't do it, and now that she is dead, I am glad I withheld the information."

Mardith snorted. "Protect good name? Hopoli Feetintheair a good name, man? Hopoli . . ."

"Enough," said Nimnestl, taking one feather between thumb and forefinger.

The ambassador looked perplexed. "Oh," he said, "but it was not the woman I was with whose name I wished to protect." He sighed a big sigh that blew his mustache into little waves. "I suppose I must mention it now, as things take such a serious turn. I did have enough presence of mind to pay some attention to the window. The only person I saw pass, though, was Maitena. It was her name, not the dead woman's, I hoped to protect. The night was dark, but I could not mistake the apron."

Nimnestl was immediately alert for a lie. Any reference to Maitena was beginning to affect her that way. "A pity you were too busy to notice what she was doing."

"Just then, yes. Not much later, though, I had reason to go to the window, and saw her talking to a man with a blue snake tattoo on one arm. Now, I never did believe she had killed her father; he was harmless. But now that this man has turned up dead as well . . ."

"You knew we were interested in Maitena's movements," said Nimnestl. "You didn't see fit to mention this before?"

Arlmorin spread both his hands wide. "I thought she was contracting for revenge on her father's killer. Even the civilized can understand that. What right did I have to interfere? I didn't know her revenge was aimed at her daughter."

"What do you mean?"

"Perhaps the girl did it," said the ambassador, with a shrug. "I don't know. In any case, having a daughter in the dungeons was bound to be an embarrassment, a check to Maitena's career. I can see that an ambitious woman would try to put embarrassment out of her way. But to do it in such a manner!" Arlmorin shuddered.

"It will bear looking into," noted Nimnestl. "Is there anything else you'd like to say to me?"

Arlmorin smiled his broadest smile. "Don't tempt me."

Nimnestl bowed and extended his letter. "Do dispose of it carefully. There are enough real forgeries at large in Malbeth without adding a false one."

"I would not for the stars further confuse the people of this city," Arlmorin replied. "Life seems to be hard enough as it is."

After a further exchange of civilities, Nimnestl was able to march away toward the stairs. "I do good, Missy?" demanded Mardith.

"Mmmmm," she replied. "You were tolerable."

"You too, Missy," said the bird.

Nimnestl wasn't sure about that. It seemed she had come away with the smaller half of the bargain. Arlmorin had learned about Aesernius, and knew of her interest in Kirajen, Harliis, Maitena, and Arual. In return, she had gotten his connection with Hopoli, which was a lie. No whisper had ever connected the ambassador with Harliis's sister, and Hopoli would never have neglected a chance to brag about that. The story of the theft of the letter might be true, with some other woman substituted.

And he had revealed that he knew Arual was dead, and how she died. But he could have passed the body in the night, before she found it, and done nothing about it.

Further, he wanted to keep Maitena at the center of things, for some reason. Nimnestl had so far avoided talking much to Maitena. Maitena was not an easy person to talk to in any event and, when upset by holiday arrangements, or murders, she lost control of words very quickly and resorted to physical conversation. Nimnestl did not want to have to damage her.

Was she avoiding Maitena for fear the woman would say something that would prove guilt in Arnastobh's murder? That was cowardice. It was obviously time to go ask more questions.

III

"MARDITH," she said, "is Maitena at the tournament?"

"I look, Missy." The bird flapped to the ceiling and slid along the shadows. Nimnestl strolled without much speed down the corridor until he returned. "I no see."

Nimnestl sighed. "The kitchens, then."

"Org," said Mardith.

The kitchens in the castle of Koanta had been big, roomy, warm. Nimnestl was always running down for a visit. The kitchen of the Palace Royal was vast, but lower, darker, dirtier. Deep under the castle, dungeonlike, usually lit only by the cooking fires, it was a place virtually no one went from choice, and few by chance.

Maitena enjoyed it, for some reason. She had had torch brackets installed in the spots she frequented, and the corner where she had cooked Arnastobh's meals was the brightest part of the cavernous hole. Otherwise, the kitchen served as a visual reminder of the destination of those who did not respect their god and king, after death.

A skeleton crew was there, keeping the fires lit and making tentative preparations for the next meal, distant because most of today's eating would come from convenient camp kitchens and booths in the courtyard. Maitena was nowhere in evidence.

Choosing a scullery girl at random, the Bodyguard took hold under the chin, put her face down to the pale one, and demanded, "Where's your mistress?"

"Please, sir, oh, Milady," said the girl, trying to curtsy and evaporate at once. "Oh, oh, I don't know."

"You might try the larders, My Lady," suggested a slightly older, bolder girl.

Nimnestl released the first girl, who crumpled to the floor. "The larders?"

"Or the vegetable cellars," said the second girl, stepping back.

On an even lower level than the kitchen were the large square storerooms where the main stocks of stored food were kept. Once they had been treasuries, the food being more evenly distributed through the castle in case the kitchens were taken during a civil war. Forokell, considering this a nuisance, had consolidated storage a generation ago.

Nimnestl crossed the kitchen to the bare stone stairs that led down to the larders, catching up the one torch lit on the wall she passed. The shadows below told her nothing worthy of notice, nor was there any clue as to whether Maitena had passed that way recently. Good thing Mardith was there to guard her back; she would have to keep her eyes on the cracked, uneven stairs.

"My Lady Maitena!" she called, perhaps ten feet down into the shadows. "Are you there?" Her voice echoed among parsnips and beets. Nothing moved.

"Good," said Mardith, as the sound faded. "We leave."

"Something may have happened to her," Nimnestl told him, taking another step down. She slid on a wilted leaf, but braked herself against the wall.

"You go no more, Missy," ordered the bird. "I check."

The next step down was a landing, so Nimnestl took up a position there. "Go ahead."

Mardith swooped down into the depths. A couple of rats dashed in the opposite direction, and took shelter in a stack of turnips that lay in the corner of the landing. Someone had decided not to make the whole trip down to the right bin. Maitena must not have been here since, or these turnips would be cleared away, and there would be one or more kitchen servants walking with a limp.

Nimnestl swung her hammer, which she had unhooked upon reaching the kitchen, not so much to damage the rats as hurry them on their way. They vanished around and behind the vegetables. Bending to look, Nimnestl saw a goodly crack in the wall just there: bad for the turnips, but handy for the rats. She straightened.

Then she leaned in again. Bringing her torch over, and setting her face nearly against the wall, she could make out a series of smaller cracks, which formed a perfect rectangle perhaps four feet high. Most of the bottom three feet were hidden behind the turnips. And that black spot at the right was no stain.

She reslung her hammer to reach for her keys. The first she touched was a wooden one, not attached to any ring. More to get it out of the way than anything else, she stuck it into the keyhole.

Reaching inside her armor again for the top key ring, she paused. Where had she gotten a wooden key? And what was it made to unlock? She gave it a little push with her forefinger. It fit nicely, with a little click as it slid in. Nimnestl shrugged and gave it a half-turn. There was another little click.

Turnips scattered as she pulled the key, bringing the door with it. Rats hissed at the light of her torch. She picked up a couple of turnips and lobbed them inside.

There was plenty besides turnips inside to interest rats. Fresh straw littered the floor. On it were a food bowl and a body. Nimnestl decided against scattering the rats. This was a bad place to enter, if she didn't know who else was around, and nothing much could be done to Arual's body that hadn't already been inflicted. But it was something to add to the murderer's account.

She pushed the door shut and kicked turnips back into a pile. This cell had been occupied by the living lately; you didn't put straw down or provide a food bowl for a pile of limbs and loose skin.

Locking the door, she pulled out the key. Nobody used wooden keys; it was easier to pick a lock or steal a key than make up a substitute like this. It would have to be some key you needed often, and one for which you'd have access to the original so you could make a copy.

Maitena wouldn't have a wooden key. She had an official key to everything below kitchen level, or had had one. Not knowing the keys would be confiscated, though, she would hardly have gone to the trouble of having a copy carved. Further, the smiths would know she was entitled to that key; they would have made her a metal copy without any argument. The smith's guild was rock solid and crystal clear; it maintained its own separate branch to track down and punish counterfeiters of keys.

Maitena could have been plotting all this for a while, getting the copy made as insurance. Trouble was, Nimnestl still couldn't see Maitena planning any farther ahead than this winter's supplies.

She took a step back and considered the cell. Arnastobh had always mentioned a cell below the kitchen, where he had put the Pearl of Adriack during the revolt. He had told that story a thousand times (without ever once hinting at the parts Eldred filled in about Jintabh). When the Minister of State, Grillon, died of his wounds, he had passed the secret and the key on to Arnastobh. After Southgate, when this key was passed on to the new Minister of State, a copy was made and presented to Arnastobh as a token of trust. This key he had long since handed on to Maitena.

Countless people had heard the story. Anyone who had listened at all would know where to find the key, if only they could find the cell: Jintabh, certainly, Kodva, Maitena, Arual, Ferrapec. . . . And, as Minister of State, Flact would know.

How tidy if all these murders could be tied to Flact. He could have had the copy made for the thief, to keep it secret from the smiths. The thief could have hidden out here, hence the straw and food bowl. Then Arnastobh and any member of the family who knew about the cell could be put away, by murdering them or blaming them for the other killings. This key was the one the pixy had given her in Flact's rooms; Chicken-and-Dumplings could have plucked it from the thief's torn pouch.

No. The pixy had held up the key before the thief came into the room. And surely the pouch had not been torn before Flact started stabbing in the dark.

Nimnestl sighed. Now she had to go interview a pixy. In its way, that could be worse than questioning Maitena.

"Mardith!" she shouted.

The bird shot out of the blackness below. "What name, Missy?"

"You go on searching here, and then go try the tournament again. Check the larders and the baker's ovens. Tell Maitena I want to talk to her. I'm going up."

"Good for you," said the bird, before winging it back down into the cavern.

Nimnestl did not have to search far. Back up at ground level, she passed a knot of courtiers whispering about the little creature with the strange mind, and what her appearance portended.

"Where's the pixy now?" she demanded.

"Up on the Main Tower, Milady," said Maniture.

That was strange. Nimnestl would have assumed she'd be down at the mock combat, as close as possible to the blood and violence. What was she doing on the highest point of the Palace? She couldn't have known the Bodyguard was looking for her, and picked out the point farthest away. Or could she? Nimnestl scowled, both for herself and to discourage curiosity on the part of the courtiers, and set off for the tower.

Nimnestl had to put her shoulder to the tower door to get outside, so fierce were the winds become. Chicken-and-Dumplings, naked and perched on the edge of the battlement, seemed to notice not at all. She squatted at one end of a long brass tube stuck in a crack. "Whee!" she shouted, throwing both hands into the air.

"What are you doing?" Nimnestl demanded.

"Oh, hi," said the pixy, not looking around. "Isn't it a swell fight? That guy just got his head bopped off."

Nimnestl peered over the stone to the little figures massed below. "You can't see that from up here, can you?"

"Use this," said the pixy, patting the tube. "It's a long-seer."

Nimnestl squatted to put her eye to the tube and saw Thrad Redhair crawling along the red ground, scrabbling for a sword he had dropped. "Where did a pixy get this bit of magic?" she inquired.

"It's mine," said Chicken-and-Dumplings. "Get away so I can see what the guy with the padded crotch is doing."

Nimnestl straightened. "Where did you get it?" she persisted.

"Oh, around. Yeah! Thrun him down! No, don't kick him there; it's full of cotton!"

Nimnestl stepped back out of a cutting blast of wind and reached into her armor for the wooden key. Her left foot kicked through a small pile of coins.

"Those are mine!" shouted the pixy, buzzing over. "You go get your own!"

Nimnestl knelt to examine the pile. The pickpocket pixy had a good haul. Naturally, she had picked out the shiniest coins, and a few brass pawn tokens were mixed in. More interesting, though, was a large wooden key.

"Where did you get this?" the Bodyguard demanded, holding it up.

The pixy, who had returned to her long-seer, glanced over one shoulder. "I don't know which one that is. Come here, quick! There's such a fight behind the beer stand! Ooh, pull her hair, pull her hair, pull her hair! Yeah, right into the keg!"

"Where did you get either of these?" the Bodyguard went on, bringing out her own wooden key. When the pixy didn't answer, she took hold of the shimmering wings and yanked Chicken-and-Dumplings up closer.

"You're a bully," pouted the pixy. "But I like that in a woman."

"The keys," Nimnestl prompted.

"That was yesterday," complained Chicken-and-Dumplings. "I don't think I remember. Oh, yes, I do so. I got one from the square sow in that horrible dress. Oh, doesn't red and gold just give you the blue hives?"

"Who?" Nimnestl demanded.

"Now, the long girl, she had the nice red dress with little gold sparkles. That was all right. I like her. I was going to switch . . . Ooh!"

Mardith had flown from the doorway. He was almost as impressed as the pixy. "What that?" he demanded, with a stare filled with disgust.

"Never mind," said Nimnestl. "You found Maitena?"

"I find," said the bird. "She say no have time. See you tomorrow. See you in hell. She no care."

"Can I ride him?" demanded the pixy, buzzing around and around the pair. She swooped away to scoop up some of her loot. "I can pay." She let something drop down Nimnestl's neck.

Nimnestl needed explanations. She needed information. She needed names. She had two wooden keys, a spluttering bird, and a cold brass pawn token with an obscene inscription.

She took these and left.

IV

NIMNESTL laughed. She took off her helmet and let the wind blow back through her hair.

"Did you see me?" the King demanded. "Did you see me, Nimnestl?"

"Who could miss you?" she retorted.

The King was showing off to a seventeen-member audience. Fifteen onlookers could remember showing off on a horse. These fifteen were smiling. Mardith could remember generations of children showing off on horses. He couldn't exactly smile, but he did rasp encouragement.

The seventeenth member of the party was Nurse. "You're going much too fast on a horse you hardly know," she stated. "The grass is wet, and that animal will fall with you if you keep turning it like a road bandit. I don't ask that you remember you're a king, but you might at least show some of the dignity of a gentleman."

"You," said Nimnestl, "are an old woman."

"And before my time," Nurse replied. "Before my time. Do you see my hair? Every grey one is a gift from royalty. And now what are you about, if I may inquire?"

The King was already off to try another trick, four bodyguards riding at a discreet distance on either side. Nimnestl hoped he did know what he was about. One slip and Nurse would be telling about it for the next five years.

There was no slip. Nimnestl was able to let part of her mind drift to the cells and apartments of the Palace Royal. Flact had certainly killed Kirajen and the Turinese thief. But he had not been waiting in the Treasury to kill the King, and she could see nothing that would connect him with the death of Arnastobh.

The leisure provided by the ride out from the Palace Royal had at least given her time to think, and she knew now who had killed Harliis. It was a tiny consolation, though, because she still wasn't sure why.

"How much do horses cost?" asked the King.

She hadn't seen him come up. "Outright purchase or with upkeep?"

The King wrinkled his nose. She explained, "To buy him, or to buy him and then feed him all of his life?"

"Oh," he said. "Both, I guess. Would it cost more than the Pearl?"

"Oh, no," said Nimnestl.

"Maybe," said Mishek, First Master of the Stables.

"He's joking," snapped Nurse. "The Pearl of Adriack is worth a hundred horses."

"Even like Morsheen?" the King demanded, looking to Nimnestl and stroking the mane in front of him.

"Well, maybe only fifty, in that case," his Bodyguard replied. "Your Majesty, I must beg leave to return to the Palace. I have pressing business."

The King giggled. He loved to be called "Your Majesty" by very tall adults. "Very well," he said, in his regal voice. Then he leaned over to add, in a whisper, "Race you!"

"Not today," she whispered back. "You don't want to give Nurse fits."

"I do, though," he told her.

He and the pixy would make a marvellous pair, she thought. Nurse suggested that they all return to the Palace Royal before this horrible weather gave some royal people the sniffles. Mishek was able to forestall the inevitable protest by asking if the King would like to discuss arrangements for the stabling and harness of his own horse. The King, as expected, jumped at the chance of such adult conversation, and the group made its way back to the Palace, Nimnestl riding slightly behind the King.

The Council Chamber, for which she headed as soon as she dismounted and handed Meriere over to the groom, connected to Kaftus's quarters via a number of doors and short halls. A guard on duty outside the Council Chamber told Nimnestl that the Regent was holding an important meeting and was not to be disturbed. He further informed her that he was a member of General Ferrapec's bodyguard, and he had had those orders from Ferrapec himself.

Nimnestl knew that, and told him so. "One thing I do not know, however," she went on, "is any reason that I should take orders from General Ferrapec. Can you think of any?" Her voice was eager and encouraging, but the way her hand rested on her hammer suggested that it would be best not to think of any. The soldier said nothing as she pushed the door wide.

The conference did not look important. Three Lords of the Treasury were in attendance, with the First Minister, several of his most important subordinates, and a contingent from the army. Forokell was there, as were half a dozen of her chief aides. Maitena was not among them. Everybody had brought enough bodyguards and sidemen to look impressive, and, further, since they had been called in from the tournament, each was dressed in holiday clothes.

Kaftus loved to do this; it confused the councillors and made it difficult for anyone to prepare for a meeting. "Besides," he always said, "the day's ruined for me anyway, with all the public functions; why not have a Council meeting, too?"

First Minister Isanten was the councillor most likely to object to the intrusion, but glanced first at his host to see if the Regent were similarly outraged. The Regent was not. He had always enjoyed watching Isanten sputter.

"Yes, Lady Bodyguard?" he inquired.

"A report, Your Grace," she said, her tone formal. She slid two fingers across the butt of her hammer, to signal that she was setting a trap. "I thought it important enough for the Council to hear."

Ferrapec did start to object, but Kaftus broke in first. "It may pertain to the subject under discussion. Does it concern the assassination attempt on the King, in the Treasury?"

"Yes and no," she replied.

"Fool," muttered the general.

"It is rather chilly today," Kaftus noted, in a tone of stupidity that no one found amusing. "Elgona, cover the windows." The guard hurried to obey. His status had been reduced to a fairly menial level since his failure to protect Harliis, but he had been lucky, at that, and knew it.

"There was no attempt on the King's life in the Treasury," Nimnestl explained. "No one in the Palace Royal would have planned such a foredoomed effort. Anyone would have known that I, the Regent, or both would have been with the King. There were also loyal Treasury guards within call. Any attempt on the King would have been futile."

There were grumbles at this, though the Treasury ministers tried to look suitably complimented by the reference to their guards. "There was an easier way for a traitor to strike at the government," she went on. "If the Pearl of Adriack were found to be missing just prior to the Birthday Oath, there would be an uproar. Some would have interpreted it as an omen, and used it as an excuse to sow panic and demand changes in the structure of the Regency."

Looking around the table to let every single councillor know she suspected each of being capable of it, she continued. "It would have been such a small thing, the theft, but a small key can unlock a box in which a whole ring of keys is kept. Such plans have been planned in Malbeth before." She turned her gaze on Ferrapec.

"But the Pearl wasn't stolen," objected Isanten, slapping both palms on the table. "The Oath was performed."

"True," said Nimnestl. "The theft failed." Unhooking her hammer, she set it in front of her, head down, and leaned on the handle. Every eye in the room was on the hammer. "The Ykenai, the Brown Robes, were behind this plot. It was just their kind of scheme: quiet, civilized, with a minimum of killing required of them. Harliis, we have learned, was one of them. Ordering his body . . ."

She had to raise her voice above an explosion of oaths and exclamations. "Ordering his bodyguard to wait at the door, he entered the Treasury, intending to take the Pearl of Adriack and exit through the rear, 'hidden,' door, telling the guards there he was in too much of a hurry to go back the way he'd come. His bodyguard, with the guards at the main door, would eventually have heard about it, but by the time he rejoined Harliis, Harliis would have had time to meet a disguised confederate, pass him the Pearl, in its bag, and move to the balcony with a second bag he had hidden under his ceremonial robes. He would 'discover' this bag to be filled with pennyetkes, and raise the alarm. If he was suspected of having engineered the terrible omen, he could slip away to shelter with the Brown Robes, and wait until the coup was accomplished."

She did not look once at Flact. "What happened?" demanded Lord Patrak.

"Someone had been studying the Ykenai, nosing out their plots. He knew Harliis was a Brown Robe and, once Harliis was inside the Treasury, disobeyed his orders and stepped inside after him. He struck Harliis down with the first heavy object that came to hand, let us say the Iron Horn of Drawziw. Then, in a high voice, he ordered himself out of the room. The guards at the door could swear Harliis had been alive when the killer backed out."

A third of the assembly was staring at Elgona. The rest were dividing their attention between Nimnestl and Kaftus. These revelations were all very interesting, but Kaftus's reaction would be even more so. If he took offense, there was a chance of driving a wedge between him and the Bodyguard, weakening their hold on the Regency.

Nimnestl, however, looked now at Flact. Moved by discomfort to speak, he demanded, "If this is true, why didn't the man announce it? Killing a traitor is an honorable act!"

"So it is," agreed the Bodyguard, with a warm smile. "But this traitor was involved in the highest ranks of government. He feared the retaliation that he knew must follow." She paused. "There was no act he would not commit to prevent that."

Elgona opened his mouth, but Nimnestl scowled at him. "I see," said Flact, who was studying the top of the big table. "So when Kirajen was about her usual prying, he killed her, then."

Kaftus blinked. "What?" he demanded. "Is Kirajen dead?"

"She did not report to me this morning," said Forokell. "I assumed, however, that she . . . oh, ah, yes." She looked very hard at Flact.

Forokell's stare could be heavy indeed. Nimnestl intervened on behalf of the underdog. "I knew she was dead. She died during a struggle with a thief who wanted her necklace."

"The man you caught in my rooms last night," Flact quickly agreed. "He had the necklace on him at the time: the one with the pearls. You know."

"Is that so?" demanded Kaftus, with a mighty frown at the Minister of State.

"Oh, yes," Nimnestl hastened to assure him. "She was strangled with it." The frown faded, but left a residue of suspicion on the Regent's face. Flact took up a corner of one sleeve to wipe his forehead.

"How horrible!" said Jilligan.

"It may have been," Nimnestl told her, "but perhaps she liked that sort of thing." She repressed a sudden thought of the pixy. "She obviously stood still for it. Her clothes were her best: Silmarian lace and frills. They were all in place, undamaged. She had her knife out, but it was her eating knife and there was no blood on it. I think now that someone knocked her down first and borrowed the knife to twist the necklace around her throat. The bauble broke in the process, and the killer—since death, rather than the necklace, was his concern—took the necklace and finished the job with something else."

"Yes, I see," Flact agreed. "You remember? I pointed out to you last night that the necklace was broken."

"You did," Nimnestl agreed. "Why? There had been a fight and his bag was torn. Couldn't what had torn the pouch also have broken the necklace?"

"It was too light," said Flact. "That is, whatever cut the pouch hadn't cut it very far, or everything he took would have fallen out. So I thought you'd used a small dagger on him. Yes, and remember? Mai . . . the handkerchief it was wrapped in wasn't cut either."

"Very true." Nimnestl nodded. "You're probably correct."

Flact mopped his forehead some more. His best chance was to throw himself on the mercy of his peers, claiming the Bodyguard was plotting to frame him. Nimnestl hoped that as long as she reinforced his story, he wouldn't think of that, at least not before some councillor made the connection between the thief working with the Ykenai and the thief killed in Flact's rooms. She might have to nudge them a bit.

"I can't follow you," complained Forokell. "Who killed Harliis? He sounds like a man of some resource."

"There are many such in the Palace Royal," Nimnestl replied. "The man who killed the thief—since my blows did not finish him—was another. That was a favor I shall not forget. No doubt I would have been bored to death by anything he might have told me about the Pearl of Adriack, had he survived."

Flact's eyes grew large and round, and his shoulders came up. "What?" He glanced up and down the table to see if he had any friends.

Frowys smiled. She never had liked Flact.

"This was the same thief Harliis was working with?" demanded Flact. "That man? Why, I thought Elgona had hired him so Maitena would be grateful enough to . . ."

Nimnestl glanced at Kaftus, but the Regent, seeing the fish begin to struggle, had already decided to bring up the net. "Did you mean to leave this with me?" he asked, raising a volume large enough to serve as both book and table. "Or did the Ykenai send it as a gift?"

He opened the book, and councillors could easily see the words "Members" and "Flact," thanks to glowing gold rings that hovered over the page. Nimnestl checked the faces of the councillors, and was satisfied. Some had been concocting alibis and defenses, since Flact was one of them, but any claim he had to their support was cancelled by his brown robes. The Ykenai would have cast out not just the Regent and Bodyguard but the Council as well. Those councillors who were also Brown Robes said nothing, noting that the Regent had set gold rings around only one name.

Flact could see all this just as well as the Bodyguard. As Nimnestl raised her hammer from the floor and motioned some of the assembled soldiers forward, he released a massive sigh. "I did it, yes," he said, raising his hands in a gesture of surrender. "The Pearl, Kirajen, the thief . . ."

His hands were level with his ears and he jerked them down. Kaftus dropped the book with an oath as it burst into flame. The Minister of State jumped back, clear of his toppling chair, grabbed out his sword, and dove up onto the Council table.

"Who follows me follows to her grave!" he warned, dashing along the table and making a dive for Kaftus's dining room.

Elgona dove after him. Nimnestl was the second one to the door, with most of the Council in a dead heat for third. Only Kaftus, who knew for certain how much chance Flact had of making an escape through his quarters, lingered, trying to salvage at least some of the Book of the Ykenai.

Jilligan and two guards pushed out of the crowd to join battle, but advanced warily, eyeing the bizarre artifacts around them. Elgona dropped back, taking Flact's sword with him. Nimnestl was peripherally aware of this. It had become a private, personal world for three: herself, her hammer, and Flact.

Weaponless, Flact grabbed at the wall behind him and found a black, diamond-shaped shield. He had just time to raise this over his head before the hammer fell. It fell with the persistence of summer rain, forcing the Minister of State to his knees, forcing him to concentrate on just keeping the shield up, giving him no time to draw another weapon.

The shield was showing cracks when Flact surrendered, not to Nimnestl, but to nature. He dropped and went sprawling across a frogskin rug, unconscious.

Elgona walked very slowly to Nimnestl's side, Flact's sword still protruding from his body. He walked as if he didn't want to disturb anybody downstairs. It surprised him when he dropped to his knees. He tried to get up. He still looked surprised when he died.

Kaftus stepped into the room to survey the damage. "Finished?" he inquired.

V

"I SUPPOSE," answered Nimnestl, leaning on her hammer to survey the scene from her end. "Anything left of the book?"

"Ashes," replied the Regent. "I hope enough remains of our Minister of State to answer questions."

"He'll do," the Bodyguard told him. She pointed at the three handiest soldiers. "You men: fetch chains."

Forokell pushed up through the vacancy left by the men. "I would like to have all of this explained now, please," she said, her voice cold with disapproval. "Are we to assume that the Ykenai have attempted to overthrow His Majesty?"

"Not so high as that, Lady Forokell," said the Regent. "Only His Majesty's government."

Nimnestl looked over the crowd and decided to move to the next business on the agenda. "I believe they had picked out a place of safety to hide the King during the ensuing turmoil," she said. "A small room lost and unused since the days of oh-one."

"Ah!" said Frowys. "And they killed Arnastobh because he knew about it."

"Killed my uncle?" demanded Ferrapec. "Nonsense. He died a natural death."

Nimnestl looked up into Kaftus's face. The Regent wore an expression of mock mourning. He nodded, and Nimnestl turned to face Maitena's assistant.

"Perhaps," she said. "More likely, it was to make Maitena look suspicious, so that any further murders that proved necessary could be set to her account."

"Then we can go back to the tournament," said Garanem, "if no action is going to be required against Lady Maitena."

"It must have been Flact's idea," mused Frowys. "He's had it in for the kitchen staff all these years, and, never expecting Lord Kaftus to confiscate her keys, he'd have chosen her to take the blame. If the cell was discovered, he could . . ."

"Of course, knowing Flact and Lady Frowys as we do," said the Regent graciously, "we would never have believed his accusations." He nodded to Nimnestl, letting her know he intended to play "friend" in this round of the game.

Frowys glanced at the Regent, and shrugged. "Who can say, My Lord? Some people are quick to judge, and only discover the truth later, as we came near to doing now with my mistress. When that cell was found, behind all those turnips, any of us could have been suspected."

"Quite so," said Nimnestl. "Quite so. You know where the cell was, then?"

Frowys looked a bit startled, but answered immediately. "Of course. I found it once while walking around in the storeroom area."

"Oof," murmured Jilligan. She knew as well as anyone in the room how likely Frowys was to set one foot on the stairs below the kitchen, or even to the kitchen. Her interests lay more in the direction of the stock pens outdoors, if they concerned anything in the food services.

Seeing the faces made by some of her listeners, Frowys went on, "But . . . but I . . . had no key, of course. Lord Flact had the only key! And I would no more have connived with a Brown Robe, and especially Flact or Harliis, than . . ."

"Maitena had a key," Nimnestl put in.

Frowys stamped one foot. "Lord Kaftus confiscated it!"

"Yes," said the Regent, stepping forward. "I have it in my possession now. Be content with having unmasked Flact, Bodyguard, and don't try to even old scores."

Nimnestl turned so she could see both him and the housekeeper. "The key was not, I think, confiscated before someone had a chance to borrow it."

"Maitena would never have lent a key to anyone," said Forokell, with finality. Everyone had to agree with that.

"To borrow it without her knowledge," Nimnestl went on, "and make a copy."

"Impossible!" Ferrapec exclaimed.

Several people echoed this and Jilligan, who was also overseer of the palace smiths, took it as a personal affront. "If you think any smith in this city, or even in this country, would make a copy," she declared, coming up next to Frowys, "you had best report it to the guild. They will tell you it is nonsense."

The word was repeated throughout the crowd. The Regent picked up on it. "Nonsense!" he announced.

Nimnestl reached inside her armor and brought out one of the wooden keys. She let it drop so everyone could hear the clatter. "I am no more attached to Lord Flact than is My Lady Frowys," she said, gesturing with her hammer to the prone Minister of State. "Yet I am not inclined to award him all of the guilt. It would take some skill, you know, to make a copy like this, in wood hard enough to serve as a key, and Flact was never known as a woodcarver. How many copies were there: one for each conspirator?"

Everyone turned to Frowys, who laughed, "Why ask me? There are other carvers in this city."

"Why ask you, indeed?" replied the Bodyguard, as the crowd pulled a little away from Frowys. "I shall ask Polijn."

Forokell was moving to confront her subordinate directly but came over to Nimnestl instead. Nimnestl couldn't help backing away half a step. The Chief Housekeeper was even older than Kaigrol, and a figure of some dread. "Now, make your accusations clearly," she ordered. "Who is Polijn?"

"A new girl," Nimnestl replied, locking eyes with the Housekeeper. "She works for Ynygyn. Einoel seems to be attracted to her. And you know, Madam, perhaps better than anyone, how a girl under stress will, at times, confide in a stranger."

"She didn't!" snapped Frowys. "I asked her . . . she wouldn't have . . ."

Forokell spun around. "Wouldn't have what?"

Frowys looked stunned, as if suddenly realized she had spoken aloud. "I don't . . . I . . . I didn't say that!"

"I was born with a cheap set of ears, maybe," answered Forokell, taking a step toward her. "It sounded from here as if she didn't, you asked her, and she wouldn't have."

"Keep her away from me!" cried Frowys, reaching thick arms forward with hands ready to take the old woman's neck. Forokell didn't move. Mitar and Gensamar, who were closest, brought their own arms up to bar Frowys's advance.

Forokell turned her piercing eyes back on Nimnestl. "I wish you would say out exactly what you think she has done."

"Certainly," said Nimnestl. "I accuse the Lady Frowys of conspiring against His Majesty, counterfeiting keys, conniving in the murder of Arnastobh, and murdering Hopoli to replace the body of Arual, whom she also killed."

"That's a lie!" screamed Frowys. Five courtiers were holding her back now. "I wouldn't kill a dog that way! Someone else cut her apart!"

"You see that she knows how Arual died," Nimnestl confided to Forokell. "As she knew where I found the cell that had been chosen for the King. I only hope she also knows where Arual was taken, so that the girl can at least receive a decent funeral."

"More?" murmured Kaftus. "Aren't you ever satisfied?"

"But you found the cell!" shrieked Frowys. "You must have seen the girl's body when . . ." She stopped, realizing she had been brought into testimony against herself again.

"No!" she screamed, and turned to run. By now, however, eight of the assembled councillors had their hands on her. It took twelve, not including four casualties, but neither Kaftus nor Nimnestl found it necessary to intervene. Frowys and Flact were chained together, a courtesy neither was awake to appreciate.

"There," said Nimnestl, as her men locked the shackles. "Now it's finished."

"Missy!" called Mardith, from the Council Chamber. "More trouble! Come quick!"

Nimnestl extemporized a verse of curse, and swung her hammer free with a vehemence that broke Flact's nearest leg. Then she forced her way back through the crowd to the next room.

Two winged creatures were dodging through the air. Each time the smaller one neared the other, it plucked a few feathers.

"Isn't this great?" she squealed. "My sisters would . . . ooh, you!" Mardith had reached in to nip her where she'd feel it.

Spectators near the Bodyguard assumed she was counting to ten. She was involved in much higher mathematics. Six were dead. Allowing doubt for deserters and casualties of the tournament, that left nine hundred forty or so. King Conan III would reach his majority at twenty-two: fourteen more years.

She felt a deep envy. When the King had nightmares, he woke up.

CHAPTER NINE
Polijn

I SENTENCE was to be executed high on a scaffold in the center of what had been the tournament field, two days later on a cloudy-bright afternoon. Polijn was allowed to watch from the Main Balcony, since the King and other dignitaries had seats closer to the action.

Iúnartar was not there to identify all the participants for her and tell their stories, but Polijn had heard them dozens of times by now. Frowys, as a former butcher, knew plenty about muscles and joints and ligaments. The experts had had to do little more than point out the questioning instruments to convince her to tell them all she knew, not once, but several times.

She and her friends had known nothing of the Ykenai plot; theirs was a private, independent affair. There were four of them, using their brains as a lever to get the muscle in the Palace Royal to handle all the heavy work for them. They had planned to kidnap the King and hide him in the cell long enough to discredit Kaftus and Nimnestl, who were to have wasted their time questioning Maitena. Frowys, besides carving any necessary keys, was to have crippled the King as well, ensuring that he would never become a soldier and thus never come under the influence of the Army.

Aleia was found in her chambers, rhythmically pushing a knife again and again into a stomach that wasn't really there any more. Frowys claimed it was all Aleia's plot, and that she had taken to herself the job of poisoning Nurse and Nimnestl just enough to keep them quiet during the abduction. Everyone wanted to know how that was to have been accomplished, but Aleia took the secret with her to the pit, unless Kaftus conducted a postmortem interview.

Jilligan had tried to make a run for it directly after the Council meeting. Mishek had been alerted to the possibility of urgent requests, though, and horses were unaccountably unavailable when the housekeeper reached the stables. On foot, Jilligan had made it no farther than the Blue Bottle. There she had tried to take cover, but was found and brought to the Palace by a company of smiths who had heard about the counterfeit keys. Under questioning, she eventually verified Frowys's account, and named two dungeon guards who had helped. These men were now missing and would probably remain so. After they had served their purpose, she had sent them to hiding places in the lower levels of the dungeon. They had not returned; Jilligan had not expected them to. Jilligan was the one who had picked Maitena to be the target of displaced suspicions, and had personally pawned the Banner of Kairor, wearing gloves to do so lest the curse undermine their plot.

The youngest member of the conspiracy handled disgrace with a degree of dignity. Quietly, gently, even apathetically, she had corroborated the other accounts before she so much as saw a cell or heard a question. She had stolen her mother's keys and returned them after the copies were made. She had slipped the poison into Arnastobh's food while taking it to Arual. She regretted neither the murder of her grandfather nor the framing of her mother. Arnastobh was old enough to die, she said, for a good cause, and she knew her mother was equal to anything adversity threw. Apparently she had intended to make it all up, after the coup, by naming her mother First Housekeeper.

The main flaw in the plan, she said, was that they had worked too hard to implicate Maitena. If they hadn't pursued the plot with the Banner of Kairor and the abduction of Arual, things wouldn't have become so complex, so hard to control. They might now be in control of the Palace Royal, and Arual would still be alive. It was the murder of her sister that drew her only show of emotion. Her fervent wish was to watch Frowys die first, for that killing.

Frowys had not admitted the murder, knowing, perhaps, that the dungeon cells were by no means impregnable, and that any death on the scaffold would be better than what she would receive at the hands of a Rossacottan mob. When the three were brought together for sentencing, however, she had taken pains to put herself as far as she could from Einoel.

The sentence called for death involving all the rigors of Rossacottan law, which had never been subjected to the process of civilization. Frowys was to die first, Einoel second, and Jilligan a distant third. On the afternoon of execution, they were marched, or carried, if necessary, to the platform in the required order. Einoel made the distance on her own feet; the guards escorting her seemed less cheerful than she did. She brightened still further when she saw the axe and the block among other props on stage.

It was Nimnestl's last favor to Arnastobh and Arual, that Einoel would not join the other two on the iron table. Her body would go to the pit, but at least it would go in only two pieces.

Some of the less well-informed spectators in the V.I.P. gallery looked for Flact, but he was not to be part of the program. The Book of the Ykenai was gone, and the books left behind in the Brown Robes headquarters had also disappeared. Flact was busy, deep in the Palace Royal, reproducing the contents from memory, with help. Apparently he had been saying interesting things, for the V.I.P. gallery lacked his four top aides. Two of the Lord Treasurers were similarly absent.

Maitena was not to be seen either. Stories about her insisted that she was a suicide, that she was out buying mourning fashions, that she had vowed to cook all the day's meals herself as a penance. No one knew where she really was, and no one seemed to care. The stories were more interesting.

The court was ready for a bit of diversion, now that the pending revolt (or revolts) had been quashed, and the bloodshed and agony would be more exclusive. And it was nice to have another holiday so soon after the King's Birthday. Many of the courtiers had new costumes for the affair, generally piled on top of the Birthday finery. Frowys, Jilligan, and Einoel also wore, at least temporarily, what they had worn for the tournament.

Polijn grew bored during the long recitation of the crimes of the prisoners. She had come to the balcony only in hopes of hearing the traditional dirge that minstrels claimed condemned prisoners always sang on their way to their deaths. No one on the platform seemed likely to sing anything, and the minstrels down in the crowd were performing bawdy songs she had known years before. She squeezed back through the crowd into the Palace Royal.

II

THE minstrel's chambers were empty. Polijn slid the door to her cabinet open and crawled inside. Closing the door again behind her, she picked up the flute and slide-whistle, and moved on back to the little hidden room. She closed the hidden panel as well.

There was no real need for all this secrecy, not now that Ynygyn knew about her flute. But the study was Ynygyn's place, not hers; she wouldn't play there unless he was present. The darkness behind the wall was her place; here she had no presentiment that someone was watching from ambush, listening.

Until today. She started a scale, but got no higher than the fourth note. Something was wrong about her hideaway today. She or it was insecure. A chill ran through her as a breeze riffled her hair. That was it: she had thought this room was shut up tight. Where could a draft get in?

She tucked the flute next to the slide-whistle and slid her hands along the walls. Behind her cabinet, except for her own sliding door, the wall was solid. But around the corner to the left, the surface slid under her hands. A second door, then, and partially open. Someone had come this way, then. While she was out? While she slept?

There was no motion in the new chamber, except for the draft. She crawled inside, and rose from her knees. Dots of light led away down a long corridor. They were just out of her reach, but she knew what they must be.

Another door opened somewhere. Polijn dropped to the floor and waited. "I should be out there, making notes for the song," remarked a familiar voice.

Polijn could also identify the voice that answered, without resort to the peepholes. "What notes do you need, Minstrel?" Aesernius demanded. "If you've seen one torture slaying, you've seen them all. And you have." She heard the sorcerer slide back the door of the cabinet and close it again. "She isn't here?"

"No," Ynygyn replied. "She'll be on the balcony, watching events."

Polijn was about to call out to them to come see what she had found. But she had a feeling about what Ynygyn would say about someone shouting in his chambers. She was starting back for the cabinet when she heard Aesernius ask, "She doesn't know about the room behind there, does she? Or the passage?"

"My dear Aesernius," Ynygyn replied, "would she have remained in my employ if she knew anything of the sort?"

But you know she does, thought Polijn.

"Good," said the sorcerer. "Then she can't be tempted to tell anyone when the King disappears next week."

"Next week, then?" Ynygyn demanded.

"They won't be expecting another so soon," answered Aesernius. "And by then we'll have these passages mapped and have hiding places chosen for the King and those of the Royal Companions we intend to keep for breeding purposes."

Ynygyn made no reply. "Oh, you'll get your share," the sorcerer assured him. "How does that line in your 'History' go? 'The noble young maids, sweeter than the apricots of Kirmith'?"

"Must you?" demanded the minstrel.

"They're your own lyrics," Aesernius replied. "Pick up your lower lip before you step on it. Where's your enthusiasm, man? Still brooding over the last one? Say, come to think of it, I've not seen your girl all morning. You haven't done for her already, have you?"

"Polijn?" Ynygyn demanded, as if affronted. "A commoner? I wouldn't so soil my body."

Polijn's gasp was lost in the bellow of laughter released by the sorcerer. "You wouldn't! You haven't been so dainty down in the Swamp. But perhaps you investigated their pedigrees carefully first. That last one was named Kronja, by the way, if you're interested. I have it on excellent authority. I do wish you could have avoided coming across Arual when . . . Did you hear that?"

The second gasp had been louder; Polijn knew she'd be found out now. She turned and took off up the sloping passage. She had farther to move than Ynygyn or Aesernius, but she moved faster and had no doors to open on her way to the end of the corridor.

But she was still on the wrong side of the door when the sorcerer reached the passage. Aesernius called out a phrase she recognized. Remembering what it was for, she stumbled through the doorway and slammed the door shut behind her.

Then she literally froze in her tracks. Cold bit at her feet like rats and, looking down, she saw the sheen of a layer of ice as it reached up to engulf her ankles. Kicking to shake it loose, she nearly toppled over forward.

The ice crept up to her knees. In the passage behind her, she heard the slow easy footsteps of Ynygyn and the heavy thud of Aesernius's boots. The ice climbed on; icy fingers began to force themselves into her body. No twist or turn did her any good.

She hammered at the ice with her free hand. The footsteps came on. Hauling her flute up with both hands, she brought it down hard on the frozen shell. Although Polijn had known the flute for a thing of value, she had taken no previous interest in the fact that it was silver, and proof against spells. The ice cracked under the first blow, but grew back to cover the damage. With rapidly chilling hands, she brought the flute down again and again, pounding it sometimes against the ice and sometimes against numb, rigid flesh.

Cracked ice was piling on the floor when the door opened. Polijn pulled free to the sound of tearing cloth and skin. This was only sound to her. She abandoned her sandals to the ice and dashed forward, around a corner. The footsteps could not be heard behind her now, but she didn't spare time to listen. Her mind was on running, and on getting up again when numbed and dripping feet betrayed her.

She hit another door. On the far side of this, she found herself behind a tapestry. Out in an open corridor, now, she turned to the stairs, but had run only a few yards before she found herself in front of the Chief Bodyguard's office. She threw her shoulder against the door and dashed inside.

The Bodyguard was in, seated at a table, her head in her hands. When the door slammed, she stood up.

There was no time to curtsy. "They're coming for me!" panted Polijn. "They killed Kronja and Olann and the others, and they're plotting against His Majesty! I heard . . ."

The door slammed open again, pinning Polijn against the wall. "Bodyguard," boomed Ynygyn, marching into the room, "when you can spare the time, I wish you'd try to find my new slavey. She's been missing since this morning and seems to have taken a valuable . . . Why, here it is."

The minstrel reached for her, but, having seen what those hands could do, Polijn ducked under them and, half-crawling, scurried away under the table.

"He's one of them!" she exclaimed, as the Bodyguard stepped around the table. "They've found a secret hall and they're going to kidnap the King!"

Ynygyn did not try to follow her, but took a step back. Shaking his head, he said, "Child, if you survive this, you were born for the minstrel trade. Your skill at impromptu tales is unmatched."

"Let's hear yours," suggested the Bodyguard.

"Another time, perhaps, My Lady," Ynygyn replied. His chin was up and his voice was chill. "Unfortunately, my stories are founded on fact, and would be a sad anticlimax to an ornate fantasy such as I fear you will hear."

"Let's submit them to an impartial judge, then," said Nimnestl, setting a hand on her hammer. "The Regent will hear yours first, if you prefer, and your accounts will bear equal weight."

"Perhaps," said Ynygyn. "But before the Council, a Council already smarting from having had to witness two of your triumphs, my word and that of Aesernius will carry more melody than that of a small drudge from the Swamp."

Polijn felt her eyes tickle. Then she jumped back as the silver flute wriggled and grew warm in her hands.

"Let's make it a foursome, then," it said, growing and

forming a small woman. "Add my testimony." Polijn took her hands off Lady Oozola's waist. To be sure, the shapeshifter had not been in evidence when the Vielfrass gave her the flute. It had all been a scheme to get Lady Oozola into the Palace unobserved.

Nimnestl's hammer was unhooked and half-raised when Aesernius entered and shouted out a spell. The head of the hammer froze to the table. The Bodyguard struggled in vain to free it, paying no attention at all to the two conspirators. She had seen what Polijn saw.

"Tut," said the Regent, completing his materialization as Aesernius started around the table to take advantage of the Bodyguard's apparent inattention. He waved a hand, and a mask of iron covered Aesernius from nose to neck.

The hammer broke away from the table. Nimnestl hoisted it and looked to Ynygyn. The minstrel shook his head, and spread his hands out wide. Polijn backed out from under the table and was the first to see the owner of the voice that cried, "Well done, well done! Excellent! I could almost hardly have done better myself."

Even Aesernius turned to stare at the Vielfrass, who was lying across the points of four dozen spears held in a rack on the wall. "What are you doing here?" demanded the Bodyguard, her hammer still lifted.

The supercilious sorcerer pointed at the Regent. "I had my eye on him at the execution. When he started to vanish, I knew he must be after bigger thrills, and I came to see what was what."

He waved. "Hi, Polijn. Nice job."

Polijn didn't say anything.

Kaftus leaned out the door to summon guards. "Yes, it was," said Ynygyn. "Aesernius was fooled completely. I knew at the time the child was no blockhead."

He stepped with dignity to a place between two men with drawn swords. "Goodbye, Polijn," he said, not looking back. "Keep practicing."

The Regent was less interested in this than in the minstrel's scheme. Hearing an outline of the story from Nimnestl and Polijn, he turned to the Vielfrass, who had jumped down to the tabletop. "How did you find him out?"

"Oh, I didn't," the Vielfrass told him. "I just thought

Aesernius was an odd friend for him to have, he having no friends up 'til now." He knelt to reach over the edge of the table, grabbing his assistant by her minimal covering and dragging her out. "I also observed him in the Swamp one evening and decided his hobby made him an unfit companion for the King. It does no good to simply SURROUND the child with misfits and perverts."

The Regent bared his teeth in a smile of delight. "How have you managed to live this long, my Vielfrass?" he demanded.

"I eat right, get plenty of exercise, and avoid sweets between meals," the sorcerer replied.

"Who's Sweets?" asked Oozola. The sorcerer kicked her in the elbow.

"She did the hard work," the Vielfrass went on, pointing to Polijn, "acting as bait. No, child, say nothing. A triumphant silence is far more impressive."

"You might try it some time," the Regent recommended. "I'm off to the King. You can give me all the details later." He faded, leaving only slightly dusty air in his wake.

The Bodyguard reached down to take Polijn's hand. "Come," she said. "Show me these passages."

Polijn led the whole party to Ynygyn's rooms, opened the cabinet, and displayed the door behind it. She stepped aside as the three of them studied the passage.

"Another maze of corridors," said Nimnestl, crawling back out. She shook her head and adjusted her clothes. "This place is a rabbit's warren."

"If it was only rabbits, you'd have no problem," the Vielfrass told her.

Nimnestl nodded. "Have you any more surprises?" she inquired. "Or is this everything?"

The Vielfrass shook his head. "If I told you, they wouldn't be surprises."

"I'd better see to it that Aesernius is properly disposed in the dungeons," the Bodyguard said, turning away. "One can never be at all sure about sorcerers. We are grateful for your efforts, though; we'll see to it that there is some reward." Polijn stepped aside so as not to block the path to the door.

As the Bodyguard was leaving, Oozola walked over and patted Polijn on one shoulder. "It has been enchanting," the little woman said. "I usually hate being an inanimate object."

The Vielfrass looked around the room. "Yes," he said. Reaching up to an instrument rack, he lifted down the slightly tarnished flute Ynygyn used for practice. "Here. He won't be wanting it, and I think he'd be glad to know it was going to someone who knew how to use it."

"But . . ."

"Foo," said the sorcerer, pressing it against her hands. "Take it before the scavengers get here."

She took the instrument, but continued to stare at his fuzzy face. "Did you really not know," she said, "that they were going to . . ."

He slid one hand to her hair and said, "I know everything, child," in what was obviously meant to be a reassuring manner. Polijn was not much reassured.

"Come, sidekick!" he called to Oozola. "You have very nearly a week of back concubinage to catch up on." He took his hand from Polijn's hair and wrapped it in Oozola's. Singing, "You're the cream in my coffee, you're the cyanide in my soup," he marched away, pulling her along. Oozola rolled her eyes, but did not try to break away.

Polijn looked around Ynygyn's chambers. Now what? She could wait where she was, or go back to the Thick Fleece. Not much of a choice.

Her status here had rested on her mission for the Vielfrass and her service to Ynygyn. Both of those were now ended, and she was only an object for the scavengers, who would lose no time in looting the rooms once news reached the tournament ground.

She rolled up her two spare shifts and, after thinking about it, wrapped the blanket around them. Imidis did not show up to protest. She looked around the room one last time, could not think of any reason to disturb anything else in place on the shelves, and moved out.

Her arms around the bundle, her head down, she shoved through the crowd to the gate. She saw a few people she knew on the way, but none moved to stop her. Arberth was still trying to explain ratifications and fortifications to spectators on the fringe of the audience.

The wind nearly knocked her off the bridge and into the moat. The sky was darkening, and winter speeding on its way. She stopped in the shelter of the guardhouse at the far end of the bridge, both to catch her breath and to check inside the bundle. Flute and slide-whistle were still safe within.

She didn't know whether she was sorry about what would happen to Ynygyn. A few music lessons wasn't much to balance against what had been done to Kronja, or Olann, or half a dozen others she had known in the Swamp. Would she have been next? She doubted it, but, of course, she couldn't know.

Anyway, for a while, at least, it had seemed that someone had an interest in her that could not be explained away by the expectation of pleasure or profit. Now she knew that Aesernius had valued her only as an alibi, or something from which Kings could be bred.

She put her head around the guardhouse to study the road down into Malbeth. She had her lessons, the tunes Ynygyn had taught her, some new clothes, a blanket, and a flute. And, of course, she still had her slide-whistle. So she had not done so badly by her trip to the Palace Royal. No reason to be so glum.

The wind had slowed for the moment. Polijn stepped out from behind the guardhouse and raised a foot to take a step.

Before the foot came down, she had turned completely around to face the Palace Royal. Maybe Arberth knew all the words to "The Hot Featherbed" and wouldn't mind slide-whistle accompaniment.